DAYS OF OUR LIVES...

CREATIVE WRITING FROM KENT & SUSSEX

Edited by Sarah Andrew

First published in Great Britain in 2002 by
YOUNG WRITERS
Remus House,
Coltsfoot Drive,
Peterborough, PE2 9JX
Telephone (01733) 890066

HB ISBN 0 75433 464 3
SB ISBN 0 75433 465 1

FOREWORD

This year Young Writers proudly presents a showcase of the best 'Days Of Our Lives . . .' short stories, from up-and-coming writers nationwide.

To write a short story is a difficult exercise. We made it more challenging by setting the theme of 'A Day In The Life Of Someone From The Second Millennium', using no more than 250 words! Much imagination and skill is required. *Days Of Our Lives . . . Creative Writing From Kent & Sussex* achieves and exceeds these requirements. This exciting anthology will not disappoint the reader.

The thought, effort, imagination and hard work put into each story impressed us all, and again, the task of editing proved demanding due to the quality of entries received, but was nevertheless enjoyable.

We hope you are as pleased as we are with the final selection and that you continue to enjoy *Days Of Our Lives . . . Creative Writing From Kent & Sussex* for many years to come.

CONTENTS

Benenden CE Primary School
Lauren Beeslee	1
Olivia Spens	2
Aruna Bisram	3
Clare Hall	4
Alison Evans	5
Timothy Scully	6
Emma Corke	7
Anna Fowler	8
Lisa Kenward	10
Georgina Corke	11
Ashley Burgess	12
Georgia Coxhead	13
Robert Aldous	14
Madeline Dell	15
James Baldwin	16
Isobel Hume	17
Rebecca Pooley	18
Caiti Walter	19

Blackboys CE School
Johannes Wolf	20
Jack Worrell	21
Liberty Paterson	22
Kelsey Martinez	23
Christopher Dean	24
Catherine Dangerfield	25
Gillian Cottingham	26
Charles Coston	27
Luke Chattaway	28
Isobel Chapman	29
Romilly Blakeley	30
Evie Broad	32

Bridge & Patrixbourne CE Primary School

Richard Day	33
James Clayson	34
Louis Conradie	35
Sophie Masterson	36
Rachel Tapley	37
Helen Bell	38
Harrey Ware	39
James Harvey	40
Richard Hartland	41
James Mackay	42
Sophie Macdonald	43
Tiffany Murphy	44
David Van Rooyen	45
Dan Keim	46
Georgia Pritchard	47
Jessica Cutter	48
Richard Brown	49
Imogen Higson	50
Elliot Denham	51
Kate Jarrett	52
Rose Markes	53
Hannah Coker	54
Thomas Goodwin	55
Suzanna Hewitt	56
Sophie Pritchard	57
Zoe Anderson	58
Ben Bostock	59
Bryony Morgan	60

Bronte School

Luke M Clements	61
Nicholas May	62
Karl Williams	63
Roberta Jarvis	64
Gary Shergill	65
Martin Verga	66
Ritwick Ghosh	67

Christopher Ramsay	68
Zoe Percy	69
Adam Skopila	70
Paramdeep Bhatti	71
Hannah Russell	72
Gursharan Dio	73

Brookland CE School

Gavid Smeed	74
Sophie Tomlin	75
Jodie Finn	76
Daisy Hannon	77
Oliver Finn	78
Michael Constable	79
Devan Johnson	80
Janet Noakes	82
Holly French	83
Steven Gilbert	84
Ben Ubee	85
Eleanor Chapman	86

Buxted CE School

Joshua McLoughlin	87
Emily Greenwood	88
Martin Hays-Nowak	89
Harriet Crawford	90
Tanya Scanlon	91
Ellen Wise	92
Adam Harris	93
David Hall	94
Karl Thompson	95
Ben Hall	96
Oliver Conaboy	97
Laura Little	98
Richard Hammond	99
Lynne Robinson	100

Cliffe Woods Primary School

Daniel Holliday	101
Ashley Earll	102
James Povey	103
Lee Heather	104
Prince Banin-Plockey	105
Sarah Lowings	106
Aimee Walters	107
Chloe Hart	108
Eleanor Prowse	109
Rebecca Darey	110
Jill Morley	111
Elizabeth Cowan	112
Michael Orvis	113
Katie Bourner	114
Paul Kelly	115
Simon Harding	116
Daniel Sams	117
Shyma Cherry	118
Elizabeth Ingham	119
Aiden Blades	120
Alouette Marsh	121
Marc Paton	122

Downview Primary School

Michelle Poston	123
Nathan Mhuto	124
Nicola Pearce	125
Tom Tyrell	126
Amy Benjamin	127
Stephanie Ward	128
Kelsey Spencer	129
Jake Lund	130
James Parsons	131
Craig Johnson	132
Emily Aird	133
Tom Stafford	134
Chris Reed	135

Gary Chandler   136
Simon Belton   137
Emily Lippitt   138
Carlie Davis   139
Christopher Ramsdale   140
Molly Turnbull   141
Becky Balshaw   142
Rayhun Aminian   143
Natalie Gillies   144
Anna Champion   145

Estcots CP School
Kelly Gunstone   146
Rachel Day   148

Groombridge St Thomas Primary School
Christopher Morrell   149
Sarah Vardon   150
Nick James   151
Madeleine Feltham   152
Zoe Neilson   153
Huw McNamara & Ryan Seal   154
Jessica Spicer   155

Harcourt Primary School
Emma Pickford   156
Ashley West   157
Jessica Campbell   158
Jasmin Cowdroy   159
Amy Thurling   160
Calum Muir   161
Rachael Martin   162
Daniel Bailey   163

Iwade CP School
Holly Fitton   164
Georgina Fairhurst   165
Paris Reeves   166

Katie Whiffen	167
Terry Brookman	168
Alissa Solecki	169
Kayleigh Grant	170

Joy Lane Junior School

Megan Crocombe	171
Ronnie Simmonds	172
Alys Scott	174
Carys Powell-Smith	175
Rebekah Crocombe	176

Knockhall CP School

Tomes Linehan	177
Jamie Jones	178
Jonathon Blackwell	179
Joanna Hares	180
Liam Harvey	181
Richard Medhurst	182
Andrew Fox	183
Tara O'Connor	184
Joanne Hull	185
Leanne Hoskins	186
Jamie Mackenzie	187
Rebecca Elliott	188
Crystal Kolsek	189
Lucy Wenham	190
Chantelle Smith	191
James Parker	192

Marden Primary School

Rebecca Boys	193
Elizabeth Adam	194

Mereworth CP School

Ben Sampson	195
Amelia Leader	196
Naomi Cresswell	197

Lawrence Puckett	198
Christopher Hall	199
Robert Astley	200
Michael Weaver	201
Hannah Hook	202
Sandy Coles	203
Sarah Burns	204
Jodie Ernst	205
Tom Clark	206
Damian Rollinson	207
Sam O'Leary	208
Tom Cannon	209
Hannah Talbutt	210
Emily West	211
James Kailanathan	212
Matthew Kiddie	213
Stuart McLachlan	213

North Heath CP School

Mohammed Hadi	215
Claire Haley	216
Danielle Harding	217
Rachel Ven	218
Gail Lowden	219
Laura Smith	220
Rikki Partridge	221
Katie Felton	222
Katherine Hilliard	223
Jake Mulcahy	224
Zoe McMillan	225
Tom Raymen	226
Georgina Warren	227

St John Fisher RC School, Erith

Sarah Britto	228
Timothy Osibo	230
Adeola Omosanya	232

Laura Faithorn   233
Jaleesa Bernard-Thomas   234

St Mary Star Of The Sea RC Primary School, St Leonards-on-Sea
Tom Powell   236
Rhianna Andrews   237
Matthew Suggitt   238
Kate Longmire   239
Dominic Porter   240
Linda O'Sullivan   241
Stuart Parnell   242
Sophie Kelley   243
Georgina Buck   244
Nicholas Webb   246
Jodie O'Rourke   247
Jacob Kirimli   248
Charlotte Moon   249

St Philip Howard Catholic Primary School, Herne Bay
Alice Starkey   250
Max Wood   251
Adam Povall   252
Bradley Harrad   253
Joanne Goldsmith   254
C J Bithell   255
Faye Fish   256
Tom Chidgey   257
Dominique Ifill   258
Matthew Khoury   259
Fiona Flaherty   260
Matthew Quantrill   261
Ben Lassman   262
Charlotte Binnersley   263
Kellie King   264
Sara Murphy   265

St Ronan's School, Hawkhurst

Jonno Ross	266
Michelle Faure	267
Marcus Hall	268
Charlotte Peniston	269
Henry Garner	270
Rosie Mockett	271
Charlotte Meyer	272
Thomas Granger	273
Dominic Smith	274
Ashley Welsh	275
Emma Cobbold	276
Phoebe Katis	277
Marco March	278

St William Of Perth RC Primary School

Stephanie Estabrook	279
Megan Johnston	280
Matt Vangool	282
Chris Jarvis	284
Imogen Robertson	286
Aislinn Hanna	288
James Dance	289
Alexander Siamatas	292
Danny Keane	293
James Mills	294
Loren Syer-Willoughby	296
Georgia Beesley	297

Shorne CE Primary School

George Gillham	298
Kezia Brown	299
Christian Purdy	300
Christopher McCann	302
Rebecca Pratt	304
Matt Clayden	306
Jasmine Hessenthaler	308
Emily Maycock	309

Emily Coode   310
Rebecca Hopkins   312
Emilie Ashen   314
Poppy Waller   315

Somerhill Junior School

Eleanor Bull   316
Sarah Parker   317
Ashleigh Knights & Rochelle Thorpe   318
Candice Parfitt   319
Sam Collard   320

West Lodge Prep School

Holly Wells   321
Helen Freundlich   322
Jemma Gurr   323
Claire Stevenson   324

The Stories

A DAY IN THE LIFE OF A TOOTH FAIRY

As I wake up in my ivy-leafed bed I turn over. Good, Baby Pixie is sleeping, his tiny chest inflating and deflating to a rhythm. I am really tired, I was up until about two o'clock last night collecting hundreds of teeth and exchanging them for fifty pence pieces; by accident I took Grandpa Chatterjjis' false teeth.

I am going to see the Queen Fairy today to have Baby Pixie christened. I went to the tailor's yesterday to pick up his christening gown. It was beautiful because you can see the tiny stitches from where Mr Stitch (the tailor) has used his talented fingers to create this masterpiece. *Bleep, bleep* - that's the fairy phone.

That was the Queen Fairy, she will be ready in thirty minutes so I better get Baby Pixie dressed and ready to go. It isn't easy to wake up Baby Pixie without being kicked or slapped at some time during the procedure.

Now that he's awake and ready we must leave for the Fairyland church in the very heart of Fairyland. It is rather chilly outside. I'm walking into the church. Oh my Fairy Lord, the Queen is looking beautiful as usual - joke! She is at the altar anointing the fairy water with perfume.

I was sweating in the fairy church as I was losing patience with the Queen Fairy because she always tuts and drops a hint, maybe she thinks that I am not collecting enough teeth for her marvellous collection. Fairy God, I am so incredibly tired I have to save all my energy for my midnight errands. So now it is back to my comfy ivy-leafed bed. Goodnight!

Lauren Beeslee (10)
Benenden CE Primary School

MY MOMENT AS A BUTTERFLY

As I hatched in my cocoon I realised that I was a beautiful butterfly. I was admiring myself and thinking that I was only what seemed to be a girl yesterday and now I am a butterfly. I began to think that I have a new life and what was in my old life has been left behind. What would I do all day? What would I think all day and what would I say all day, seeing as I have no one to play with or talk to?

Throughout the morning I got lonely and realised that being a butterfly isn't that much fun after all. I sat down on my tiny legs and wished to be with my family. I remembered all the good times we had had together and thought that I might never see them again. I tried my hardest not to cry but water kept dripping down from my eyes.

A few minutes later I had calmed down and decided to make the most of the time I had as a butterfly, seeing as no one else would have an opportunity to be their favourite animal, or would they?

I was feeling tired and wanted to go to sleep, so I laid down on the petal of a flower and made one more wish to wake up in my own bedroom, but even though today hasn't been much fun, my favourite animal is still a butterfly.

Olivia Spens (11)
Benenden CE Primary School

A Day In The Life Of Jade, My Sister

It was quite a hectic experience. I picked a very busy time seeing as she had GCSEs.

I woke up in my bed as usual, hang on, wait a minute, I'm in my sister's bed in her 'wicked Odeon' room. It's only called that because it's the same colour as the Odeon cinema in Tunbridge Wells.

At first I was scared and worried, and then I realised that revenge was mine and it smelt so sweet. Ha, ha, ha! Then there was her music as she was getting dressed and doing all her wonderful make-up. But let's fast-forward.

9.00am- Assembly, which his what we call boring, but not today. No, not today, not with me there. I found some old tissues in Jade's . . . I mean my pocket. I tore them up and flicked them everywhere, even on the Scottish teacher from hell, Mrs Stracken. Boring, let's fast forward.

Stooop - 10 o'clock, right maths. Maths is my best subject but not when I'm in year 11 doing level ten mental arithmetic. Ow, maybe this isn't so good after all.

Ding-a-ling-a-ling - 12 o'clock. Now I can find out what Jade's life is really about. My guess is that we are off to the kebab shop for some *really* healthy food, but I decide not to go or I would have had a fat lump for a sister.

I thought Jade's life would be more interesting, but however miserable I make it, it's still boring. Before I end my day as Jade, I just have to get her a detention and to do that I'm going to skip school.

Aruna Bisram (10)
Benenden CE Primary School

A Day In The Life Of A Cat

I hate being in this cage; it's so poky and small.

Oh, I'd better start at the beginning.

This morning I woke up, as usual. I had breakfast, as usual, but I wasn't hungry so I left some. I went back to sleep and guess what woke me up five minutes later, an annoying little mouse and it was eating *my breakfast!* That was too much. I prepared to pounce and then Miss Sweetheart, my owner, picked me up.

Well, I wriggled free and ran after the mouse that had disappeared into the skirting board. Miss Sweetheart saw it and ran around the house screaming her head off, jeeze! What a fuss about a little mousy.

I didn't catch it but I managed to bite its tail off.

When Miss Sweetheart calmed down she picked me up and exclaimed 'Has Pussykins caught a nasty disease from that vile rodent?'

Oh boy, here we go again! Every time she sees me catch or bite any creature I'm in for a trip to the vet. That's why I'm here in this horrid little box of a cat carrier.

Today I'm going to catch it no matter what, so I got up early and found a pot of glue. I pushed my saucer outside the mouse's house and knocked over the pot of glue.

The mouse came trotting out and got stuck, or I thought it had. I lunged forward and the mouse ran to its hole, but *horror!* I was stuck. Eventually Miss Sweetheart cut me free with some scissors and I never caught another mouse again.

Clare Hall (10)
Benenden CE Primary School

A DAY IN THE LIFE OF EASTER BUNNY

Some people don't believe in me, but I don't believe in Santa Claus. It's a delight when my part of the year comes - Easter. The children, who wake up full of happiness, see the chocolate eggs I have brought them.

A trip to the nearest Bunnyworths to buy all the eggs I can possibly find, then to sort out who gets what. Seeing all the eggs stacked up on the cart ready and raring to go. Finding comfy cushions to sit on, a lovely seat just apart from the Easter eggs.

The next decision is to find the quickest route, to find a place where there are no mole hills or bumps! A route where there are no traffic lights and people's houses are easy to find. A nutritious supper to fill me up, for a starter - carrots, for a main course - carrot soup, and for a dessert - a delicious carrot cake. To end with a freshly grated carrot and biscuits.

After my rounds are done late at night, I travel back full of happiness knowing my job is done! A tasty carrot to nibble on and a cup of home-made carrot stew. I sit down and put my feet up and just imagine the children's faces the next morning, when they see all the delicious eggs I have delivered for them.

Alison Evans (11)
Benenden CE Primary School

A DAY IN THE LIFE OF THE INDIAN IN THE CUPBOARD

Creak! There I sat in the corner. I looked up. 'Aahhh! It's a huge giant.'
'Wow!' said the giant.
'You touch, I kill,' I shouted. Then the giant tried to pick me up and I stabbed him. He was called off by someone and he shut the cupboard. 'Uh oh, another 12 hours drained out of my life.'

12-13 hours later

'Hi, welcome back. I'm real, now let's hope that doesn't happen again.' And so I gave into the giant, whose name was Omri I had found out and let him pick me up. 'That's a long way down.'

'Me want horse,' I shouted. He must of heard me because he gave me a wide selection to pick from. I picked my favourite and he made it real! A while after he took me outside to give me a run on my horse but when I was being carried back on the horse, he got frightened and it bucked and hit me on the leg. Omri, in the cupboard, brought to life an army doctor who nursed my cut back to health and afterwards made it plastic again.

Later on that day Omri told his friend Patrick who, after he was told, wanted one as well so when Omri was getting me some food, Patrick made a cowboy called Boone. Omri was really annoyed with Patrick.

I have many adventures with Omri in my later life (including getting a girlfriend.)

Timothy Scully (11)
Benenden CE Primary School

A DAY IN THE LIFE OF NICKI

It was a normal day, the sun was shining. I couldn't really see anything, it was kinda blurry. I rubbed my eyes and then I knew it. I wasn't in my own room. I wasn't even in my own body.

I ran to the mirror and then realised I wasn't in any old body, I was in my sister Nicki's body. 'Nnnoooo!' I couldn't believe it. I was in my worst enemy's body. I saw the time, it was 7.30. I would never have enough time to get ready by 7.55.

I grabbed Nicki's uniform, putting it on as fast as I could. 'What if she had homework?' Wait a minute, who cares, that's her problem not mine!

I remembered that Nicki was going round to Becca's house. She said she was going to the graveyard to do something. Spooky, huh! Back into reality, I heard the bus pulling up, ran downstairs and grabbed my bag . . . wait a minute, Nicki's bag, and ran out the door.

After school we waited outside for the bus home. I could see the bus approaching from a distance. When we got on everyone was flicking bits of paper and singing to the radio.

We finally got to her house and went straight up to her room. She asked me if I had bought the earring. 'Huh!' I replied.
'You know ice, needle, ear!'
'Oh yeah!'

It took us three hours but we finally finished. My mum arrived an hour later and asked me what I did today. 'You don't want to know,' I replied.

Emma Corke (11)
Benenden CE Primary School

A Day In The Life Of A Maori

I woke up this morning in the sleeping hut. I knew it was Saturday so I didn't have to get up early. Jon, Liam, Ruby, Heather and Jo were still asleep (it was Liam and Ruby's birthday today.) Oh no, I do have to get up. Mum has to bake the cake and put up the decorations. I dressed quickly. I realised my Tiki was missing so I searched my compartment and soon found it.

I better tell you what a Tiki is; a Tiki is a shape like a fish hook because legend has it that long, long ago, off the coast of New Zealand, a man called Maui (pronounced Maw-ee) fished up one of the New Zealand (it depends on which tale you listen to) islands. Nowadays Maoris wear them to remember his bravery; it is usually made of whale or cow bone, it is said that it is only lucky if someone buys it as a present for you, talking of presents, I need to go and help Mum with the cake and decorations!

The rest of my brothers and sisters, apart from Heather, were still asleep by the time everything was done. After an hour or so of waiting the rest of them were all up except Liam and Ruby. I was sent in to wake them up.

Everything was ready, the chief sent everyone to hide; as I slowly and gently pulled back the door of the hut. Liam and Ruby walked out and said almost at the same time 'Where is everybody?' Suddenly the biggest roar in the world broke out. Ruby and Liam looked scared but soon cheered up when they saw what it was. The sight was magical! The whole camp was blurting out the words of happy birthday and thrusting presents and roses at them.

This palaver went on for the rest of the day; usually at the end we would all sit around the camp fire, tell stories and sing to Rima's guitar, but tonight was different. The chief had managed to get hold of some fireworks. We watched them from outside the hut and after the biggest one it was time for bed. We all crept slowly back to bed, clambered into our PJs then straight under the duvet and that's how it was, we all zonked out into dreamland.

Anna Fowler (10)
Benenden CE Primary School

A DAY IN THE LIFE OF A DOLPHIN

The day was Friday 15th. I woke up feeling very cheeky so I ventured out on my own. I got into a bit of trouble but I am OK. By the way, my name's Fin and I have blue skin and it looks all shiny in the water. Anyway, you want to hear my story so I will tell you.

It all started early one morning and I felt very cheeky, so I went out on my own and all of a sudden I was being chased by a pack of sharks. Those big, fat, bloodsucking bullies, they don't care who they scare just as long as they get their meal. Selfish huh! Anyway, I swam as fast as my fins would take me and I managed to escape.

Unfortunately, as soon as I got away from the sharks I got into more trouble with some humans and their stupid fishing nets. As I was going out the water my mind went blank. The next thing I knew I was back in the water. I looked up and I realised a small boy had freed me. Without warning a harpoon was fired at me!

I swam away. Soon I could see I was being followed by the boat. I realised if I was ever going to escape I would have to go deeper under the water. I went under the water and escaped when I eventually reached home. I was so glad and no one knew where I had gone which was extremely lucky for me.

Lisa Kenward (11)
Benenden CE Primary School

A DAY IN THE LIFE OF A DOG

I woke up as usual with my regular day's plan - to get fed, chase the neighbour's cat and go to the park for a game of frisby.

I get up, have a big stretch and go to my owner for some food. My owner, who is called Lily, is the nicest possible owner anyone could have. She does anything for you. She takes you for walks, plays with you, lets you lay on her bed, anything you want really.

I went outside to look for the neighbour's cat so I could chase it around the garden. Then I heard a familiar voice calling my name. Lily! I bounded up to her and licked her. Was I going to the park now? What if I was? I would miss my game of chase. Hang on a minute, what if the cat thinks I'm not going to chase it anymore? Then it will be easy tomorrow. I don't need to worry about the cat anymore, so I can enjoy my game of frisby at the park.

As I set off for the park with my leather lead and my fancy frisby, I see the cat at the window. It starts to hiss but I just ignore it and carry on trotting along. We had our game of frisby and were coming home for some dinner. Lily opened the door . . . oh my doggy word. What had happened to the house? Then I heard the dog flap. The cat . . .

Georgina Corke (11)
Benenden CE Primary School

A DAY IN THE LIFE OF NODDY

I woke up with a bang. This bed's too small, I deserve better. Hang on, I'm not myself, I'm Noddy and I've got that dinky little bell on my head. I do hope the person inside me is smart. I'm in the middle of SATs.

If I remember correctly, Noddy has a car and I'm inside Noddy's body . . . Let's hit the road. Man this car's slow, let's go to Mr Spark's garage, he'll fix it in no time at all.

5 minutes later

'I've finished.'
'What's the charge?'
'Two nods for you.'

Nice! My car's complete with rocket boosters. I'm off to the bookies. Three minutes later - I'm here at last. I've got to place my bet of a N1,000,000 which is a lot more than £1,000,000.

Oh yeah, I put my car into auto-drive and the race was on. An overtake on the first corner, that auto-drive works a treat. Oh, past three cars and into 6th, pure skill and swiftly round the next corner. Crash! Someone's down and brought another car with it and into 4th. Zoom into 3rd. What a skid! Into 2nd and it's 1 on 1 to the finish line and turbo knocks in and zooms into 1st and wins. Yippee! I'll collect my money, go to the pub, then go home and nap. See you tomorrow.

Bleep! Bleep! Bleep! 'Big Ears where are you?' There was a laugh, my two brothers were giggling. I was in my own world again. I ran down to get my SATs exam grade marks from the post . . .

Ashley Burgess (11)
Benenden CE Primary School

A Day In The Life Of Teddy

At the end of Melbourne Drive, in the small beige coloured cottage lived Bailey Seven, his younger sister Rosa and their mother, and in Bailey's bedroom was a shelf. I am an old teddy bear and I lie on the shelf.

By no means could you see me hidden behind a pile of old books. I looked at my hands, thick layers of dust cover them and the intense, musty smell was overwhelming.

A shrill of excitement split the air. I heard Bailey bound up the stairs. By this time I had figured out that this meant he had just got a new Action Man or something like that. He hurled through the door and I looked at his hand. A large box was neatly wrapped, though not for long as Bailey ripped off the paper.

He placed a shimmering go-kart on the floor and examined the room for something. 'Small, but big enough to sit at the steering wheel. Aha!' Bailey walked closer to me, his emerald green eyes focused, he picked me up off the shelf. Time stopped, everything frozen around me and I felt like the happiest teddy alive.

As he placed me on the plastic seat, the synthetic seat belts and fake upholstery were fabulous.

I have never felt more loved, more elated, more surprised as I have today. I'm the proud new owner of a silver Mattel go-kart and better known to Bailey as Teddy Schumacher.

Georgia Coxhead (11)
Benenden CE Primary School

A DAY IN THE LIFE OF BULBASAUR

Hello, my name's Bulbasaur and I'm a Pokémon. I'm Ash's favourite Pokémon. I forgot to mention what a Pokémon is. It's a cartoon creature that has these special moves. My best attack is 'solarbeam' which I learnt at Level 65. My favourite time is dinner time because I am let out of my Poké ball and I get some scrummy, yummy bulba beans which enter my tummy. It's fun for me when I'm battling and prancing around places like Ilex and Viridian forest. At the moment my trainer called Ash has got three badges. He has got six Pokémon including me, Pikachu, Squirtle, Charmander, Abra and Pigey.

Now onto the story. I was up against a Weedle when it used poison sting. As I was only Level 17 I used a vine whip. I forced the Weedle to faint as it was super effective. Ash won the battle and I grew to level 18. After that I grew another 7 levels which put me to Level 25 and I learnt Razor Leaf and poison powder. Then Ash defeated the Elite four in supreme style growing all 151 Pokémon to Level 100. After all the trouble, excitement and fun, Ash is the Pokémon champion of the world.

Robert Aldous (10)
Benenden CE Primary School

A DAY IN THE LIFE OF A TATTOOIST

I wake up at 6.00 to open my tattoo shop called 'Carla's Tattoo Parlour'. My first client called Lee Harvet came in and wanted a tattoo saying 'I love Ken'! (I think he must have been drunk the night before.)

Last week Sandy came in wanting her belly button pierced and she came back this morning saying the stud wasn't clean and has now gone septic! (Of course I will have to give her a refund.)

That's now sorted. Now onto the delivery of ink for tattoos and I need to get some more needles. I'll be back soon, just going to the sewing shop down the road, bye.

The ink delivery came to £59.99 for three tubs of blue ink. The sewing shop only had one needle left. There was a big knock, knock on the door, it will be Lisa. She wanted her ear pierced for the seventh time in one ear (she is a pain free girl.)

Now back home to Chelsey, Emma, Matt and Becky and, of course, my husband Paul who will hopefully cook the tea.

That reminds me, Sandy's refund cheque. Hopefully tomorrow will not be like today!

Madeline Dell (11)
Benenden CE Primary School

A DAY IN THE LIFE OF BART SIMPSON

Hi man, how are you doing? Bart here, I'm having the worst day of my life. First I got told off for waking up late, then earlier in school I got beaten up and had my dinner money stolen off me. Still, Homer said he would take me to the arcade after school so that should be quite fun. Tonight there is a film on so that should keep me occupied.

The bell rang and as usual everyone stampeded out of school, as well as me. Everybody ran on the bus as if they had rocket booster shoes on. As soon as I got home I ran to my mum and asked where Homer was. She said he was going to be back late from work. That spoilt my day even more. I asked her what time Homer would be back, she said he would be back around nine o'clock. (That's what time Die Hard starts.) Great, I won't be able to go to the arcade now. I walked into the front room, switched the TV on and plunged myself into the couch, with a grumpy face on. I watched TV. I flicked through the channels until I found a channel with something good on to watch.

James Baldwin (11)
Benenden CE Primary School

THE SQUEEKS

I am a harvest mouse and I live by a railway track, in a wheat field. I live with my husband, Mr Squeek. We live in a nest that I built. I had gathered tall stems of grass and bundled it into a big ball making a lovely cosy nest. This nest would need to be big enough for as many as eight baby mice. I had only been born thirty-five days ago, but I was already thinking about being a mother and having my own children!

Mr Squeek was out searching for food, preparing this for the babies. He was searching for seeds, berries and insects such as grasshoppers, moths and caterpillars. He was taking food back and forth to the nest, he was also getting hungry and looked for the closest flower which wasn't far away. Climbing to the top of the flower and using his tail as an extra limb to balance, Mr Squeek licked the flower's nectar to give himself energy.

Mr Squeek was thinking about me. I would need plenty of energy, not just to make the nest, but also to give birth to our babies and to feed them with my milk. It was going to be hard work because our babies would be blind when they were first born.

Mr Squeek scurried home to me, we were so tired, closing our little black eyes, we went straight to bed in our beautiful nest, that swayed in the wind, rocking us to sleep.

Isobel Hume (11)
Benenden CE Primary School

A Day In The Life Of A Wild Rabbit

I jumped out of my hole and chewed on some wood to clean my teeth. Now for some food. Wait a minute, I forgot something, the tea party! I will be late, but first for a little chase from Mr Fox. Weee, weee, isn't this fun! Okay lost him. To the tea party.

'Good morning Marigold and today we have Tom and Peter Rabbit. So Tom, where's Jerry?
'At home.'
'Oh right!'
'Yum tea, biscuits anyone?'
'Yes please, yum biscuits.'

Two hours later . . .

'Bye Marigold, bye Tom, bye Peter Rabbit. Right, now for another chase. Who is it now? Mr Weesel. I'm so fast for him great, lost him! Now, for supper. I can eat one of the human's lettuces, in we go the cat still fast asleep. Ah nice, juicy, crunchy lettuce, better leave before the humans catch me. We have had a good time but now it's time to say goodbye. Would you like to share this blade of grass with me? No, oh well then more for me. Well goodbye then, it was nice to meet you.

Rebecca Pooley (11)
Benenden CE Primary School

THE NIGHT WE DANCED TILL MIDNIGHT

Today was a very exciting day for me. It was my ballet performance. We were performing Cinderella. My best friend, Jemma, was playing the part of Cinderella and I was the Fairy Godmother. I was extremely nervous. I had to lead a dance. The dance was with Cinderella and the little rats.

It was actually a very easy dance, but the costume I had to wear, yuck. I couldn't even walk, let alone dance in it. Anyway, it was half an hour until the performance Then a horrible thought struck me. The hall would be full. I would be leading a dance; if I got it wrong I would be laughed at forever. I got so scared. I told Jemma. She gave me some good advice. I felt much better.

After what seemed like forever, the time finally came. I went backstage to get my costume on and to do my make-up and then I was ready. My heart started pounding. The music started. I peeped through the curtains. Jemma was dancing on stage.

Five minutes later the dance finished. Next up were the stepmother and the ugly sisters. At the end they had 'boos' from the audience, but everyone wanted to clap. Then, it was my turn. I was so excited but so nervous, in the end I had to be shoved on stage. Then finally the music started. I began dancing around. I was doing it right. I was so proud. I just couldn't believe it! Another achievement completed.

Caiti Walter (9)
Benenden CE Primary School

A DAY IN THE LIFE OF A SPIDER

'Spike, get down!'
'Okay, okay.'
'We're out, we've skived school again.'
Oh, I forgot to introduce myself. I'm Sid and this is my friend Spike.

Suddenly, the school roof got lifted off and a human head peered over. Luckily me and Spike scuttled behind a leaf and managed to avoid intervention by a group of school children. I heard the whistle go in the distance followed by teachers shouting. We crept out and peered around all I saw was the school, then an ant army jumped up and fired their big rifles at me and Spike. We ran and ran and ran until we had lost them, but we were lost ourselves. Spike heard something. We scanned around, after that we gazed up and there was an orange and white rain cloud. 'Poo, this smells. It will attract the flies . . . did I say flies?' Then the rain cloud fell down and a cat unfolded himself. For a split second he looked me right in the eye, then he pounced. We both ducked. It flew over us and into a brick wall. After all of that we heard a buzz, it was the flies. This time we had to run but the flies didn't follow us. We saw teacher and relieved we said 'We won't ever skive school again!'

'OK,' shouted the teacher, 'get into the temporary classroom.'
'What a day!'

Johannes Wolf (9)
Blackboys CE School

A DAY IN THE LIFE OF A SCIENTIST

Welcome to my top secret lab five miles under the ground. Let me introduce myself, I'm Professor Scuagbullonmike (scuag-bull-on-mike) and this is my lab of *horror, ha ha ha! Please come in.

OK, this is my lab of *horror, ha ha ha.* Sorry, I really like saying that. OK about today. I'm sorry about today, it's just an ordinary day for me, not like when the world was being invaded by giant rats with chain saws from the plant of cardboard boxes. It is very boring there, as you can imagine, just a bunch of boxes. All I'm really doing today is checking up on my new discovery on bringing dinosaurs back to life and please don't ask how because it is very complicated.

Now there is something I want to introduce you to, another chemical I have been working on for about two and a half years now . . . smash. Oh no! Sparky, that's my cute little dog, you smashed the hydro-acid chemical, now the whole world will explode and all civilisation will die, no! Oh no, that's the wrong chemical sorry. No, I really do mean it. Oh well, let's get on with the day.

Oh well it has been a very long day but . . . oh no! Sparky you just knocked the chemical through a dimensional port hole. Oh no! It has just landed on someone's head. Oh no! They are mutating into an evil alien slime, the world is doomed!

Jack Worrell (10)
Blackboys CE School

A Day In The Life Of The Statue Of Liberty

Hi, I'm the Statue of Liberty and I'm going to tell you about my day. I start off with a tickling wake-up call from the first few people climbing up me, and a couple of foot pains from annoying children walking all over my feet. Sometimes I don't know why I bother, I could always walk around the city rampaging, causing chaos and havoc. Actually, I think I will - *boom, boom, boom!* Don't worry, that's only my feet. I'm getting a bad tummy ache from the people jiggling inside me.

Before I go back to my place I think I'll just do one thing. Here it is, the Empire State Building - bash, bash, bash! Crash! Well not anymore, that cocky arrogant skyscraper has been my arch rival for years, always bragging about how tall he is. Well, he won't be bragging anymore. Anyway, I better just make sure none of the other skyscrapers will be bragging. Actually, just to be safe I'll destroy all of the buildings too. Oh don't worry, this isn't my normal day. You can't even imagine what goes on in a statue's normal day. But anyway, just remember the words of us Yanks 'Have a nice day!' Oh and Liberty by name takes liberties by nature.

Liberty Paterson (10)
Blackboys CE School

A DAY IN THE LIFE OF CUDDLES THE CAT

Yawn! Oh sorry, I'm Cuddles, Cuddles the cat and I am very sleepy but I have to get up and go outside and do my stuff. Oops! I forgot breakfast, can't miss that. I went upstairs and opened Laura's door. Boing! 'Cuddles get down.'
'Miaow!'
'I'll feed you in a minute. Hold on, I'm coming.'
So we went downstairs and sat in the living room. Oh now where's that food.
'Miaow, miaow!' I purred and rubbed my fur against her leg. My fur went static. She scooped a can of food onto my plate, not the crunchies, no, no! Is she deaf? Oh anyway, I'll just have to eat them, humph!

I forgot to tell you, I like food, sleeping, hunting and scratching.

I walked outside and sharpened my claws on Laura's sun bed. I walked along the path to the forest.
'Squeak, squeak, squeak.' It was coming from the tree hole.
'I've gotcha,' I said skidding on my belly through the rustling leaves. Ouch my head! I banged into the tree, fudge sticks. Oh back home then.

I sat on the couch and watched Sabrina. I like Salem in the show, he's cool. Oh sugar sticks, what happened to the power. It's gone out. Laura came running down the stairs. She tripped on the hairbrush. Ow, crash! I burst out laughing, teehee! Where's the torch? Oh there it is. There's a bit of light.
'Are you all right Cuddles?'
'Miaow!'
'Okay, now let's try and find the power box. Ouch!'

Kelsey Martinez (10)
Blackboys CE School

A Day In The Life Of A Black Panther

Yawn! Oi, get out of my territory. Oh sorry, please forgive me. Let me introduce myself. I'm a shadow cat, as the native's call me, or a black panther in your speech. It's really hot out here in the rainforest, so I come out at night where the cover of darkness acts as my camouflage, as well as my ebony black coat. Anyway, let me tell you about my normal day . . .

I start off by getting up at about 9.00pm to get a drink from the local watering hole. It's a perfect place to hunt usually so I always keep my eyes and ears alert to hear approaching warthog. I'm a loner so I don't have to share my kills with anyone else except scavengers. It's easy to get a good drink, all I have to do is walk up and roar and all the other animals scarper.

After I've finished my drink, it's time to go hunting. The usual prey is capybara (a giant guinea pig.) I have to swim to get at this since they sleep over the other side of the river. It's rather annoying because all the splashing I make usually wakes up at least one who wakes up all the rest. Luckily tonight it worked and I managed to get a semi-adult. After I've killed it I drag the corpse up to my hideout (a hollowed out tree trunk) and eat my fill. After eating I store the kill (which will last me another week) and then settle down for a good day's sleep.

Christopher Dean (10)
Blackboys CE School

A Day In The Life Of An Elephant

Hi! My name is Tusks. I like to carry people on my back because that's what elephants do. I'm big and grey and I like to work for my owner, whose name is Raj. He is not nearly as big as me, so that's why I help him push down trees in the wood. It is fun, really! Normally I would be carrying my owner around but today I took a break so I could tell you about a day in my life.

Okay, where do I start? Oh yes, it was about eight o'clock when I went down to the stream to have a nice, cool bath in the blistering sun. This is a daily routine. I splashed about and sucked water up my trunk and sprayed it all over me, then went back stumping up the hill as I went. It got to about ten o'clock when I was really bored so I went for a walk in the forest. That cheered me up! I walked and walked until I ended up where I started.

'Tusks, Tusks!' Oh no, look it's Raj. Hey, I've been looking for you. Oh I forgot, you can't understand me. Look, I'm coming.

I spent a long time that day with Raj. We played and walked for hours.

Then it came to the end of the day when I went to cool off in the stream once again because it was very hot. Anyway, I better go now, Raj's calling me.

Catherine Dangerfield (9)
Blackboys CE School

A DAY IN THE LIFE OF A POSTMAN

Oh no! 5.30, I'd better get up. Ooops! I forgot to introduce myself. I'm Phil and I am a postman. I'm scared of dogs, *most unfortunately*. I hate my job. Guess why, because of the dogs. Also partly because it's so lonely. I don't see a soul till evening. I'll tell you a little about myself. I've got such a tiny mouth. Also, I've got a tiny green nose with a one inch wart on the end of it. No! I'm not a wizard! I wish I was though. Maybe I could get a new job. Anyway, I must stop nattering now and get onto the next paragraph.

I gobbled my cereal and rushed to work. Uh oh! House number 9, they've got a massive Alsatian. It's barking already, help! I rush up the drive and shove the letters in and ow! What's that? Phew! Now that's over I'll just open the post box. Oh bother, I've got the wrong key. I'll drive back. Got the key now, Eeek! Yes! It's opened, *no post!* After all that, I'm going back to bed.

Oh goodness, I'm starving! I'm going to get a cookie. Crumbs! I must have slept for ages. It's dinner time. Goodbye roast dinner, fish and chips for me. Yawn! I'm tired anyway. I must get the afternoon post done. There were no dogs thankfully. I'm tired. Yawn! Goodnight buddies. Snore, snore, snore, snore!

Gillian Cottingham (10)
Blackboys CE School

A Day In The Life Of A Crab

As usual the normal life of a crab is walking sideways crunching its pincers together, trying to get a shell cracked. The crab hadn't eaten for days.

It was just lying there, doing absolutely nothing, by the sun apart from looking from side to side watching a fish trying to escape from fishing tackle.

The crab had nothing else to do, that was the only thing that interested him, it made him watch for hours till he laughed so much he finally broke the shell. All there was in the shell was a bit of sea water.

The crab finally started to move in the water, just then a massive rock appeared before his eyes - he just walked past, then another rock - he walked past again.

Millions of rocks came this time, the crab climbed up all the rocks. It took the crab ages to climb up them all.

At the last rock the crab could see the sea. After all that a fisherman kept swerving around because a fish was trying to escape.

As soon as the crab got past the fisherman, he finally came to the sea. All the crab wanted was to go to the sea because he was invited to a barbecue. They were having swordfish, the crab's favourite fish. After the barbecue the crab fell down drunk and he never rose again.

Charles Coston (9)
Blackboys CE School

A Day In The Life Of Barney The Cat

Time to sleep for the day zzz zzz zzz zzz

Yawn! Big meanie! Why did he have to wake me up?
Huh! Oh hello, I'm Barney the cat. I hope you like my fur, I heard orange and white is so fashionable.

My sister says I'm fat, but personally I think she's jealous of my long whiskers. Grr! I hate these fleas! I think my flea-collar needs changing.

'Barney, Fluffy! Puss, puss cat food!' a male human says in a high voice. That's what he always says just before he feeds us.
Did I say feed us? *Yahoo!* I love food! Here I come! Chomp, scoff, munch. Now to go hunting.

Shh! Be Quiet! I've just spotted a mouse. Creep up slowly then . . . pounce! Yes, got it! I'll take it into the house to eat. I don't know why humans get mad at me when I leave innards everywhere. I can find nothing tastier than a freshly killed rodent. Yum. Oh look there's Fluffy, I'll just go and spoil her hunting.

'Hey Fluffy look what I caught.'

She's giving me an 'evil' because the mouse she was stalking just ran away.
'Barney! Out!'
Ouch! Cat's don't always land on their feet you know! Oh well. Chomp, scoff, munch. Mmm that was nice. I'll just go inside to find a nice comfy spot. Found one! Time to sleep for the day.

Goodnight. zzz zzz zzz

Luke Chattaway (10)
Blackboys CE School

A DAY IN THE LIFE OF A LIONESS

'Come on Simba!'

Hello, I'm Zera the lioness, I live in the middle of Africa right near the Equator which is really hot. I have twins called Narla and Simba. I want to tell you about today.

I woke up nice and early to a cool summer's day. I woke up early to go and hunt for breakfast, lunch and tea. I went out with the lionesses for the hunt but before I went, my children came out of the cave. They were whining that they wanted to come with me. I had to take them with me otherwise they might run away. I carried them on my back and set off. The twins kept on whining that it was too bumpy on my back and also hot.

It was so hot and the lionesses and I decided we would head for the waterhole. It was quite a long journey down to the waterhole and it took us about half an hour to get there.

When we got there, it was already packed, Simba went down to the edge and a wilderbeast who was next to him was startled by a noise and rose up and started to fall. It was about to fall on Simba. Simba jumped into the water and I rose up and started running towards the edge, I jumped into the water and managed to get Simba out. I carried him on my back and I went back home to put him to bed.

Isobel Chapman (10)
Blackboys CE School

A DAY IN THE LIFE OF A SHOPKEEPER

Boring! Another day at work.

Sorry, I forgot to introduce myself. I am Kelly, a shopkeeper in Brighton. I work at Miss Selfridge and I've worked there for . . . mmm I think it's three years now.

Oh gawd! Look at the time. It's already a quarter past eight and I'm not even dressed. Oh where're the keys for the shop? I never can find them. I hope the new stock's here today, we're running a bit low.

'Hi Kelly'
'Hi Mel, hi Lisa'
'Kelly?'
'Yes Lisa'
'Stock's here.'
'Mel will you help me put this stock away? Lisa can you mind the till?'

I forgot to tell you Lisa and Mel are my shop assistants and I have another one called Amy, but she only works here on Saturdays. It's been a bit quiet and I've been bored.

Oh look it's twelve o'clock, time for a lunch break.
I'd better just go and tell Lisa and Mel that I'm going for lunch and if they want a coffee. I wonder what shall I have for lunch?

That was tasty, I decided to have a salmon salad.
'Mel, Lisa I've got your coffees.'
'Thanks'
'Thank you.'

'Lisa and Mel, you can go and have your lunch as it's very quiet.'

'Hi Mel, Lisa, have a nice time?'
'Yes we did, we went to Starbucks cafe.'

Look at the time, it's only an hour until I'm off work.

'Bye Mel.'
'Bye Lisa.'
'Bye Kelly'
'Bye, bye.'

It's good to be home. I'll have a bath and then go to bed.

Romilly Blakeley (10)
Blackboys CE School

A DAY IN THE LIFE OF A STEWARDESS

Oh help! I'm in the wrong lane. Oh, there is no room in the staff car park I'll have to park in the overflow car park again. Ouch! My stupid high heels, I think I've broken my ankle.

A typical start to a typical day, the next thing I know I'm in the plane pointing out the nearest exits and the captain is saying 'Cabin crew doors to automatic.' We're off!

Once we level out I've got to serve breakfast like I normally do.
'Hello Sir, would you like a salmon starter or straight into a full English breakfast?'

I've just finished serving breakfast and I've spilled someone's tea down Jennifer Lopez's top. Oops! Well never mind.

After a long time of serving people drinks and peanuts. It's time for lunch. I didn't get to serve lunch, instead I had to give the crew their lunch and guess who was in the cockpit? Jennifer Lopez! I gave them their lunch and ran downstairs. We are descending and the captain's saying 'Cabin crew doors to manual.'
Wow! Ouch! We've landed in Israel. Hotel bed . . . here I come!

'Hi Natasha. Do you know where the crew bus is?'
Trust Natasha to know where it is.
Here we are at the Hotel Dackard. My favourite hotel in Israel.
The porter is asking me if these are my bags.
'Yes, they are' I answered.
I've just booked in and I'm going to bed.

That was a typical day for a stewardess.

Evie Broad (10)
Blackboys CE School

A DAY IN THE LIFE OF ELVIS PRESLEY

I am Elvis Presley and I have been asked to give one day of my life to Mr R Day. Well I thought and I decided that I would give a day where I had to do *everything* in one go.

It all started when the President of the United States asked to see me.

'Ah Elvis sit down,' said the President warily. 'Now I've heard that you're quite a hit with Rock'n'Roll.'
'Yeah, that's me!' I replied.
'Well I wondered if you could do a concert for me?'
'No problem, when?'
'Today!'

As I left in my limousine, my face turned more and more grim as I was taken to my estate. At about 7pm I was in my dressing room putting on my white suite. I looked okay on the outside but on the inside . . . I thought this will be bad. Suddenly my thoughts were shattered by someone calling my name.

'Elvis hurry up, you're on now!'
Quickly I gathered up my guitar and waited then I heard it . . .
'And now the king of Rock'n'Roll Elvis Presley.'
Smiling I strode on stage, then a burst of song exploded inside of me and before I knew what I was doing I starting singing 'Since the day I left you!'

Afterwards I felt the same satisfaction I always did when I had had a successful concert.

Richard Day (10)
Bridge & Patrixbourne CE Primary School

A DAY IN THE LIFE OF A GIBBON

A gibbon is a large monkey.

In the morning the male produces a loud musical solo which begins with a 'tuning up' practise so that it can loosen its throat and mouth.

The next stage is alternating by taking turns with the female gibbon. The main part is the great call of the female when the male does hardly anything in the song.

One breed of gibbons is called the Kloss they usually sing separately rather than together when the male does his morning musical he may continued for up to two hours. The females' song is usually shorter but even more impressive. Every three or four days she climbs to the top of a tree using twenty different phrases of song and her great call. There is a great deal of rushing about as she launches herself into the air, ripping off leaves as she goes.

The gibbons' diet is two thirds vegetarian consisting of flowers, buds, shoots and leaves. They have to travel great distances to gather this. The rest of their diet is made up of the occasional insect or other small animals. Fruit provides most of the water they need, but they also lick raindrops or dew from leaves.

In a typical day a gibbon spends about three hours searching for food, some four hours eating and the rest of the time resting, sleeping, grooming, playing and calling.

James Clayson (10)
Bridge & Patrixbourne CE Primary School

A DAY IN THE LIFE OF HARRY POTTER

Harry Potter was woken up at 7am by Aunt Petunia banging on his cupboard. He went downstairs and had dry toast for breakfast. As normal, Uncle Vernon shouted at Harry for doing things wrong and about his owl screeching at night, followed by Dudley, a greedy boy, asking for more food. Uncle Vernon continued to shout at Harry. Dudley's annoying friends would come around later and chase Harry around the house. Then later Harry might sneak into the kitchen and steal some food and hide in his cupboard to eat it.

Later in the day he would go and sit on the garden bench and maybe tease Dudley by saying he was going to turn him into a frog, but he would get told off by Aunt Petunia and be given a whole lot of jobs to do like cleaning the windows, washing the car, mowing the lawn and trimming the flowerbeds, pruning and watering the roses and repainting the garden bench, and those were only some of the jobs he did. Then without having any lunch, he would stop at about 6pm and lay exhausted on the ground thinking of Hogwarts with all its food, his friends and playing Quidditch.

At last he would be called to come in and have tea, not a particularly nice sort of tea, with a slice of toast and a cold tin of soup and a glass of water. Exhausted he would collapse into his cupboard and would fall asleep immediately.

Louis Conradie (10)
Bridge & Patrixbourne CE Primary School

A Day In The Life Of A Rat

I scampered amongst the chicken houses trying to see which one contained the most eggs. I was hungry. I hadn't eaten a thing all day so I expected at least five good eggs, but if not, I wanted lots.

After ten minutes I found a hut containing seven eggs, I was feeling hungrier than ever so I started to nibble through the chicken wire, I was more eager than ever, this was my lucky night.

I bit the last bit of wire and dived inside ready for my meal that I had been waiting hours for. I sprung up on the first egg ready for a feast. I ate for ages and lost track of the time. When the feast was over I crept back towards my heap of garbage loaded with food for my thirty-five young rats who were just starting to enjoy living in the lap of luxury with the hen houses nearby.

Most of my brothers and sisters live near the rubbish dumps and they say it is paradise with all the shelter and all the food.

I would love to live in the city, we would never starve there, not in one hundred years.

It was getting early and I was getting tired, so I scurried home past my sleeping babies to get to my cardboard box, ready for a long day's sleep.

Sophie Masterson (9)
Bridge & Patrixbourne CE Primary School

A Day In The Life Of My Dog Oscar

Hi, my name's Oscar! I'm one and I'm a Tibetan terrier. I am white with black spots.

When I woke up this morning, I heard footsteps down the stairs. Someone opened the door. It was Rachel. I was already up and out of my bed when the door opened, I hid from Rachel and she couldn't find me. I got a nice 'good morning' stroke and then she opened the front door to see if I wanted to go out. I didn't! I just looked at it hoping she'd get the message that I wanted to play, not go out in the garden. Rachel snuggled down on the sofa and watched boring old TV (she always does that on weekend mornings). Jack came downstairs. This was much more promising! Then Jack sat down and ignored me - reading his Beano again!

Daddy then came down and made a big fuss of me, this was more like it. We went off to feed the chickens together and then we went off to the farm. I saw my friends Kate and Rosie, they're Collies. They are much older than I am, but they are my best friends. I annoy them sometimes because I want to play so much. My daddy came to pick me up in the truck and put me in the back, I like this because the wind blows in my face and I can see where I'm going.

I get home exhausted after playing all day with Rosie and Kate.
I want to go home and sleep until it's time for my supper.

Rachel Tapley (10)
Bridge & Patrixbourne CE Primary School

A DAY IN THE LIFE OF A DOLPHIN

A world of water, sapphire blue, diving up and down through the crashing waves squeaking happily. I dive under . . . brightly coloured fish playing around the glowing coral. I see friends and join them swimming and squeaking. I need air. Like a bullet I surface and breath in. I see a boat they used to bring me food now they bring poison.

I warn the others, but where is Mother? I glide through the shimmering ocean but I can't find her. I feel a sudden jolt of the heart. She couldn't be . . . she wasn't . . . I didn't like to think what could have happened to her but she was probably all right. I go on swimming and I decide to go and visit the mermaid, people go to the mermaid to hear her sing. When the mermaid sings, all your worries go away, she also knows everything.

I glide through her cave and see her on her silk bed, she has golden hair, golden eyes and a long glittering tail. I ask her where mother is. She answers in her strange echoing voice 'Your mother is beside Seashell Bay.' So off I swim to Seashell Bay, but when I get there she's in a net. She isn't alive. I stare for a few moments, squeak sadly and dive back down to live my lonely life trying to make it happy again, but I find my wife and children waiting for me and I think that my life isn't so bad after all!

Helen Bell (10)
Bridge & Patrixbourne CE Primary School

A DAY IN THE LIFE OF A LION KING

He woke on a sunny morning in the middle of an African plain and stretched his long body and spread his massive claws in readiness for his day ahead.

The king of the pride was hungry and thirsty and decided to wander down to the water's edge for a drink. He lapped up the cool water for a few minutes until he realised just how starving he was. He hadn't had a decent meal in days. In a month or two there won't be wildlife around to catch and the lake will soon be all dried up and the animals will be off in search of water. He slowly made his way back to the pride and told the lionesses to go and get his food. It was their job after all. He watched as three of them stalked their prey, it was a big juicy zebra who was quietly drinking at the water's edge. Before the zebra knew what had hit him, ten big claws were sticking in its thighs. He kicked and kicked but there were now two of the lionesses on him, each side hanging on for grim death. The blood was pouring out from between the stripes.

The Lion King was watching, drooling, and waiting. They ripped the zebra apart and ate it. Later on in the day, the Lion King yawned, which means that all the pride should go to sleep. So every lion went to sleep.

Harrey Ware (10)
Bridge & Patrixbourne CE Primary School

A Day In The Life Of Farmer Joey

In the morning Farmer Joey got up at 5 o'clock to start work. First he made his breakfast and then he got ready to feed his cattle.

The only problem was Farmer Joey couldn't talk, so he would call his dog by hitting two clogs together and his silky black and white dog would come wagging his tail. Farmer Joey would then make a sign and his black and white shepherd dog would go out and collect his sheep and cows.

Then he would put some food in a bucket and tip it into a big silver tray filled with all sorts of vegetables. Farmer Joey would then go and check on his five pigs.

The pigs just rolled around eating, sleeping, rolling and leaping. This was quite weird for a farmer to see but Farmer Joey just smiled and walked on.

As the day drew on, the sun started to set on the horizon and Farmer Joey knew it was time for his tea. The orange glow wasn't something he always saw, and he watched it for a while until it went down. When the sun had nearly gone, Farmer Joey started to walk home where he fed his dog and fed himself. When he got home, he yawned a big yawn and fell asleep.

James Harvey (10)
Bridge & Patrixbourne CE Primary School

A Day In The Life Of Robin Hood

The horn sounded. This meant trouble. Robin Hood jumped to his feet, grabbed his bow and ran to gather his friends. They made their way to where Little John was standing. He was the lookout. He made sure there was no trouble on the road. Today there was trouble.

Sir Guy of Gisbourne, Robin's enemy was looking for his camp. Sir Guy often did this, but he never found it. When this happened it often meant a fight, so Robin and his men got ready to fight if they needed to. They were all very good fighters.

This time there was a fight and everyone drew their swords and knives or took their bows off their backs. Robin climbed up a tree with his bow and put an arrow in the strings. Back came the strings, he let go and the arrow flew through the air, hitting a bad knight straight in the heart, which killed him.

Will Scarlet, another of Robin's good friends was fighting with his sword. He was fighting against the head knight. Will soon overpowered the knight and he fell down dead. Soon all the baddies were getting very tired and some started to run away. Now only a few of Sir Guy's men were left and he ordered them to run away which they all did. Robin and his men had won the fight.

On the way to camp Robin shot a deer and made a fire back at the camp to roast it on. They had a feast.

Richard Hartland (9)
Bridge & Patrixbourne CE Primary School

A DAY IN THE LIFE OF ALAN SHEARER

Match day, Newcastle are tenth in the league, still in with a chance for a UEFA cup place. I wake up and get dressed in a tracksuit and I go downstairs, have a quick breakfast of cereal, call goodbye to my wife, jump into my Mercedes and I drive off. On the motorway I can see the ground. Fifteen minutes later I'm inside St James' Park and getting changed once more into a Newcastle tracksuit and thirty minutes later we had done our training and the manager was giving us tactics. We had our last warm up outside and then the match was on. We had some good chances and one of them fell to me, a header into a corner. The second half was similar with us winning chances and from strong words from our manager we got two more goals, one from Gary Speed, a great volley from twenty-five yards out. The other team, Middlesborough, put up a fight but when the ball fell to me from a great move involving twenty-two passes and when I got the ball I had a quick instinct to score and I did in a nice way. I put the ball in the top corner and if I may say so myself, it was a good goal. After the match I was really tired and I drove home and had a good rest.

James Mackey (10)
Bridge & Patrixbourne CE Primary School

A DAY IN THE LIFE OF MR PUCKWELL

Mr Puckwell was very worried. He had organised a pet day. More like a stress day. The bell rung. Class 5GB entered the room with fluffy kittens and hair-raising dogs. Then came in Charlie, the smallest quietest boy in class, he was carrying a, oh no! a hairy frightening black, Mr Puckwell's worst nightmare, a spider!

Mr Puckwell started the register, Hannah, there was a rattle and a cackle and the hairy Bertie the spider was out! There was a great rush which ended up as most students standing on chairs and Mr Puckwell standing on the display table of nature and its wonders. Charlie, however was trying to calm the hysterical class down and wasn't doing a very good job. When Mr Puckwell jumped on the display his beautiful wedding ring had fallen off. Bertie had got it on her hairy leg.

Charlie was crawling on the dirty ground trying to catch Bertie. Charlie cornered Bertie, Bertie's beady green eyes were looking straight at Charlie. Nervously Charlie made a quick grab, taking off the ring and giving it proudly to Mr Puckwell. Just then the fat Mrs Wiggle, the headmistress, came in. There were great applauses for Charlie. Mrs Wiggle was stunned when she was told the story. Next assembly Charlie got a medal. He thought to himself, just wait Mr Puckwell, just you wait, pet day will be here again soon!

Sophie Macdonald (10)
Bridge & Patrixbourne CE Primary School

A Day In The Life Of John Lynx

'Ring, ring, ring, ring, ring, ring, ring, ring.'
'Ah please be quiet!'
John Lynx is a chimney sweep, a gambler and a young, full of life, twenty-two year old. He gets woken every day by his alarm clock 'Ring ring!' He struggles out of bed and puts on his doggy slippers. While cooking fresh toast, John Lynx looks for his old scruffy chimney uniform, but as usual fails to find his chimney sweep.
'Oh great where can it be?'
John unexpectedly found it in his room mate's bathroom. He quickly ate his burnt toast and set off to work.

Today he was working at a local chimney and so he could just pop home to get some lunch. It was a dirty and sooty chimney, so John came home covered in black soot after a hard morning's work.
'Right now I have five pounds I can go to the casino and try to win some more!'
He went to the nearby arcade with a hopeful heart picked a reasonable machine and started to gamble . . .

'What! All that money gone just like that, well, no change there.'
He went home to the living room and had a good doze. When he woke, 'You've Been Framed' was on. While he slouched on his sofa he silently drifted into his dreams, hoping tomorrow would be better.

Tiffany Murphy (10)
Bridge & Patrixbourne CE Primary School

A DAY IN THE LIFE OF A BEE

First let me introduce the main character of this story. His name is Bee (that's because he is a bee.) Anyway let's get on with the story. When the sun starts to rise Bee and all the other bees begin to get up from their long night's sleep. The first thing that the bees do is to go out looking for food. They normally go to flowers to get the nectar and that is what they have done today. All the bees try and go for the best looking flowers which is normally the colourful flower. As Bee was flying back to the hive to eat his food, there was a very loud noise behind him. Quickly he spun around to find himself looking at some sort of machine and a very big person pushing it towards him. As fast as he could he sped away with the rest of the bees. In absolute panic hid behind a large bushy oak tree and waited in silence for the big noisy thing to pass by. Then he slowly crept back to his nest. As soon as he got there he told the other bees (by vibrating his silvery wings) what had just happened. All the bees were buzzing with excitement. Soon the word got round to the Queen, but all the Queen said was,

'You silly bees that was just a lawnmower.'

They were so depressed they fell asleep.

David Van Rooyen (9)
Bridge & Patrixbourne CE Primary School

A Day In The Life Of Squadron Leader Ames

Oh not another air raid. There have been so many since I came to the underground hospital here in Dover. The hospital's already cramped. Now isn't it about time for breakfast? When will that nurse bring it, that wretched woman.

'Nurse, could I have some breakfast? Thanks.'

Porridge again. I've had it for the last two weeks. Arghh! The pain where my leg should be.

I see it again, the Messerschmitt behind me. Bang! Down I go. I need to act quickly. My landing gear, it's been destroyed! I will need to crash land, crash land.

'Squadron Leader! Are you alright?'

'Yes, Nurse.'

'Time for your medication.'

She gave me an injection but the pain was nothing compared with my leg being amputated. All I remember is the pain. I was still in my plane . . .

'Doctor! My leg! My leg!'

'Er . . . I think it will have to be amputated. Pass me the chloroform. Thank goodness there is some, and the scalpel. You'll pass out while this is over your nose.'

'Tea, Squadron Leader?'

'What about lunch Nurse?'

'You missed that, I'm afraid.'

The last time I had tea this bad was at the cricket club. Can't wait to play. But my leg. I can't play with one leg. What will I do, in the future? Everyone says take it one day at a time.

Dan Keim (9)
Bridge & Patrixbourne CE Primary School

A DAY IN THE LIFE OF THE DOZY DOG

I wake up early in the morning, have a stretch and yawn. I hear footsteps coming. I get ready to pound and I'm off. I leap on the bed and I lick the adults' faces, then I walk around and with a great thump, I lay down. The grown-ups get bored of me laying on the bed, so they go downstairs. Ahh . . . just as I like it on my own at last, wrapped in this comfy feather nest.

I am woken by voices saying
'Walkies, walkies, time for walkies.'
When I get downstairs I am welcomed by a pat on the back and voices saying
'What a good dog, what a good dog.'
When I get back from my walk I find that the upstairs door is open. I see nobody is looking, so I will just creep upstairs. Nobody will hear me.

I just get to the top of the stairs and I hear
'Come down here, come down here this instant you cheeky dog.'
I go downstairs with my head down as if I was ashamed of myself, but I'm not really. Then I see them standing in the kitchen making a cup of coffee, so I sit patiently for my dinner. About five minutes later I get it. After I have finished it's time for bed. I slowly but surely drift off to sleep and I dream of what tomorrow will bring. I think it will be exciting, don't you? zzzzz . . .

Georgia Pritchard (9)
Bridge & Patrixbourne CE Primary School

A Day In The Life Of A Lizard

It was another hot day at the zoo and another tiring day of sitting in front of glass with people staring at you. In the Californian zoo over one thousand people visited each day and stared at the lizard. Every day the lizard woke up, drank and ate, then he went up to the glass and stared out at all the people who were walking past him.

As he looked out at all the people he saw one who was eating lunch, suddenly a man jumped on the other man and stole the apple which went flying through the air into the glass of the lizard's house.

The lizard thought
'Well he's just made my life better.'
As quick as lightning that lizard ran away.

Later that day he had hopped on a lorry and fallen asleep, little did he know that the lorry was going far from the zoo to the desert where the lizard belonged.

When the lizard woke he was in a barren desert where he belonged, so he jumped off the lorry into the baking heat. When night fell the lizard walked right into a hole with more lizards in it. He thought to himself and said
'I will stay here with all these other lizards.
And so he did. Meanwhile back at the zoo the keeper had a small amount of food, for who?

Jessica Cutter (10)
Bridge & Patrixbourne CE Primary School

A Day In The Life Of Our Cat

If I tap on this window a little bit harder I might just wake them up. Tap, tap, tap . . . It worked, she's opening the curtains and she said good morning. She opens the bedroom door and I run to my cat flap and in I go. She opens the kitchen door and immediately I start to purr and rub her legs and beg for my food. She opens the cupboard door and pulls out a sachet of cat food. Then she puts it in my bowl and I start to pace around her legs and the chairs. She walks to my spot next to the cooker and puts my bowl down. I then race to my bowl and start eating. When I have finished I walk under the kitchen chairs and plod into the hall. Then I go into the lounge and jump on my favourite chair. Mmm a nice sleep I think. So I go to sleep and before I know it the boys are stroking me, so I jab them. I stretch and jump off my chair, race back into the kitchen, fly out of my cat flap and belt straight across the grass and into the hedge. Then I find my boyfriend called Musty. I play with him for about half an hour and when I'm tired I just go back indoors to bed.

Richard Brown (10)
Bridge & Patrixbourne CE Primary School

A Day In A Life Of Mr Corfield

One day a baby was born called Simeon Corfield. He had a great sense of humour and always got Bs in secondary school, so he got a job as a teacher!

The first day back from Easter was super. He quickly got dressed and went down the creaky stairs to breakfast. He was wearing his purple shirt and beige trousers. He dyed his hair blond! He . . . well said goodbye to his children (Daniel and Nathan) and his wife (Alice). He moved to the cupboard to get his books out, gave his family one last kiss, opened the door . . . and hopped into his car.

When he got to school, children were playing. Zoe was skipping, others, hand-stands. He jogged up the brown stairs and went to put his bag and green books down. He trundled over to the board, then handed round the red books. Drr! The bell rang. He walked back to bring his class indoors.

First it was literacy. He was teaching prepositions.

Drr! Playtime! He gave a sigh of relief. He paired up with Mr M and jogged into the staffroom.

Time passed and it was time for maths. 5/SC were learning fractions!

Twelve o'clock, lunch! Mr C had made his own lunch.

Drr! History! Mr C Liked the Victorians best!

When he arrived home, Alice had made tea for the four!

Imogen Higson (9)
Bridge & Patrixbourne CE Primary School

A Day In The Life Of A Rabbit

Hello, my name is Elliot and I will be telling you about a rabbit that had an extremely long journey and narrowly escaped.

Here goes. There was a rabbit called William and he was ten years old. He had a sister called Claire. One day they went out to explore the forest. They were hopping along as they would usually do when suddenly from out of nowhere came a large red fox. He chased after the rabbits excitedly. Then a rabbit ran just in front of the fox and he was getting closer to a tree. Quickly the rabbit got out of the way and then *bang!* The fox had just run straight into a tree. Thankfully William and Claire both managed to escape. When they got back it was past their bedtime. Then their mum said 'I hope you were not attacked by anything.'
'No, we weren't,' said William.

The next day they went out to explore more forest. They came across a large grey fluffy thing. They thought it was something a human had dropped. It was really a badger. He was asleep, but then he woke up and chased after the rabbits. The rabbit was caught but then William bit its ear and the badger ran away. The rabbits were safe.

Elliot Denham (10)
Bridge & Patrixbourne CE Primary School

A Day In The Life Of Florence Nightingale

Every morning I wake up at 6.00am and check on all the patients. I get really depressed, looking at all the poor men fighting for their lives, but I don't show my sadness because it will make them sad.

I wake up all the nurses and we make some healthy breakfast. The men that can walk go to the kitchens and eat their breakfast. The men that can't walk get their breakfast in bed.

After I do the breakfast I go and clean the wards, because if I don't it will cause infection. Then I start to bandage up the wounds, making sure I keep them clean.

More soldiers are arriving with terrible wounds. I help the men bring in the soldiers and put them in comfortable beds and get them clean sheets. I have hired a new chef to cook more appetising and nourishing foods instead of broth (boiled bones). For lunch they have healthy meals. When they start to drift off to sleep I walk through nearly four miles of corridors.

Sometimes I sit with them and watch them die. It never really bothers me watching them die because I see it all the time. After all the checking of the soldiers is done, I sit with them. Sometimes they dictate letters to me that I write down and send to their loved ones.

After all the chores of the day are done I sit in my chair and drift off to sleep.

Kate Jarrett (10)
Bridge & Patrixbourne CE Primary School

A Day In The Life Of Tony Blair

I woke up in my soft comfy feathered bed and went downstairs, to find my darling wife making breakfast. I got dressed in my smart suit and tie ready for my day and saw my children off to school.

I walked out my front door, thinking about why the Queen wanted to see me, and suddenly lights everywhere, I had a flash of cameras shooting at me, asking me questions like 'Why does the queen want to see you?' etc.

My security guards made way through the river-like crowd so I could get through. I climbed into my Limo, and got driven to Buckingham Palace. We drove slowly, for there were crowds of people swarming round my car amazed at what they were seeing.

I finally arrived at Buckingham Palace, we drove through the big gates and into the courtyard. I was sent up to the Queen and told she wished to express her feelings about foot and mouth. When I got to her she said 'Now I don't usually interfere with your government stuff, but I feel you are not making a very good job of stopping foot and mouth so please make it one of your priorities!'

After that I got driven to many different meetings, to try and sort out this terrible problem. When I had finished, I got driven home tired and worn out (to put my feet up) to the smell of my lovely wife making dinner. While eating it we were discussing what I'd have to do tomorrow!

Rose Markes (10)
Bridge & Patrixbourne CE Primary School

DAY IN THE LIFE OF A SEWER RAT

The rat scampers down to the sewers. Gasping for breath, running away from the wild cat, who holds claws as sharp as razors cutting through the strongest metal and teeth as fierce as tigers. The rat harmless, but deadly, enormous teeth, knock-out, soon dead in one bite. Slow, painful death. Sleeping, while over his head the busy city, raging like the enemy, the wild cat purring fiercely and loudly. While the poisonous rodent sleeps he dreams ratty dreams. He dreams of his sleep, his food and his drink, but most of all he dreams of the crazy creature that tries to hunt him down, his deadly arch enemy, the wild cat. Is this a dream or a nightmare? Tossing and turning, the rat can't sleep, through this horrible but extremely realistic nightmare. As the tiny creature sleeps his surroundings are changing. The walls are caving in. The slimy river which the rat drinks from, starts to splash around making the walls wet and weak. While all this is going on the rat remains silent and still. Blackout. Suddenly the sewer rat is in the city. He wakes, he is puzzled. How did he get here? But now there is no time to think. He is faced with his enemy. The deadly, fierce, wild cat. To the cat the chase means nothing, but to the rat the chase means life or death. The race has come to a sudden end. The tired rat remains silent and still.

Hannah Coker (9)
Bridge & Patrixbourne CE Primary School

NOAH'S ISLAND

A day in the life of a monkey called Rocko who lived on an island which belonged to a polar bear called Noah.

Noah has a lot of animals on his island like elephants, ant-eaters, monkeys, tigers and giraffes.

Rocko had learnt to be a healer because there were a lot of poisonous snakes like cobras around. He had to make a lot of potions using trees and leaves in case the other animals were bitten.

One day Noah was walking through the vines and trees when something bit him on the leg and it hurt him a lot. It was Hiss. Hiss *sssaid*
'It's your fault for *ssstepping* on my tail.'
Hiss took Noah to Rocko but Hiss used his most powerful venom so Noah might die and Rocko said that he needs to go to Diamentina to get the magic plant. The vulture squadron flew Rocko over to Diamentina in search of the plant by a waterfall. When they took off they went back as fast as they could go back to the island. When he got back, he turned the plant into a potion and gave it to Noah. The potion woke him up and Rocko saved the day.

Thomas Goodwin (10)
Bridge & Patrixbourne CE Primary School

A DAY IN THE LIFE OF A PONY CALLED STAR

I am Star. I live on a farm with my owner called Suzan. I will run you through what I do in a day. Let's start. Well, first I would wake up and wait until Suzan would come, meanwhile I would eat my hay and drink some water. When she would come, I would look for an apple in her pockets and always found one. She then put on my head collar and led me down to the field along the road, so I could have a run around and eat some grass. After that Suzan would take me back and would get me tacked up with my black saddle and my black leather bridle. We would then go for a long ride around our village and back again. She would untack me, take off my black saddle and my black leather bridle. Then she would put on my rug and my head collar and she would take me down to the field, along the road and let me graze in the field. After that she would take me home and groom me with my body brush, my dandy brush, my curvy comb, my face brush, my hoof brush, my hoof pick and she'd brush out my mane. Then she'd put me in my stable, give me some fresh water and a bowl of pony mix, then kiss me good night. To show I loved her I would nuzzle her arm and when she was going I would neigh because I wanted her to come back to me for one more kiss.

Suzanna Hewitt (10)
Bridge & Patrixbourne CE Primary School

A DAY IN THE LIFE OF A POP STAR - KASSEY BROWN

I woke up at 5.30, my alarm clock buzzing in my ear. I stretched my arms after a night of sleep. I heard footsteps coming from the hallway.
'Come on Kassey, get up and get dressed,' shouted my mother flying my wardrobe door open.
I had to go to a photo shoot with my manager, Nick. I put on my clothes and went out. I'm one of the most famous pop stars in England.

When we got there Nick said 'Go through that door, your fans will not see you and the children are waiting.'
The children were three comp winners of a show hosted by Sam Jeny.

When I got through the door there they were, Jill, Suzy and Ben eating toast. They ran up to me and asked for my autograph and gave me some toast.

The photographs were taken by a famous photographer called Terry Hagan. I had some taken with Suzy, Ben and Jill. After that we went to a recording studio in London. Jill, Suzy and Ben all went with me to record a song for Comic Relief. The music producer was called John. We sang lots of songs then went to a restaurant. After that we went shopping in Harrods, Jill bought a dress, Suzy bought a couple of dresses and Ben bought boy things. I bought everyone a necklace and Ben a big bag of sweets.

We dropped all of them off at nine and I went straight home to bed.

Sophie Pritchard (9)
Bridge & Patrixbourne CE Primary School

A DAY IN THE LIFE OF A GUINEA PIG

In the mornings my cage is covered up with a blanket. I wait for my owner to uncover me. Finally my owner comes to uncover me and takes out my food dishes. I make a funny noise because I am hungry then I hear my owner's footsteps coming to give me my food. She puts my dishes into my cage then shuts it. I gobble down my dinner.

Then I have a rest. Then my owner comes to my cage and picks me up and gives me a cuddle. Then after a little while my owner takes me back up to my cage and puts me away. I don't want to go away but I have to. I bite my owner's arm but she still doesn't take any notice of me. Slam! She shuts the cage door. I go to my water bottle to have a drink. It is nice and refreshing. Then I go into my hay. Then something fell off the shelf. Then I hear my owners coming up the stairs to go to bed. They come up to bed and give me a handful of food and cover me up. I eat all of my food and then I go to my hay and snuggle up and go to sleep.

Zoe Anderson (10)
Bridge & Patrixbourne CE Primary School

A Day In The Life Of An Actor

First, I have to get up early in the morning to get to rehearsals in time. Once I am there, I go straight to the dressing room to get changed and maybe put a bit of something on my face if I need it, (nothing *too* dramatic!) After I have finished in the dressing room, I would normally go to the director for him to tell me when we will be practising my performing parts unless I am told to do something different.

While I am waiting to go on stage I would probably either practise my lines or watch the people on stage. And after that, when I'm on stage; you can guess what I do . . . act! After I have finished all of my parts on stage then the director would tell us how well we did and what needs improving and other things like that.

After that we go right through the whole performance from the start, right through to the end. After we have finished the performance then we are allowed to go back to the dressing room to get changed back into our ordinary clothes and to take off our make-up if we have any on. We then say goodbye to the director, (if we are polite) and then go back home. We don't get back too late; it's normally about six or seven o'clock on ordinary days. By then, you are usually sleepy, exhausted and tired so you go to bed. Goodnight!

Ben Bostock (9)
Bridge & Patrixbourne CE Primary School

MRS PEYTON RANDOLF!

A lady from Colonial Williamsburg, Virginia, 1720, Mrs Peyton Randolf was woken by her maid, Emily. Emily was a slave girl who had been with the Randolfs since her birth. It was very hot! She sat on the side of the bed and chose a lovely dress out of the three which Emily had brought over. It was pink satin with white lace frills. She put on her pearl necklace which Mr Randolf gave her and some long white gloves. Hanging from her arm was a silk pull up bag. She went over to her dressing table and Emily did her hair, then she put on her lace cap and went to breakfast. Then she went to the kitchen and checked the menu for lunch with the cook, Hannah.

She went out for a small walk to talk about a poor family and what to do with their thirteen children. When she came home she sat down to a six course meal with Mr Randolf. Then she went shopping and met Mrs Wythe and they went walking and shopping. She was very glad she had put on her wide brimmed hat to keep the sun off her skin around Williamsburg. When she came home she sat in the parlour and rested, then had the leftovers from lunch and then feeling tired she called Emily to get her undressed and into her nightie, then she got into bed and went to sleep!

Bryony Morgan (10)
Bridge & Patrixbourne CE Primary School

A Day In The Life Of A Spider

One day I was spotted by a frog. He jumped on top of me but I laid him out for good, or not. I knew he would be back to hunt me down and chew me up. So I made a huge web in a tree watching over the pond. I was extremely careful with my footsteps or else it could be my last. There he was. I pushed him in the grubby pond of mud. I ran to escape from the beast that calls himself the frog the king of the playground for frogs. It was a very daft thing to do because I made him very mad and very very very fast which isn't good. That very evening he was on my tail or should I say hot on my web. He saw my leg sticking out. I didn't realise that I lost my leg. That freak will pay for this. A few minutes later I felt someone following me. I stopped, looked around and carried on walking on and on and on until he appeared. I ran and ran and saw a tin can and a cat. I ran through the tin and cat gobbled up the frog.

Luke M Clements (11)
Bronte School

A Day In The Life Of A Mouse

I woke up, got to my feet and looked out of my hole, I jumped in fright. I saw a cat walk past my hole.

I crept up to the entrance, I saw the cat in the next room, so I ran to the kitchen, horrified the cat might see me.

I went into the kitchen to look for food. Luckily there was some cheese by the oven. I ran to it and ate it as quick as I could. Once I had finished I tiptoed back to my hole.

As I turned round the corner, I saw the cat, I crept up to the cat and bit its tail. The cat chased me but I hid. The cat soon found me and we were on the run again.

The cat chased me into the lounge where I hid under a rug. The cat could not find me, so I crept round behind it, swung my tail and hit it, then ran. I ran into my hole. *Bang!* The cat hit its head on the wall and was dead behind me. I was still horrified to move.

After a couple of minutes I was fine, and was able to move round the house without feeling scared.

Nicholas May (11)
Bronte School

A Day In The Life Of My Dog

My dog is called Timothy. He lives with me and my family and animals. I have decided to spend a day as my dog Timothy. Timothy is a Yorkshire Terrier, he was born in a magnificent city called England. He had a mum and dad who were as big as he was. He also had lots of brothers and sisters.

Every day Timothy would wake up and stretch, then slowly clambering out of his cosy, fluffy basket and would scamper over to his watering dish in the corner under the counter, by the bins. Then not long after he had taken stock of his surroundings, he would be scooped up by two enormous, muscular hands and gently placed in the great outdoors.

Out in the outdoors Timothy would feel free, more free than he had ever been. Out here he could chase after tiny sparrows, sniff the tortoises and chase his tail. Until he heard a kind voice call his name. Then he would run as fast as his legs could carry him to the door, take one last sniff and leap the step and onto the kitchen floor.

Here he would lay and watch the morning bustle of his family. After things went boring and quiet, Timothy would carelessly follow anyone or thing that moved and breathed until he got tired of watching soles of people's feet. Then he would trot into my bedroom and play with any socks which were slung anywhere.

Then after his long day of work and play, he would jump onto a bed or armchair and crawl into someone's arms and lay his head down, listening to voices, or music. He would then be carried to the very place where he started his day. I hope you enjoyed hearing the tale of my dog Timothy.

Karl Williams (10)
Bronte School

A Day In The Life Of A Golden Eagle

The warm, later spring sun was warming my feathers as I sat on the cliff edge preparing a nest for my young. It had been a long, cold, wet winter in the Highlands of Scotland, for us golden eagles.

My long, brown and golden feathers rest and my big, round, brown eyes, set on the ground and sky, watching for prey. My hooked beak was longing for something to grab onto. My claws gripped the edge of the cliff. Then, out in the sunset I saw something scurrying along the floor. I swooped silently, the prey scrambled into the bushes and out of sight, but not quite. A tail was trailing out of the bush. I dived sharply into the leaves. My favourite a big, fat, juicy mouse. I gobbled him up in one big gulp. My other favourite food are voles, birds, mice and lots more.

This year is really important to me. This year is my first year as a mummy. I've got to practise getting the right food for the babies and protect them thoroughly. I'm making my nest out of twigs, moss and dirt. I'm three years old and my partner was killed in a fight, so I've got to handle everything on my own.

It's tough, but I'll cope.

Roberta Jarvis (10)
Bronte School

A Day In The Life Of A Snake

Morning came and I woke searching for food. I saw a squirrel eating nuts. I struck it with my fangs and injected venom into it. It slowly ran away from me but then it died by the venom. I then swallowed it whole. Then I went to find some more. I slid along the path searching for squirrels. It was very quiet. The trees were silent, afraid of my presence. I had found my prey. As quick as a blink I had already struck the poor rat. After I had eaten that I went back up my tree.

The type of snake I am is a green mamba.

I had a rest for an hour then I heard a loud noise. I went down to see what it was. A big grey African elephant stood just in front of me. I slid along as quickly as possible. It was right behind me. I went into a hole and escaped.

The elephant went away and when I came out of the hole it was out of sight. I went out to find some more food. The place was deserted. There were not any rats or even squirrels. There were no lizards either. But then I saw a small gecko lizard. I sneaked up on it from behind and bit it. My fangs dug right into it, then I swallowed it. I had my dinner.

I went back to my tree and slept till morning.

Gary Shergill (10)
Bronte School

A DAY IN THE LIFE OF NEIL ARMSTRONG

At six o'clock the alarm clock rang and Neil Armstrong woke up to find out in the post if he had been chosen in ten months time to become and passed his test to be an astronaut. That meant that he would have to start his hard training today.

He jumped into his car and started to drive to the NASA station where he would begin his training. When he arrived there he saw Roger Moore the training instructor coming towards him. Roger talked about what times he would have to do written work and which times he would have to meet himself in the NASA space rocket Apollo II.

Neil first had to study a giant book about the space rocket and it took him hours to study the whole book. He then had to learn about the thousand buttons which would surround Buzz Aldrin, Michael Collins and himself.

Neil then came home to tell his family and kids about what he had to learn and that he would try hard to be the first man to touch foot on the moon. This would give him great fame and make him very rich.

He still had to do a lot of training in those ten months and he couldn't sleep at all.

Martin Verga (11)
Bronte School

THE DAY IN THE LIFE OF A DOG

Hello, my name is Snoopy, and I am a Labrador. I live in a little house with an old man who needs me as a guide dog. I like staying with him and he takes care of me. At 8.00am he wakes up, then he has breakfast and so do I. At 9.00am we go shopping at the town centre and he uses me as a guide dog. We later go to the park where I like playing.

My owner is very kind and is like a father. He feeds me and strokes me and I do the same for him. In the afternoons, he takes a nap while I watch the television (he always turns it on for me). He always sleeps like a baby, and I don't turn the television too loud. My favourite programme is 'Woof'. In the evenings I don't do much. My master has tea and gives me dog biscuits which I love very much. Sometimes I go to some children's house to play with them.

When it is time for dinner I bark three times which means time for dinner. He usually has roast turkey, and smoked ham and juice while I have guess what? Dog biscuits. When it is time to eat (I mean sleep) he tells me goodnight. I love living with my master because he is so caring and that is the day in the life of me.

Ritwick Ghosh (11)
Bronte School

LUCKY ESCAPE

The siren wailed and I leapt to my feet. I ran to my aircraft which was sitting on the tarmac ready for take-off. I jumped into my tiny cockpit and started to taxi out onto the runway. Then I pulled the lever slowly back into my stomach and gradually rose into the pale grey sky tinted with the rays of the early morning sun.

As I approached the enemy lines, the anti aircraft guns started to blast great quantities of shells at my Sopwith Camel. I had to climb higher to avoid the ever closer shells. Then I spotted five German Albatrosses coming towards me firing bullets. I automatically jerked back the lever and soared upwards narrowly missing them. I shot back and miraculously hit one of the Albatrosses on the propeller which made it spin earthwards hitting the ground with a huge bang.

I shot down two more planes but somehow the leading plane got behind me and began destroying my fuselage. I lost control of my plane and spiralled down to earth but luckily landed safely on my wheels. I bumped over the field and just came to a halt centimetres before hitting a tree.

I struggled out of my cockpit and set my plane alight but I couldn't get very far away because my ankle had twisted as I fell from my cockpit. As the German soldiers advanced my friend George dived out of the sky and shot at them.
'Quick,' he shouted, 'hop on board.'
So I scrambled on his wing and held onto the struts as he lifted the nose of the plane skywards. What a lucky escape I had that day!

Christopher Ramsay (11)
Bronte School

A Day In The Life Of A Show Dolphin

The sun is starting to appear and my trainer, John, should be here soon with brightly coloured buckets which contain my breakfast.

The sun is shining brightly into the crystal clear waters. The spectators are starting to arrive so it must be nearly time for my performance. I'm just going to have a little peep above the water to see all the people. The crowds are gasping as I jump out of the cool water and dive back in.

I see John out of the corner of my eye with his buckets which surely must contain fish treats. Oh look, John's calling me over, it must be nearly time to start. I'm a bit worried in case I do something wrong and disappoint the children.

John has just signalled for me to do a turning jumping dive and I'm tearing from one end of the pool to the other for the jump. I'm hoping everything will go right. Here I go . . . *splash!* Yes I've done it! and all the crowds are cheering.

I finished the show and didn't make one mistake. Now I can relax in the cool waters of my home under the blazing sun.

Here comes lunch, I'm starving. I've got my next show soon so I'd better hurry up.

I'm about to do my final jump, the hoop jump. I'm going to try my hardest to do this jump as it is extremely hard. The whistle goes and I soar through the air and through the hoop. The crowd cheers as I hit the water and receive my reward.

It's getting late now so I must go to sleep as I will have a busy day tomorrow.

Zoe Percy (11)
Bronte School

A Day In The Life Of A Horse

I was minding my own business and all of a sudden everyone wanted to ride me.

My name is Hippy the horse. One person who weighed eleven stone, jumped on my poor little back. I was gasping for air when he flattened me. Someone else leapt onto me and kicked my leg at a very fast speed. 'Neeaaee . . . !' I cried and went flying down a hill very rapidly. I thought, how dare he kick me that hard. After the ride I went to the vet and they started examining my bruised bone. They wrapped a long comfy bandage round the broken leg. I was in so much pain, but after I was cured by the vet, my owner and I went home and had a snack. Then we went to bed.

Adam Skopila (10)
Bronte School

A DAY IN THE LIFE OF A RAT

I am a rat. It is hard when a cat is about, it has large claws which are very sharp, frightening things. Mean eyes and a dirty grin on his face.

We rats normally live in the sewers or streets. We love the stinky smell. In the sewers or the street are smelly welly stink and things. The streets are good to find food, especially in the junkyards and bins.

Some rats try to get in human houses to make a home. It is dangerous, most rats do not escape, but me, I live in the busy streets, finding drink and food, sleeping in a hole, chasing my brother and learning how to get about. By the way, humans can be frightened of us, but we think they are the threat. Lots of people call us mice, but we're not!

I am a brown rat. I find it hard to escape from owls normally. Sometimes they chase us, but mostly chase the mice that lurk about.

I hate being a rat. It's hard to get about. I wonder why humans are so unkind to me and my family? All we do is sleep most of the time. I'm the fast one in my family. A rat's life is very difficult compared to a human's life!

Paramdeep Bhatti (10)
Bronte School

A Day In The Life Of A Squirrel

'Oh, it's so cold up here,' thought Squiggles. 'Where did I put those nuts for my breakfast? I will go and find them.' So off Squiggles went to find his nuts. 'Oh, I remember now, they are by that big oak tree.'

He started to dig but all he found were worms and then Squiggles eventually found his nuts. He carried them to his house and started to break and eat them. 'Yum, now I feel much warmer. What shall I do now? I know, I will go to the orchard to see what the people have left for me to go and hide.'

So off he scurried to the orchard and hid behind a bush, but some children saw him and ran towards him. 'Oh no, I must run, but not home because they will find where I live and where I leave my food and I won't have anything for breakfast tomorrow.' So he ran over the fence and into the nearest field. I must get home before it turns cold. So off he went to his cosy hole in the tree. 'I am getting very sleepy, the sky is getting very dark. I am going to go for my night run from tree to tree before it rains and then go to sleep.' So off he went, jumping from tree to tree. 'I am tired after all that exercise, I am going back home.' He went back home and laid in his tiny, comfortable bed and fell asleep. 'Goodnight everyone.'

Hannah Russell (11)
Bronte School

A Day In The Life Of A Baby

Hi. I'm Gursharan Dio. I'm eight months old. I'm so smart, in fact I'm smarter than my parents. Most people think that being a baby is the best thing to be, because it's all play and no work, but people smother me with toys and kisses and disgusting baby food. But I have to pretend to like it so I don't hurt their feelings. Also, if I could tell them, they would go away.

I'm playing with a noisy car and crawling around. The door bell rings and Mum opens it. Oh no, my aunty is here! She gives me huge kisses and it's horrible. She comes up to me and gets my cheeks and squeezes them and gives me a horrible kiss. Luckily my mum says it is my nap time, so she takes me upstairs. I fall asleep. I'm not tired, I am just bored with looking at the ceiling.

Soon after, I am awake again. My aunty has gone. Mum starts giving me some food. It is mashed bananas again. My mum gets it all over me. After, my dad gets my teddy bear and we play peek-a-boo. Boring!

Mum and Dad take me up to bed. My mum sings me a lullaby while I look up at my mobile. That has music and teddy bears on it. Soon, Mum leaves the room.
'Ga, ga, goo.'
Who says babies can't talk?

Gursharan Dio (11)
Bronte School

A DAY IN THE LIFE OF FRANK BRUNO

The day starts when I gaze up at the pictures above my bed. After that, I stroll downstairs to have my breakfast, then I do my morning workouts before going on my jog around the back lane. After that, the time is twelve o'clock. Then I think to myself, 'I have got a fight in six weeks.' At one o'clock, I set off towards the boxing ring, then when I get there I start practising for the match. Then I have a drink and something to eat. I have to stay here for six weeks to get used to the heat, also the lights. Then I have a rest till I have my dinner.

Gavin Smeed (10)
Brookland CE Primary School

A DAY IN THE LIFE OF MRS SWIFT (MY TEACHER)

On one scorching hot Wednesday morning I woke up and thought to myself, 'What grief will I have from the children today then?' I was meant to be at school by now. I usually leave around half-past seven. I was late.

I raced out of bed and started to get everything sorted. At the same time, I was trying to get dressed, brush my teeth and have some toast. Finally, by half-past eight I was ready to leave. I went out of the house closing the door behind me. I jumped into my car and set off for work.

When I got to school, Mrs Hill had a go at me for being late. I had to make up an excuse. In the end, I just said the first thing that popped into my head, which was, 'Well, I didn't have em . . . a, em, tooth brush and em . . . I didn't want to come to school with dirty teeth, so em . . . I went to the shops and got one.' Mrs Hill was not impressed. I walked slowly to my class. They were waiting for me, I was teaching them fractions. Then it was break.

In the staffroom, we had a right laugh, while Miss Adams was stuffing her face with chocolates. The bell rang.

The next lesson I was teaching was English and the children had to write a poem. Then there was lunch. There was three hours left. It was hometime in no time.

Sophie Tomlin (10)
Brookland CE Primary School

A Day In The Life Of Mrs Swift

I woke up at 8 o'clock, I was rushing around because my alarm went off at 8 o'clock, when it was meant to go off at 6 o'clock. I'm normally at school by now. I looked at my clothes. I couldn't choose, so I picked my daisy dress and a white cardigan. I arrived at school at 8:30. I made toast then started planning today's history lesson with Class 4. I thought, 'Wonder if the Year 6 will give me any grief?' The school bell went. I saw Michael talking in line, so I said to Mrs Jones, 'Michael has five minutes at play time,' and I walked with my books to maths. They were doing decimals and fractions.

I started marking Class 2's RE and History. When the bell went, Mrs Macafer wanted a word with the girls, so they stayed in while the boys went out to play. I went to the staffroom for herbal tea. I spoke to Miss Adams about Michael's behaviour towards the teachers.

During English, I stayed in the staffroom marking homework. Time flew by, then the bell made me jump. Miss Adams came in and we had a roll each and watched the children play. Mrs Eastwood said, 'I will have Class 4 this afternoon.' I gave her my plan. I helped Mrs Giles in the office. Time flew by, it was 4 o'clock. I went to the gym to work out till 7 o'clock, then went home to start all over again.

Jodie Finn (11)
Brookland CE Primary School

A Day In The Life Of Britney Spears!

I leapt up and mumbled to myself, 'This is not my bedroom (too tidy) or my body.' Looking puzzled, I looked around. I was in a posh hotel! I jumped off my (or should I say someone's) bed and in a second, I was in front of a mirror . . .

'This is not my face, but the face of *Britney Spears!*' I shouted in surprise.

Suddenly, the doors pushed open and in came a strange man in a suit, pushing a trolley marked at the side 'Breakfast Trolley' and sure enough, there was breakfast laid on top the trolley. The mouth of the man opened and he said, 'Hope you are ready, Britney Spears.'
'For what?' I replied.
'Your trip into town,' he said. 'Now then, your bodyguard is waiting, so hurry up.'

I told him to leave while I got changed and ate my breakfast, so he left. I thought that I might as well enjoy the day. I found my way through the enormous hotel to the bodyguard and we climbed into the limo. We reached town and gazed around and I asked the driver, 'Is this France?'
'Yes,' he replied.
I sat back, thinking, 'I am in France.'
After about half an hour, we stopped. The driver stepped out of the limo and opened my door and we stepped out and went shopping. Then, for a treat, we had ice cream. I started choking and closed my eyes. I opened my eyes again, I was back! Was it a dream?

Daisy Hannon (10)
Brookland CE Primary School

BMXING

On Sunday, I had to get to the BMX race in half and hour because the time was 8 o'clock. I went to have a wash. Before I had my breakfast, I put my BMX bike on my trailer. I got in my car and went, it took fifteen minutes. I got there first and I looked at a letter, it was about the race. The time was 10 o'clock. I went to look at my BMX bike. 'It's raining,' I said, so I covered my BMX bike and I got into my car and waited for an hour and ten minutes. One hour went and the sun came out and the others came to set up and make sure the track was not too wet, but you can't go ninety miles an hour. The race was gong to start, so the drivers went to the start line. I was on my last lap and I came first. The race finished and the racers went home. I had thirty minutes till my favourite TV programme and I got home in time. The programme finished at 11 o'clock, so I had a wash and then I went to bed.

Oliver Finn (9)
Brookland CE Primary School

A DAY IN THE LIFE OF TONY HAWK

Tony woke up with a start. Today was his first competition. 'Waiter, make me some breakfast while I have a shower,' ordered Tony.
'OK, Master.'
He had a nice, refreshing shower and the breakfast was laid on the unmade bed.
'Thanks,' said Tony in a tone of ingratitude. There were two slices of burnt toast, they looked like charcoal. Once he had gulped down his breakfast, it was time to get dressed, so he put on his pair of black combat jeans and his greyish, whitish T-shirt which had 'Birdhouse' in red writing. Birdhouse had sponsored Tony since he had mastered the art of skateboarding.

After he had got dressed, he went down into the garage. 'What board should I choose?' Tony had ten skateboards to choose from, so he chose the Ed Birdhouse board with white wheels, even though they were his unlucky wheels, but they made a good combination together.
'Tony,' called the waiter, 'it's time to go now.'
'OK,' said Tony with excitement. 'What car shall I take?' Tony muttered to himself.

Tony decided to take his Porsche, which cost him £1,000,000, but he didn't care because he was a millionaire. The phone rang, it was the announcer. He said, 'Get your butt down here now Tony, the crowd want you badly. All I can hear is 'Tony, Tony, Tony!''
'OK, I'm coming,' and he dropped the phone as if it was a poisonous spider. Tony was there in five minutes.

'Alright, Andrew my man.' Andrew Reynolds was a skateboarder too. He had liked Andrew since he had done his first ever run in a ramp. It was Tony's favourite series. 'Heaven is a half pipe.' Tony stepped into a half pipe. He picked up speed and pulled a 720° Madonna.
'Amazing,' said the commentator.
Then he made his finishing move, 900° kick-up to Indy, and Tony won the competition and celebrated with Andrew all night long.

Michael Constable (11)
Brookland CE Primary School

A Day In The Life Of Harry Potter

In the morning, I wake up and reach for my glasses. I hear Neville's loud snores. My best friend, Ron, is slipping on his jet-black robes and tidying up his red hair (even though it's always a complete mess.) I slipped on my robes, said good morning to Ron and headed for the great hall.

Hermione was at the Gryffindor table. I looked up at the enchanted ceiling and saw the clouds moving across the sunlit sky, glowing in the golden sun. 'Morning, boys,' said Hermione, 'How are you?'
'Fine thanks,' said Ron. At that moment, a huge flock of owls soared into the great hall. Hedwig landed on my shoulder, holding out her leg. It was a letter from Sirius and it read . . .

> Harry,
> Fantastic Quidditch match. Dumbledore kindly let
> me watch the game. Can't wait to see you play
> again, how you glide across the sky dodging the
> bulgers.
> Please send next Hogsmede dates.
>
> Sirius.

'Harry,' cried Ron.
'What?' I said.
'Quidditch!' roared Ron.
Within a flash, I dashed out of the hall, summoned my new Firebolt and straight into the arena. Oliver Wood (our coach) was there talking to the team. 'Harry, nice of you to join us!' said Oliver.

Quidditch practice over, first lesson Potions. Professor Snape. Detention again. Dinner, fantastic roast. Next lesson Herbology, Professor Snape. Greenhouse blew up.

Dinner in the great hall - a choice of Pumpkin Pie, Frogs Legs, Roast Leg of Lamb and Chicken Pie. Dumbledore sent us to bed by finishing off with a speech.

'What a day,' I said.

Devan Johnson (11)
Brookland CE Primary School

A DAY IN THE LIFE OF A TEACHER

The day starts out like every day. The teachers are wondering who is going to give them a good day and who is going to give them a bad day. They get into their new, shining, silver cars and they have to get through the London traffic, which is terrible for the drivers. The teachers have to get to school, but they are late again because of the traffic. The school they teach at is called Brookshoe School for four to eleven year olds.

My name is Miss Clare Noakes. When I get to school, the time is 9:30 so I am late for my class. The first lesson my class has ICT. ICT is when the children get to find out things on the computers. If they have been good, they get to play games, but if they haven't, they don't do anything but sit there. We will go into the next lesson now, which is maths. In maths we have to listen to the teacher who tells us what to do. If we get stuck, they will help us by making the sum easier, but they do not tell us the answer. If different people get stuck on the same question, the teacher will go through it at the end of the lesson to help us understand it more. The next lesson is English and in English, we write stories. The last lesson we have is PE. Thank you for the day.

Janet Noakes (10)
Brookland CE Primary School

A Day In The Life Of Hannah From S Club 7

Hi, I'm Hannah and I am twenty-four and I'm dying to get to the sun, sea and surfboarding. Every morning, I wake up trying to pick what to wear, like summer dresses, crop tops and shorts. I'm wearing a pair of shorts and a crop top. I haven't the slightest idea what they are wearing. I'm going to Los Angeles (known as LA) to film our new TV series called 'LA Seven.' We're there finally and I wanted to go straight to the pool, but I couldn't. We had to film the first shot of 'LA Seven'. I told the director to tell the producer to tell the stylist to put tons of make-up on me, to make me look hot! I had to put water on my face to stop it from itching. It was a scorching hot day and after we had shot the first part of the first programme, we were working in Miami, but we changed. I hit the pool really quickly to cool off. In the night, the band go and perform our songs in the restaurant called 'LA Seven', The band's favourite songs are 'Stand By You', 'Don't Stop Moving' and 'Never Had A Dream Come True.' In the night, we go into the boys' bedroom and play spin-the-bottle. My dare was to kiss Bradley, Jon and Paul all at the same time. It was so embarrassing. I was crying last night because I missed my mum and dad so much, I wanted to go home, but then Rachel and Jo came in to comfort me.

Holly French (9)
Brookland CE Primary School

A Day In The Life Of My Hamster

Hi, I am Salty. Three weeks ago, my owner bought me. Every week he had been down to the shop to see me, until he saved up enough money to buy me. Now we love each other dearly. I have got a daily check-up and here it is:

1. Clean my water bottle once a day.

2. Check for illnesses. He feels my belly for lumps (it tickles!) He feels my tail for wetness, which makes me jump. This is to check for tummy upsets.

3. He checks that I am storing food in my cheeks.

4. He looks for veruccas and mouth ulcers.

5. He has to cut my nails, brush me and also brush my teeth. At the end of all this, I fall asleep.

Anyway, where were we? Oh yes, I am a Siberian hamster and that means that I am a very rare type of hamster, because I am white with black ears. The white body camouflages me in the snow, although I have not quite worked out yet why I have black ears.

Last week, I went on a motorbike. There was a little box on the back made out of perspex, so that I could see where I was going. My owner, Steven, put me in cotton wool, added some food and water and even made a woolly hat for me, then we went down to the shops.

The shopkeeper was really confused with the fact that there was a live hamster in a motorbike helmet!

Steven Gilbert (9)
Brookland CE Primary School

A DAY IN THE LIFE OF A DOG

As I waddle through my own back yard, I run to the front door and wait for my owner to bring me dinner. My owner comes out and looks at me and smiles, my tail is wagging rapidly as I tuck into my feast. He clips the lead onto my collar and takes me for a lovely walk. When we are far into the fields, he lets me loose and I'm like a mad beast. When it is time to go back, I get on the lead and he takes me home. When I get back, I waddle to my bed and have a long rest. I wake up with a shock in my tail. I open my eyes and the farmer's children are home from school. Oh no! They rub my tummy and stroke my head really hard. The farmer tells them to get changed and sort out their lunch boxes. Suckers. I quickly run outside, because I cannot bear children. I hide in my secret hiding place so they will never find me. I lay down and lick myself until I am nice and clean. The farmer's children come out looking for me but they still cannot find me. The unfortunate thing is that I sneezed and they heard me and came over to stroke me. The day has finally come to an end, so I gently stroll in and lay by the burning hot fire. The farmer and his wife finally go to bed.

Ben Ubee (10)
Brookland CE Primary School

A DAY IN THE LIFE OF MY CAT

The continuous dripping of the leaky tap in the kitchen woke me up from my deep slumber on the warm, freshly ironed washing. My owners woke up too when they heard my pitiful miaows and miaows to be fed with a bounty of cat food. After my meal of squashed game, I miaowed again trying to speak their tongues, but with no joy. I was picked up by my neck and was thrown outside in the crisp cold of the morning breeze. After all I've done for them, that's gratitude for you! I lay on the ironing while it's still hot, I scratch sofa legs till they're in tatters, I bring them dead mice and birds as a present, what more do they want? Want me to eat my food from a bowl? Fat chance of that happening!

I went on my daily prowl to see what's happening on the estate. Suddenly, I saw something black fluttering out of the corner of my eye. It was a fat, plump, juicy raven (not a raisin, they're disgusting things, but I was thinking of going vegetarian a month ago, or so) and I was starving hungry. I was getting ready for the kill. My body was flat to the ground, I took aim and pounced. Blood spattered everywhere. My chops were stained with gore and blood. I didn't fancy eating, so I went inside and napped again on the ironing, dreaming of scrambled eggs. I love eggs.

Eleanor Chapman (10)
Brookland CE Primary School

A DAY IN THE LIFE OF A WOOD-ELF ARCHER

I woke suddenly. It was my watch in the magnificent forest of Glothorien. I crept to the side of the talan, picked up my bow and crouched, listening intently. Suddenly, I saw a troop of Orcs marching on the ground. I fitted an arrow to my bow.

'What is it, Ragomar?' whispered Leon.

'Orcs,' I replied quietly.

Arrows whistled from the trees at the Orcs. I fired at who seemed to be the leader. Leon rose and shot at the leader too. I carefully took aim and fired. It hit the leader right between the eyes! The other Orcs fled, some getting hit as they fled. Several elves from surrounding trees jumped down and gave chase silently in their cloaks of Glothorien. Several Trents* also gave chase, their root-like legs stomping up and down, the earth trembling beneath their feet. The birds chirped in the Trents' branches, eating berries. I drew my Elven-Smith** sword, leaped down and gave chase, sprinting after what was left of the foul creatures' company. I saw my sword was bright blue. I caught up with an Orc, which I slashed with my Elven-Smith Orc-hunting sword. Leon followed. My sword glowed bright misty blue with content.

'Ragomar!' came Leon's voice from behind me.

'Yes, Leon,' I replied, turning around.

'These are Orcs from The Shadow Land. The Dark Lord's magic is upon them.'

'I know,' I said with a sigh. 'What I want to know is how he got his hands on Orcs!'

I pulled out cordial and some wafer bread***. Then we sat quietly and ate.

*Trents are tree-men
** Elven swords turn blue when near Orcs
*** Wafer bread is a type of cake

Joshua McLoughlin (9)
Buxted CE School

A Day In The Life Of A Door

Hi, I'm a door. Every day I stand there bored, lonely, that's all I ever am. You need a special card to get through me, otherwise I stand strong and do not give in. No strange people, no smelly boys, no wellies, but don't storm me because it hurts. Come on, I'm getting stiff just standing here and I need some fresh air. This boy keeps kicking and punching me. It really hurts and he might break my glass.

Emily Greenwood (9)
Buxted CE School

A Day In The Life Of A Hair

When I wake up, I am sticking in the air. My owner puts gel on me. It makes me jelly-like and slippery. My owner's brother flicks jam at me, so he washes me and gels me. I go to school with him, the wind blows me. I reach the playground with my owner and someone pulls me and I start to bleed. You might not think that hair bleeds, but it does. I do nothing much all day. I start feeling tired. My owner goes home and watches TV then goes to bed. That night, I fell out of his head and got brushed outside and I made a living on a hare.

Martin Hays-Nowak (10)
Buxted CE School

A Day In The Life Of A Chalk Board

7 o'clock 'til 3:30 and something bright and white and dusty smothers and tickles me in different places, making me short-sighted. Non stop, five days in a row and sometimes at what they say are these 'leak-end' things. I think they mean Saturday and Sunday, but I'm not sure. No one hears me, perhaps they're deaf. They have no love or care for me. I haven't a clue what shape I am or what anyone thinks of me: it's just like they take me for granted, like I will always be there for them. I've heard lots of swearing and rude words in my life, nothing will ever be fun. Why, why was I invented, when I don't have a proper life?

Oh sorry, don't mean to be rude or anything. I learn a lot in my life, seeing as I've been in different classes, different schools even.

Harriet Crawford (9)
Buxted CE School

A CREATURE'S DAY

Don't dislike me. I'm really not that bad. Everyone hates me, even from 8am everyone shies away from me and tries to believe I'm not there, but in a way, I can believe why they do it.

I'm an ugly little thing. I'm a gritcher. Oh, and if you don't know what that is, it's an ugly little green thing that looks like a troll. I'm nocturnal. Well, should be. I'm the only gritcher that wakes up during the day, that makes it even harder to make friends. My days are always terrible, but today was an exception.

I woke up still half-asleep, but today felt different, somehow I felt different. Maybe even happy! Today I was out all day because it was the day when all gritchers stay awake all day to worship our king. Our king lived near a stream. He was called King Minimus. He would bellow, 'Little Skim, little Skim.' I hated it when he called me little, I really wasn't that small.

Today is the day! I'll make new friends and after today, I will be nocturnal. I'll try hard to be like everyone else. Oh no! They are leaving without me. Hey, don't leave me behind! 'Come on Skim!' shouted Kimu. He is the leader. It would be a long walk.

When we got there, we did what we always did - worship him, then go home. But I was normal, just normal.

Tanya Scanlon (9)
Buxted CE School

A DAY IN THE LIFE OF A DOOR

Hi, I'm a door, a lonely little door. Poor old me. I have no one to play with. Oh here they come. You see, I am the door on the rocket Apollo. I heard that I am one hundred feet from the ground level and I hate heights. A good thing is there is no gravity in space. Oh, here comes the countdown. Ten, nine, eight, seven, six, five, four, three, two, one, lift-off! Americans return to space as the Discovery clears the tower. I'm going. Right, we've gone! It is cold. Everyone has been talking about how to get there and how long it will take. Oh no! I am breaking in half. Arrrgh. Wait! They are leaving me behind. No, wait, come back! Oh, now I will never see another doughnut again and I will have been up here ever since. What's a space door's favourite game? Knots and aeroplanes! Er, yes, I know I made it up myself but I have been up here for about fifty years. So boring up here, you don't have anything to do, only play with the intergalactic earthworms and meteors. So very, very boring.

Ellen Wise (9)
Buxted CE School

A Day In The Life Of A GameBoy

Ping! I've been turned on. Yes, I have waited in my case far too long. Somebody's finally bought me, they can play on me for hours and hours, non-stop. Sorry, I forgot to introduce myself, my name is GameBoy Sam. All my other mates are with owners like me. Well, as I was saying, it's my job to tell you what I do in a day. Sometimes my owner flicks the side of me and I spring into life. My owner has got one game, it's called Super Mario. You have to kill evil monsters. It's painful for me when Mario gets hurt. It doesn't hurt him, it hurts me which triggers him to die. Well, about 8:30am he turns me off and goes to school. The whole family disappears till my owner gets home. Today there's a meeting for GameBoys. I've been invited. It's at the Town Hall, well that's where I think it is. It's past the church, across the school field and past the junk yard. By the time I got there at about half-past one, they had started. All of it was boring, but when it came to questions, I asked 'How come I was bought today.'
They said, 'You're lazy.'
I shouted, 'Be quiet GameBoys,' and left the room.
Well, that was that. Uh oh, they'd come home early. I was in trouble. I decided to jump through the letterbox and went to sleep.

Adam Harris (10)
Buxted CE School

A DAY IN THE LIFE OF A SNAIL

I wake up and slither across the lid of my pot and down the wall to my food. I eat for a while; my friends come down the walls to the food too. A big hand comes down and grabs me by my shell and lifts me up.

The hand put me down on a long, cardboard track. There were other snails, but I didn't recognise any of them. I started crawling forwards and then turned and climbed up the wall. The hand grabbed me and put me back on the track. I slithered up the wall and across the top. The wall was rounded at the end so I popped into my shell and rolled down the slope. The hand picked me up and put me on his shoulder. I slithered down his shirt; he pulled me off and put me in my pot. He took out another snail called Vodafone. He left the lid off the pot. I could see a bird circling overhead and warned Phat Slug (another snail) that there was a bird above us. The bird started coming lower and lower. The bird came down, picked me up by my shell. I instantly popped into my shell. I thought if the bird drops me on some stones, I am going to be a slug. Arrrgh! I could feel the wind on the outside of my shell. *Crack!*

David Hall (10)
Buxted CE School

94

A Day In The Life Of A Football

Beeep goes the whistle as my early match starts. I get kicked hard, people don't know that footballs have feelings. The goalkeeper *boots me out* onto the centre of the field. The view to the floor is tremendous and very exciting, then *bang!* Suddenly the lights go out for a minute or two, then the light comes back on again. I see me blasted into the net and then the final whistle blows, then the match is over and I am glad.

Then I had another match.

Beeeep the whistle goes. I have still got another match. I get booted really, really hard! I wonder what they would feel if I went round kicking them? Then *ouch!* I hurt myself. I hit the post and I ache at the end of today I am going to be black and blue.
Ow! Aw! Ouch! I went in the goal and I hit the camera. Suddenly, *beeeeeep* the whistle goes and I said there must be someone up there. Then the moment I have been dreading, the last match of today.
Beeeep the whistle goes. *Ouch!* I was smashed! 5,000,000,000 feet in the air I could see America and my house and then *blast!* I got kicked in the goal.

We had 2 minutes left and then I said I hate this job, then I burst myself! That is the end of my day!

Karl Thompson (10)
Buxted CE School

A Day In The Life Of A Dolphin

Oh you may think all I do is swim, swim and you think my life is fun and sometimes boring. It is quite dangerous because of a game called Shark Slamming but the whole point of it is being dangerous it's like being on a motorbike going two hundred miles an hour. We were swimming one day and met a diver called Oliver Conaboy and he said, 'Why don't you go to a chocolate ride?'

I said, 'What's a chocolate ride?'

Then Oliver Conaboy said, 'It's like a chocolate go kart, do you want to go now or later?

So we said, 'Later.'

So he went awwww doh. Then we had to go on the ride because he really wanted to and he wouldn't shut up, it was like well, I don't know how to describe it, but it was real fun because you fell off the carriage and into this chocolate lake and you were allowed to drink some.

Then we went to get some water chocolate which is like caramel. After we'd eaten it we went on a roller coaster that took an hour and a half. When it had finished we played a game of shark slamming, then we went to sleep.

Ben Hall (9)
Buxted CE School

A DAY IN THE LIFE OF A CHEETAH

Well how do you do folks. Bill's the name. I am a cheetah. I've just woken up and had my breakfast, the remains of a llama I had for my dinner. Here is Africa. It's a desert, no water, no shade, nothing but creatures to eat and long grass to lie in wait to ambush a herd of wildebeest. In the long grass my family and I lie very still and pounce at the last possible moment.

Roar! Sorry, but me and my family are fighting over the meat as we do all the time when we catch a meal.

Sigh! My big brother got the meat. It's hard to get something to eat, if it's as big as a wildebeest if you are on your own. Today we are going to take a break down at the river.

Ah this is the life, lying in the summer sun. Our spots as you call them reflect the sun. The reason we are resting is we have a hard life, catching breakfast, lunch and dinner for a living. It's a hard life. If you think we hunt lions, think again. They're much bigger and fiercer than cheetahs. But we keep an eye on them just in case they attack. They have once, but we're much faster than them and we got away.

Well, see ya, bye. We need to go to bed because the sun's going down.

Oliver Conaboy (10)
Buxted CE School

A Day In The Life Of Laura Little

I woke up late and I quickly got dressed and had breakfast. I kissed my mum and I went to school. When I got to school there was nobody there so I went back home and I shouted at my mum because I was so hot. Steam came blasting out of my ears and I stomped upstairs. I pulled my hair out and when I went down my mum said to me, 'What have you done to your hair?'

I said, 'It fell out.

But Mum said, 'You pulled it out.'

On Friday I went to the hairdressers and the girl said to Mum I had to have a wig and I looked like a clown. Mum laughed at me and I was really embarrassed and my cheeks were going all pinky-red.

Mum said, 'It's time to go home,'

I said, 'Good,' because Mum had said 'When you get home you can have a chocolate cake,' and I said 'Yes, yes.'

The next day I went to school and Tegwen my friend laughed at me and the bell went and we all lined up and I was so embarrassed I wet myself.

Laura Little (9)
Buxted CE School

A Day In The Life Of An Explorer

Crumble, aaaahhhh, ouch, I hate falling ice in Antarctica. Oh well, at least it woke me up. I'd better get going if I want to find that mysterious and gleaming Antarctica jewel, that's the only thing which keeps me trundling through the snow. I have the worst job ever. Whoa, nice polar bear, nice bear, go fetch the snowball. No, well, well, what about this. He's going and so am I. Crunching through the snow again almost twelve hours have gone by and no jewel still. I feel like death rolled up in a ball and in a corner. A storm, oh I wish I was in Jamaica exploring. Ah, lightning and snow, can't walk, snow powerful. Oh no, the bear's back. Go fetch the red lighted candle. Phew, he's taking it. Red candle, aaah, aaaaaah! I just hope he doesn't come back. Aaah, bang! No wonder the bear population is going down. Hey, that's the cave with the jewel. It's dark, I'll give it that. That's a sk . . . sk . . . skeleton and it's human. They weren't lucky as usual, there's ice crystals blocking the way. This looks like a job for dynamite, bang! Forward I go, there's the jewel. It's stuck in the ground, it came out. I'm rich, I'm famous, I'm cold, I'm out of here!

Richard Hammond (11)
Buxted CE School

A DAY IN THE LIFE OF A PENCIL SHARPENER

Hello! I'm the pencil sharpener, I'm in the pencil case which is my house. Oh no, here comes someone else who wants to use me again. I never get a moment's peace. I only get a whole day off at home when someone's left me at home or I've fallen out of someone's pencil case.

One day it did happen, a boy used me and put me down so I scuttled off to hide. I heard someone coming and say, 'Where's that blooming sharpener?' I let him find me and we had a good time sharpening pencils, doing other things. And I will never hide again! No one knows what a life is like for a pencil sharpener. But it's super-dooper, triple super to be a sharpener doing what sharpeners do best, they sharpen, sharpen, sharpen, to make pencils really sharp that is what I do best.

There's a very dear friend of mine called Ruler, she is called Ruler because she is the leader of the pencil case and she has not got a crown so I made her a beautiful crown with paper and ribbon and she is still wearing it. She has a secret place where she hides it, under her pillow and you and me only know where it is, so don't tell anyone. And I was put back in the pencil case.

Lynne Robinson (9)
Buxted CE School

A Day In The Life Of The Letter 'Z'

I woke up in my book when it opened and I was added to zebra and then to size. The book I was written in was slammed shut, squashing me. It was suddenly opened and I was scribbled out. I was being cut out of paper and glued to the wall. I was at the end of a line with twenty six other letters and I was the bright, lime green one. The children were making sounds of different noises of insects and are now doing a bee. I was worked off my feet, me and about thirty other letter 'z's' were added to buzzzz. I've recently been added on the front of the 'zoo' and on the front of the 'zebra's' paddock. A lady was peeling the 'zest' from a lemon to give to a chimp in the enclosure next door. She was talking to a 'zoologist' when she was finished in the primate 'zone'. In the elephant house a large, yellow 'zigzag' line was painted on the wall in the muddy paddock. A mural of the 'zodiac' system by Babbon Hill. Some people say that the 'zoo' caretaker is like a 'zombie' in the early morning shifts.

Daniel Holliday (10)
Cliffe Woods Primary School

A DAY IN THE LIFE OF A FRONT DOOR MAT

Oh no, what's the time. Oh my God, it's the morning, here comes the postman. Ow, he always dumps the heavy load right on top of my head. I wish he was a front door mat, so I could dump the heavy post right on top of his head then he'll see what it's like. Eventually they've lifted the heavy post off my head. About an hour later the children are going to school and they all run out the door at the same time. Ow, ow, ow, ow, ow, then after them comes their mum with the bags and while she shuts the door she drops the bags on my head and stands on me and shuts the door. Half an hour later Dad comes out with his heavy briefcases and drives off. Eventually peace and quiet. 3.20pm, oh no. Everyone's back, ow, ow, ow. Great, just as I was having fun, they had to come back. Then about two and a half hours later Dad comes home from work with his heavy briefcases and paper. Ooo, this really gets on my nerves. Then comes the children's horrible cousins. They're always running in and out the door in their football boots. I absolutely hate it when they come round. Hooray, they've gone and about time too, they were really getting on my nerves. Eventually the day has passed and I can have some peace and quiet, but I'm dreading the morning, goodnight.

Ashley Earll (11)
Cliffe Woods Primary School

A Day In The Life Of A Teacher

Aah, what's the time? 8 o'clock, 8 o'clock! Got to get to school, must get dressed, what should I have for breakfast? Oh forget breakfast I've got to get to school!

I'm late, it's 9 o'clock, the kids will already be in school. What should I say? Oh I will think of something. 'Oh, hi kids.'
'Why are you late sir?'
'Well it all started when I woke up late because my alarm clock had broken so after I had thrown it out of the window and stamped on it I rushed to my car but it wouldn't start, so after the neighbours had helped me start the car I was off. But when I got out of the road I was attacked by aliens and they pulled me and my car to their spaceship. I arrived on this planet that was made out of chocolate. I was really enjoying it until I remembered I needed to get to work. So I tried to go but they wouldn't let me. I saw the spaceship so I secretly ran to the ship and climbed up the entrance into it. It was all written in some alien language, so I didn't know what button to press to get started. I just picked the first button I saw and pushed it, unfortunately that was the alarm so I pushed another one which was fat and red and I was right. So I made my way to Earth and here I am, unfortunately the aliens weren't happy I took their spaceship.'

James Povey (11)
Cliffe Woods Primary School

A Day In The Life Of A Dog

Hi, I'm a loveable dog. Boy, I hate having to pretend that I like doggy treats and acting all lovey-dovey towards my dumb owners. I have to wake up in a freezing cold kennel with a bowl of sludgy dog food, ugh!

The only good thing about being a dog is when I go walkies, woof, woof. I get to chase rabbits in the field and dig great big holes which all the hop, hops, (rabbits) fall down. Ha, ha! Whenever I always go past the big green thing, which I think my owners call lace (lake), they always tug on my rope thingy and pull me back from running to the lace and getting wet, Ohhh!

When my stupid owners have their dinner they always shout at me when all I want is a bit of yicken (chicken).

The absolute worst thing about being a dog is being sent to my kennel when I chew my dad's hat. I only want to have a bit of fun, *howlll*!

I've never actually seen my mum because I was separated from her at birth by some people who I think are my owners. Anyway, I better get on with my time schedule which I've been working on for two days. Firstly, I get up, secondly I have breakfast, thirdly I sleep, fourthly I have lunch, fifth I sleep, sixth I sleep and I sleep.

Lee Heather (11)
Cliffe Woods Primary School

A Day In The Life Of A Clock

There I was hanging up on a wall and around 9 o'clock people were staring at me. My hands were aching and I couldn't bear the pain, my long hand was turning every minute and my short hand was turning every hour. Oh and I also have another hand which moves every second. I have 12 numbers painted on my face. It's 12 o'clock and a whole load of kids were staring at my face again. Hours passed and my hand was aching more than ever. It was 3 o'clock and I could see people leaving to go home. There was a teacher marking a book and she was staring at my face. Tick-tock, my arms were aching and my shortest hand is going round and round. The rest of the day went by, my arms stopped aching but it was still moving. I can see another teacher walking into the room helping the teacher mark her books. They were there for some time marking the book. It got to 10 o'clock and they were still there. My arms were beginning to ache again. Wow, what a day! Now I definitely know how it feels to be a clock.

Prince Banin-Plockey (11)
Cliffe Woods Primary School

A DAY IN THE LIFE OF A HEAD TEACHER

Oh no, it's nine o'clock and that means children! I hate my job, oh well I suppose I could tell the children off for nothing.

'You stop running, you detention!'

Ahh that's much better, now I feel much more in charge. Ring, ring, oh there goes the telephone. Hold on, 'Yes Hogwarts Primary School. Oh Mr Mayor how lovely to hear from you. Oh you're not coming tomorrow, oh well never mind!'

Yippee, now we don't have to impress the mayor. Yes, oh it's time for lunch. Mmm I always love lunch. I always get a bigger plate. Yum, 5 long fish fingers, 25000 beans and a great big dollop of mash. I wonder what's for desert? Ah yes, apple crumble and loads of custard.

I'm bored, I know, I'll tell some more children off.

'You child, eat properly, and you - get your elbows off the table.'

Ahh now that is better, now I've got the office to myself. I can have some real fun. I can mess up all of the children's files. And now, I've got a meeting with the school council. Oh great, now they want new things for the playground, how demanding can they get? Wohh, that meeting has taken us right up to 3 o'clock, my favourite part of the day, home time!

Sarah Lowings (11)
Cliffe Woods Primary School

A DAY IN THE LIFE OF A TREE

I wake up by the bright, heated summer sun. My crisp, green leaves turn warm from the ball of fire, creating my food. Then all of a sudden I hear 'Ahhh.' It's the kids, the kids that play in my fresh, green field. Now they have relaxed and are sitting down under my long, thick branches to eat their lunch, cheese sandwiches.

Now they have gone and I go to sleep to the sound of singing birds and the light of the setting sun. Being a tree is great. I'm glad I'm a tree and not a human. Humans have to put up with lots of trouble. But being a tree is fantastic, you get to stand in the blazing hot sun and relax whenever you want.

Sometimes I do want to be a perfect human but I think I would prefer to stay the way I am. Being a tree can be lonely, because you have no one to talk to. Human beings just think of trees as a plant that provides oxygen for them to live. They think we trees don't have feelings but we do, just like everyone else.

At night I stay awake and stare at the starry sky and wait for the sun to come up so a new day can begin.

Aimee Walters (11)
Cliffe Woods Primary School

A DAY IN THE LIFE OF A DOLPHIN

I can't sleep a wink, lots of noises. Toots of boats. Every night is a danger zone with fishing boats everywhere spreading out over the rippling blue water. I can't wait till morning when I can leap under and over the dazzling blue and white waves to impress the boat tour. I could have people, glorious people looking at me gazing with marvellous grins of happiness. Cameras flashing as they get fabulous photos of me leaping all over, it makes me feel happy to think that they have all come to see me the one and only 'Danny the Dolphin'. Oh, it really does make me so happy.

As the light dims, the day dawns I just like to slowly swim, it's very tranquil to think about it. I think I need a rest I might have a small sleep before the boats start to come. I soon wake up, I feel really uncomfortable. I really need to swim. Oh no, I'm stuck in a fishing net. I can't get out, I'm going to die! No, I can't let this happen. I must get out of here. Ah, look a hole I can swim out of this net. Right, here I go. Whoosh, hooray, I'm free. I hope this doesn't happen again.

Chloe Hart (10)
Cliffe Woods Primary School

A DAY IN THE LIFE OF GERI HALLIWELL

I wake up at 6 o'clock. Or more like I'm woken by the blaring of 'Wannabe'. I feel a sharp pain when I hear my crackling voice. Then I remember my hair and believe me, I'm over it. The Spice Girls was just a phase. Anyway, back to my glamorous solo star life. I'm picked up in a silver limousine and cute little Harry sits on my knee.

After a long, sweaty ride, we finally arrive on the set of 'It's Raining Men'. Then coffee, toast and I'm raring to go. Firstly a long session of backflips and ow - splits!

My back aches, my legs ache and my head aches. Earlier on I was nearly killed. I had to be picked up by this man in a black leotard (yum, yum) and he dropped me. Also, when we were filming outside, it was snowing. I very nearly froze. Anyway, after a long, hard day I went back to my home. I turned on the radio in time to hear a recorded interview of myself on Heart 106.2. It was followed by 'Spice Up Your Life'. I feel slightly sick and turn off the sound of Mel B in my ear.

So now it's clubbing time (yippee!) To the Forum (my favourite club). The speakers are pounding. Suddenly 'It's Raining Men' comes on. I see everyone dancing and every ache I've ever had melts away. It was worth it.

Eleanor Prowse (11)
Cliffe Woods Primary School

A DAY IN THE LIFE OF ALAN TITCHMARSH

Today we were filming Ground Force in Essex. It was a hard job. First we put down new turf and took out all the dead and dismal plants, it was a dreadful job. Next a tea break and biscuits.

Tommy, as usual, was cracking jokes with Charlie, her ginger hair glistened in the golden, round sun whilst she grasped for the deep, red rose bush to put in the multicoloured border. The lush, light green grass lay flat on the ground. Quickly, grey clouds filled the sky.

Soon we had nearly finished the garden just for a few more finishing touches. The garden was for a young couple who were on their honeymoon and the parents wanted to surprise them. It was going to be big. The job was finally done, I was exhausted but the look on the happy couple's faces cheered me up.

Quickly we picked up our things, had a glass of wine. Charlie and Tommy and I squeezed into the van and drove off. Tommy realised that he had left Willy back at the house. We stumbled back and loaded him into the van and were finally able to go home and rest in peace with a cup of tea.

Rebecca Darey (10)
Cliffe Woods Primary School

A DAY IN THE LIFE OF A RADIO

Early morning, I get turned on and lots of sound comes out of me. All of the morning I bang away playing Hear'Say, A1 and Atomic Kitten. I get listened to and sang to all the time and advertise concerts, places and albums. My volume gets turned up loud and soft as I keep banging away. Now I'm turned off as my best friend the CD player starts to play, I just sit waiting and waiting. As hours pass it soon becomes lunchtime, yummy, yummy.

A hand comes towards my mouth with delicious, smooth, shiny tapes. The hand puts it in and presses *play*. I start to chew, as the delicious tape goes round and round minute after minute, hour after hour, I just keep chewing. The tape stops and I start go get hungry again but no more tapes. 'Oh no', the hand starts to turn me on again. I start to get hot all of a sudden. I stop. My switch no longer works, I no longer work. The hand grabs my plug and starts to slot it back in place. I start to play. The dark sky comes over and the light gets turned on. Now it is night and I am turned off until dawn.

Jill Morley (11)
Cliffe Woods Primary School

A Day In The Life Of A Pointe Shoe

Ouch, that hurt! I'm Penelope the pointe shoe, and I absolutely hate being stuffed in this stupid ballet bag for hours on end! It's pitch-black and there is definitely an awful stench hanging around *my* corner of the bag. You see, I have slimy, smelly socks squashing me totally into unnatural shapes, totally bending me!

I think it's about 9.00am so I will be taken out of my owner's bag soon. I can hear her coming now and I think she is going to open the zip! Yes! The light, the glory, the world is flashing at me, so bright and beautiful, I love it. She is reaching for me and I am finally out from her bag, fresh air smells gorgeous. I think I can hear someone saying that the show is starting in 5, 4, 3, 2, 1, up goes the curtain, I think! And I'm on, *weeeee, wahooo, swing, swosh,* the joy of dancing! Oooh and I'm up (with a few wibbly wobbles first) ouch, you're squashing me, how could you do this to me?

You see she has just decided to go up on her points which really hurts when she does it because it *squashes me* completely! Ouch, ooh, ahh (Mummy! Well I would say Mummy if I knew I had one!)

Phew, I'm back down and off, I think she is using my best friend the ballet shoe next.

Well, that's me done for the day; I'm off to bed. Well, the back of the awful bag anyway!

Elizabeth Cowan (11)
Cliffe Woods Primary School

A DAY IN THE LIFE OF A MAGNIFYING GLASS

Michael took me to school today, well he took his pencil case, which just happens to be my home. It was about 9.45 when he reached into my humble abode and grabbed . . . wait for it . . . the pencil, *big* let-down! By 10.17 (Michael's loony tunes watch always told me the time, which was usually annoying but it's begged me to tell you the time), he had used everything except for poor, lonely, forlorn me. Things got even worse at lunch when I got germinated, er evaporated, er confiscated, that's the word. I was in that desk for 3 hours with only a packet of Haribo and a plastic eyeball to talk to (the eyeball didn't say much, I don't know, cat got her retina?) before Michael had the courtesy to free me. Oh well, at least I can now go home and go to sleep zzzzzzzzzzzz!

Michael Orvis (11)
Cliffe Woods Primary School

A Day In The Life Of A Rabbit

I wake up in my warm and comfortable hole and have a lick wash. As I peep my head out, I smell the fresh lettuce on a freshly cut field. I hop over to the fresh, green lettuce, and have a little nibble, then I eat more. The farmer comes out with his broom and chases me away. I run down to my hutch - hipperty-hop, hipperty-hop. As I hop out again I get an irritable itch, my foot goes thump, thump, thump. As I hop around the field I see another rabbit, love comes into my eyes as I see her beautiful, brown, loving eyes staring back at me. Her pure white fluffy fur attracts me to her straight away. Her teeth crunching into a carrot, me drooling over the sight of it as I drift closer to her. As I do she runs away. Just my luck, I think to myself with tears coming to my eyes, then a sudden sob. Perhaps I should follow her, maybe she wanted me to, or perhaps I'm paranoid. As the sun goes down, I feel a little sleepy, I get weak and tired. I go back to my cosy hutch and have a nibble on a carrot, then go to sleep.

Katie Bourner (11)
Cliffe Woods Primary School

A DAY IN THE LIFE OF A WATCH

One lovely morning I get put onto the wrist. Every day I feel like I'm being haunted by the eyes. I shake all around when the boy runs about. Oh not again. The eyes came glaring down on me, I closed my eyes very quickly and opened them again after a while. After a few hours I was being looked at again and now, ow, my buttons are being pushed over and over again. Now I'm being rubbed because I'm a bit dirty. Oh no! I'm going into the dark and horrible jewellery box while he goes and does some games. I hate being put into the box, it stinks. Oh, oh, I'm being put back onto the wrist. Ah, he's pulling me tight. Ouch! Someone's saying 'What's the time?' So down came those glaring eyes again, horrible they were. Oh no, not the stop watch. I hate running very quickly to time something. My buttons are going to get pushed again very hard. My buttons are very sore now. He's looking at me and now he's walking away. Yeah, we're going home. I might be able to get some rest. Yes, I'm being taken off and I've got bruises all over. I'm definitely going to have another nightmare tonight. Then tomorrow it will happen all over again.

Paul Kelly (11)
Cliffe Woods Primary School

A Day In The Life Of A Television

I am playing happily away to myself when I realise that no one is listening. It makes me feel very sad but guess what, a comedy is on. Ha, ha, ha.

My owner's woken up so he better come and turn me off so I can have a nice rest while he goes to boring school so he says. It is always boring when he goes to school but today felt different. And so it was, in came the most worst sister around. She turned me on. Oh no, Teletubbies. I knew that that was going to be on for half an hour. Boring.

Suddenly I had a brilliant idea, I would turn myself off and so I did. She went down to tell her mum. Her mum came up. I tried really hard to turn me on and it worked. What's happening? I was being unplugged but then I realised I was going to the mechanics. Nooooo! Of course I worked for the mechanics so it was another trip home. Granny round, that's bad because all she watches is the Discovery Channel all the time. My owner's back and the best children's programme is on. Night time, am I going to be turned off? I hope so. Click. Goodnight, I'm off.

Simon Harding (11)
Cliffe Woods Primary School

A Day In The Life Of A Cat

Hi, I'm Alfie and this is my everyday life. I wake up to a beautiful morning and start scratching at the door until my owners let me in.

I get my breakfast, yummy, goose, chicken and fish, what a selection! I'm full, I think I'll go and relax on the sofa. This is nice, just sitting here doing nothing. What, oh yes, he's picking me up, I wonder where I'm going, it's so exciting . . . no wait, we're going to the door. Let me go! Let me go! I struggle to get free, but I've been chucked out and the door's been slammed in my face, what a bummer!

I know, I'll go see Peter and Charlie (my brothers). Hey, there's a black thing following me, it's getting closer, come here you little . . . Wow, I'm dizzy, who would have thought that it was my own tail, I think I'll lay down.

Arrgh! That was a nice nap. Now what was I going to do; oh yeah, I was going to see Peter and Charlie.

Well, they're not in the garage. (That's where they usually are). There's a woman over there maybe I'll get a grooming. I'm not filthy. Look, there's the owner's car! I'm going home.

Finally back, quick, no one's looking, maybe I can sneak upstairs. This bed is so comfy I could just stay here forever. Someone's coming - hide! It's only one of the kids, he won't chuck me out, hopefully. Wrong again, well back to the great outdoors.

Daniel Sams (11)
Cliffe Woods Primary School

A DAY IN THE LIFE OF A GUINEA PIG

I woke with a start, there was a big hand in my hutch grabbing my food bowl. Then there was a rustle in my bedding. Truffle had woken up and she began to squeak. Suddenly the big hand appeared again, this time with a bowl of my yummy food.

'Mmm,' I began eating, then came Truffle, she was hungry. I climbed down the wooden slide into my run and began chewing on the fresh, green grass. But next door's dog saw me, I started squeaking and ran as fast as I could back into my bed. Truffle lay near me, her warm fur touching my cold ears. Once the barking stopped I peeped out of a hole to see if he had gone. Yes, he had. Down the slide I went, munch, munch, munch, the grass was lovely. By now I was quite thirsty I started drinking from my bottle. I was so hot and I felt very tired, I laid down and fell asleep. I began dreaming, it was weird I was in a box with Truffle and there was straw everywhere. I ran around trying to get out, suddenly the box opened and in came a hand trying to grab me. In the end she grabbed me and I squealed. I woke up with a jump, I remember what the dream was about when my owners first got me. The big hand came back into the cage and picked me up again and put me back in my bed.

Shyma Cherry (11)
Cliffe Woods Primary School

A Day In The Life Of Anne Robinson

I woke up this morning in America, a huge American breakfast waiting outside my door. The tray was packed with things like: bagels, croissants, a huge mug of coffee, bacon, eggs - sunny side up and not forgetting pancakes with maple syrup. I looked up at the schedule above my bed. Thursday - photo shoots and a show of American The Weakest Link.

After breakfast I stepped outside my private apartment, not before applying my make-up and doing my hair. Camera flashes blinded me - I walked briskly to my black, chauffeured car. I climbed in. Soon we were driving along the road towards the set.

I arrived at the set and no sooner had I stepped outside the door I was whisked to the make-up room. The make-up artist started applying mascara while her assistant chose my costume, a PVC cat costume. I stared at the costume and asked the assistant if she was mad. I would not wear that. She then saw sense and pulled out of the rack a casual trouser suit, that was more like it!

Soon I was sitting in an open-topped convertible, it wasn't going anywhere because it was for show for my photos. It took ages for them to finish. Flash after flash after flash, and shouts of 'Can you move to the left or move to the right?'

Later on at the studio for The Weakest Link, I looked over the top of my glasses and thought back over the day. It had been easy compared to other days!

Elizabeth Ingham (10)
Cliffe Woods Primary School

A DAY IN THE LIFE OF AIDAN BLADES

Early morning, I awake, always at 7.40am. I make my cereal, frosted Shreddies, my favourite, then I will and watch 'Trouble' for quarter of an hour. I get washed and dressed into my school clothes and get back down the stairs to put my Kickers shoes on ready for Josh to knock on my door. He usually comes at 8.40. Then we walk to school. I'm in Year 6 and he's in Year 4, quite a difference. When I get to school I meet up with Lee, Simon, Ashley, Mark and sometimes Jill and Georgina plus Aimee and Katie. Then we go and have literacy following assembly, me and Lee chat but don't tell the teachers though, we'll get in trouble. After our assembly we go and play football out in the playground. Cool. Then we come back into the school building and on Mondays we would have science. Boring! And then we have, are you ready, Creative Writing. That's kind of alright I suppose. And then lunch, I have ham sandwiches, crisps and a digestive chocolate biscuit and then we muck about in the playground again. Now it's the end, bye. Oh yeah, I forgot that my name is Aiden Blades.

Aiden Blades (10)
Cliffe Woods Primary School

A Day In The Life Of A Remote Control

Morning has come and the house is filling and she slouches on the sofa and here it comes, this is going to hurt. She's going to press my button, here it comes, ouch! That hurt, the television turns on like a flash of lightning and it blared out making her (my owner) screech and again my buttons are being pressed and my insides are going crazy with electric running through me. Suddenly, oh no, my batteries have gone flat! Here we go again, ouch! Stop pushing my buttons, not my back, now ow, I've got my back coming off, eventually I'm free, no turning of my buttons, just lying here on my own. I'm bored, on my own with nothing to do and nothing to watch on the new TV. I'm just waiting for my batteries to be put back in. Thank you Lord. An hour later my batteries are being put back in and my case is being put back on, here we go again. On with the TV but I'm not going to moan. It's getting late now and she's getting tired. Come on, turn me off and do it before you go to sleep.

I need to turn off, it looks like you're going to have a big bill. I'm off to sleep now. Wake me up in the morning and turn the television off otherwise it will keep me awake and bored.

Alouette Marsh (10)
Cliffe Woods Primary School

A Day In The Life Of A Question Mark

I often wondered what it would be like to be something different, maybe an exclamation mark or something, something abnormal. So then I decided that I would become something different. A question mark.

My first day of being a question mark was very confusing, people kept asking me things that I didn't know how to answer. Why, what, if, where and then I realised these people could be talking about anything and that was my answer to them. They asked me why and I answered: because. They asked me what and I answered nothing. They asked if and I replied what. They asked me where and I replied somewhere over the rainbow. Well, I didn't actually it was just somewhere. I suddenly realised that there were lots more of me and I just kept appearing again and again. Before long my whole surroundings were just me, a lot of question marks.

My second day wasn't as bad as my first although still a lot of questions, but overall a very enjoyable day. A few hiccups along the way, some very serious like once I couldn't answer a question I was asked so I suddenly disappeared and appeared again halfway round the world on a scrappy piece of paper.

My third day was just too much and I had to ask myself that very important question, was I in the right place? No, so now I'm back to normal being something different.

Marc Paton (11)
Cliffe Woods Primary School

A DAY IN THE LIFE OF MICHELLE POSTON

It was my birthday and I was having a brilliant day at the Regis. It was the end of my party and my family were having a drink while me, April (my sister) and my cousin was playing in the slide. Suddenly my cousin pushed me down the slide backwards. I flipped round and there it was, a nail sticking out right in front of me. *Bang!* I fainted. I can remember my mum screaming and my dad shouting at the manager of the restaurant. My dad and my mum carried me to the car, put me in the car and away we went.

The next thing I knew I was in a hospital bed. I saw doctors and nurses rushing around me. I felt like my forehead was going to explode. I looked up. *Aaarrrhhh!* A bump, all I could see was a bump. It took me a while till I realised that it was going to be there for a long time.

The next morning mum and dad, Sam (my brother) and April came to visit me. Dad said 'We have got compensation,' then they gave me the money. That night I decided that I would take my family to Malta. I stayed in the hospital for another week to recover and off we then went to scorching, hot Malta.

Michelle Poston (11)
Downview Primary School

A Day In The Life Of A Spaceman

I nervously walk past the new, sparkling spaceship glinting in the sun. The speaker goes off telling me to get on the spaceship. I'm sitting in my seat, strapped down, thinking I'm going to be sick.

The next minute I hear 3, 2, 1 . . .

I feel the huge spaceship rumbling as my stomach turns upside-down. The spaceship takes off at an incredible speed. I can finally get out of my seat and float. I feel so magnificent and wish that my family could share this great experience with me. It is really hard eating and going to the toilet because I have to eat out of a special container and go to the toilet through a tube.

After eight hours the moon seems to be close. I look back at Earth, my heart is beating with excitement. I think 'I hope I get back safely for everyone to greet and welcome me home.' I orbit the moon looking curiously at the big holes in the ground called craters and atmosphere. Once I have circled the moon I make my way back hoping I have enough fuel.

I get ready for my landing in the sea.
By now I have been sick because my guts wobble constantly around. I get in my space capsule and soar down to Earth. I am extremely glad I made it back.

Nathan Mhuto (11)
Downview Primary School

A DAY IN THE LIFE OF RACHEL WOOD

Rachel decided to start playing for the USA ice hockey team. A week later she got to the training session and started to panic. It was half an hour later. 'Yes!' Rachel scored a goal, she didn't stop smiling until the coach, Grill, walked over and then in a flash he came out with, 'You're on the team!' For a minute Rachel was speechless. Fifty weeks of training had finally paid off.

The big day came, the last match that they had all been waiting for, USA against GB. 'Here we go!' Rachel started to panic and then her name was called. 'Oh no!'

'What?' coach replied eager for her answer so that she could join the game quickly.

'I forgot to have my chocolate boost. Now I'm going to start getting mad.' So Rachel quickly looked in her pocket but the chocolate wasn't there.

It was time to go on the ice. There was only fifteen minutes to go. 'Wow, chocolate!' *Bang!* The puck went straight into her forehead. Rachel got sent to the hospital right away.

An hour later Rachel woke up. 'Where's my chocolate?' she asked. All of the family and doctors started to laugh.

'Rachel, I'm so glad that you're all right. By the way, we won the game and the rich Prime Minister promised you would get to play another game in a week's time,' coach explained.

So Rachel went home to rest and said to her mum, 'Well, I think I'll go and visit the Chocolate Box.'

'Oh no you won't. You'll stay right here!' Mum replied sharply.

Nicola Pearce (11)
Downview Primary School

A DAY IN THE LIFE OF JAMES BOND

'Move, move, move!' Boom! A massive explosion just went off. I ran to the safe. Sir Robert King was dead on the floor. His assassin was in a boat down below on the River Thames. I ran down to the Q division, jumped into my boat and flew out the wall after the assassin. I put the after-burners on to catch her up; she shot me with a chain gun but the bullets bounced off the boat's armour plating. I fired two torpedoes but she crashed the boat on the shore and ran out before the torpedoes hit.

I parked my boat near hers. She climbed into a hot air balloon and started to go up. I gripped onto the rope attached to the hot air balloon. She shot me twice but the bullets missed. I told her she would be protected by MI-6 if she came with me but she would not have it. She shot the gas canisters. I let go of the rope before the balloon exploded. I smashed into the Millennium Dome. Two police helicopters picked me up and took me back to MI-6 HQ. The doctor gave me a sling for my arm.

The next day I went to Sir Robert King's funeral. After that we went back to the HQ. Agent got an information booklet, but me, I asked one of the superior personnel but he said that M pulled me off the assignment.

Tom Tyrell (10)
Downview Primary School

A Day In The Life Of Cher

It was the day before the 'big day'. I was deciding what I was going to wear. I choose my sparkly dress and my gold high heel shoes. I had an early night because I didn't want to fall asleep on stage.

When I woke up it was quarter past six. I was late. I was supposed to be at the practise concert. When I got to the hall my agent said to me, 'Where on earth were you? You should have been here half an hour ago.'

'OK, I'm sorry. My alarm clock didn't go off,' I said angrily. After me and my agent had finished arguing we got on with the practise concert. Finally after two and a half hours, it came to the proper concert. I went to the dressing room to get on my dress and shoes. It took me two hours and ten minutes to get through twenty of my songs. Then it came to the final song which was 'Strong Enough', that was it. It was over. No more dancing or no singing for four whole weeks!

Amy Benjamin (11)
Downview Primary School

A Day In The Life Of A Wannabe Pop Star

I woke up early feeling excited. I had a wash and got changed. I rushed out the door grabbing a piece of toast. I got in the car. I was all set to drive to London for the auditions.

I arrived much later. There were a hundred people there, it was great. I sat down and waited till I had to go and sing. I was the second person to sing. I sang 'Reach' by S Club 7. It went really well, even though I was a bit scared singing in front of all those people. I sat down and waited for everybody else to sing. There were loads of good singers. It was the end of a really hard day and I had to go and see Nigel. I opened the door, walked the dreaded walk over to the table to be told that he wanted me to come back next week for the next stage of the auditions. It was loads of fun. I can't wait for next week. Will I survive another day?

Stephanie Ward (11)
Downview Primary School

A DAY IN THE LIFE OF HARRY POTTER

Hi, I am Harry Potter and this is all about my day.

First, double potions lesson. All Snape did was torture me and Ron and tell us to make us 'beauty spell'. Ron put in too many frogs' legs and *bang!* Cleaning the trophy cabinet for us! Then we went into the Great Hall for lunch. I wasn't hungry and all I could do was stare at my plate, the thought of either helping Snape cut up frogs' legs or cleaning the trophies in the cabinet wasn't good. I heard Malfoy come out of Snape's room sniggering. Then he came over to us and said 'No visit to Hogsmeade for you boys.'

Now, we had been told that we couldn't go on the visit. I just wanted one bag of those webbed spiders or beetle squirts. I went to the house and muttered the password and grabbed my Quidditch robes, changed into them and shuffled out onto the pitch. 'In line Harry.' That's my teacher's way of saying 'Stop being silly and messing about and wake up.' I entered the stadium and the crowd roared. I got on my broom and floated upwards. The whistle blew and the game started. I caught the golden Snitch in the first five minutes. Then disaster struck! My broom lost power and plummeted to the ground in 0.3 seconds. My ankle was broken and I had to go to the person I saw most often, the nurse, I had to stay in the ward for twenty-four hours. Everyone came to check on me, well everyone apart from Slytherin. And the star visitor Cho-Chang, she had just got back from the visit to Hogsmeade and had bought me a pack of webbed spiders. I asked her to the dance and she said 'Yes!' Ron and Hermaine are going together, a perfect end to a disastrous day.

Bye.

Kelsey Spencer (11)
Downview Primary School

A Day In The Life Of Link

Pulling down my green tunic, I checked my blonde hair in the mirror and thought about the day ahead. I buckled on my newly polished sword remembering past battles and how trusty it had been. My battered shield could have yet more dents by the time today ends I thought.

I set off to the lost woods. Mido, one of the most selfish Kokoris, stopped me and claimed that there was a new law. 'Anyone who heaadss . . .' before he could finish his sentence I put him to sleep with Zelda's lullaby. I arrived at the entrance to the lost woods I was confronted by a skell kid. I pulled out my sword and, well, that was the end of it. I crossed the bridge and ended up in Hyrule field.

Then a young girl called Malon ran up to me and gave me a horse called Epona. I leapt onto it and galloped towards the battle. When I arrived nothing was there, not even a soul, then out of the blue appeared Ganon. 'I knew you would come Link,' Ganon roared. I didn't reply.

We had a long and bloody battle. In the end I gave Ganon a mighty blow, he fell to the ground, his last words were; 'We would have been a good team.'

Jake Lund (11)
Downview Primary School

A Day In The Life Of An Alien

Hi, I'm Gorka. I come from Saturn. Well, I don't really come from Saturn, I come from Earth. I've been ordered (on my life) to return to Earth as a spy by my leader Nak! You see, Saturn has declared war against Earth because Earthlings recently smuggled two hundred million spies, reportedly for a magazine.

A few light-years later

I landed back in Shakle, my home town. I'm a German. I've been on Saturn for ten billion, two hundred and thirty-five thousand years. (I had an operation to make me this old!) I've developed many Saturn features such as having a blue body, green hair and purple ears. I don't think they will count me as an Earthling, so I've got my old skin, hope they take me for an Earthling. Cross my fingers, hope not to die and return to Saturn with lots of information and not even a finger lost.

The last few light-years

Travelling at the speed of light, I finally got to Earth and got a ring on the telephone.

'Nak speaking.'
'Nak,' I replied.
'We are sending reinforcements.'
Bang!'
'Oh, that's nice of him to slam the phone down on me.'

The reinforcements are here. Let's go.

James Parsons (10)
Downview Primary School

A DAY IN THE LIFE OF A CRICKET BALL

I'm still waiting in my box, to be chosen for day one of the Pakistan v England Test Match. This will be a chance of a lifetime if I'm chosen. Although I'm not looking forward to being smacked all round the park, it should be interesting. Oh no, here come the umpires to pick me up.

England elected to bat, it's hot in Waquar's hand. The roar is huge. The first ball is ready to be bowled. I hit the ground with a thud and, owww, Ather's hit me for 4. Before I knew it I'd been hit for 150 runs. A headache is beginning to wear in. 40 more overs and they have the option of a new ball.

Pakistan and England have gone in for lunch and I'm in the umpire's pocket, my head is throbbing. England declared at 436-7. People don't think about us cricket balls getting hit backwards and forwards all day. It's not much fun for us you know. We're going back out after a 45 minute lunch break. 12 more overs and then they'll choose the new ball and then the only use I'll be is a training ball. Boo hoo!

We're out and Goughy is ready to send me down at 90mph. Owww, clunk. Saeed Anwar smacked me for 6. I can see everyone in Lords. 1 more ball and the new ball if they want it. I'm smacked for 4.

What a great day, painful but fun.

Craig Johnson (11)
Downview Primary School

A DAY IN THE LIFE OF DOZY DOG (TOY)

Yet another boring day sat on the shelf of no return. No kisses, no cuddles, no nothing she used to give me.

If only it could be the days when me and Jo were inseparable again. Thoughts from the past drifted into my head.

'Weee, come on Dozy your turn!' she picked me up and held me against her.

'Jo, come on darling, time to go home.'

Grabbing me by the paw she ran. I felt myself slipping, eventually I fell. *Splash!*

A great muddy puddle went all over my fur - Jo didn't care, she laughed and ran. My head dropped. The murky water ran over my head. For hours I lay wondering what would happen.

I felt a pair of warm hands pick me up. Gazing into my eye she said 'Dozy, Dozy, Dozy. What are we going to do with you?' Jo's mum had come to take me home.

We got home, she put me in the washing machine. Where was Jo? She was always at home and if she wasn't, she would always take me with her.

Water poured in, spinning in circles. I was wondering if Jo still cared about me. Jo got me out and hung me on the washing line to dry. I hung there trying to decide if I was the favourite toy any more.

Once again I fell.

'Dozy, what are you doing on the floor?' She picked me up, hugged me and placed me back on the shelf where I belonged.

Emily Aird (11)
Downview Primary School

A DAY IN THE LIFE OF A BILLY CAN

Ah, a minute's peace . . . *boom!* Oh my head, what a thumping headache I've got and all this disgusting mud, it's all moist and bumpy, it's giving me a cold! A shattering scream came from a crowd of soldiers, a bomb had just landed on them and had made a gigantic bang!

Thank goodness John wasn't over there. Oh yeah, I forgot to tell you about John, he's my owner, I know because he has written his name on me in permanent marker pen in bright yellow. Yellow's my favourite colour. I really, really like John because he treats me really well. Take for instance all the other Billy cans, they are old and rusty, but I'm clean and shiny.

Yawn! All that talking's made me sleepy but before I could shut my eyes another large grenade was thrown into the trench. A few people jumped out of the way to dodge a bomb! I felt myself being lifted up and being carried over to another trench. I looked around to find nothing more than a thick green gas surrounding us. We were going to have to be fast because the gas was deadly poisonous. We were losing the war, the Germans had knocked out our communication's radar and most of our tanks. John jumped over a half-hit tank, he slipped on the tank and fell over. He was knocked unconscious. I flew up into the air and landed with my handle stuck right in the soggy mud right behind John's head and I got jammed there. Maybe it will save him!

Tom Stafford (11)
Downview Primary School

It's a Dog's Life

'Uhhh,' I groaned as I yawned a gargantuan yawn. I trotted out of my small bed of hay and had a good stretch. 'Grrah!' I barked.

'Dogmatix, here boy!' I heard Obelix call. The sound of Obelix's voice makes me happy and I sped like rocket towards my owner. 'Getafix has asked us to gather wild boar for a feast tonight,' Obelix stated. 'Asterix is waiting.'

I bounded outside, waiting for either Asterix or Obelix to appear.

'La la la la!' came a deafening melody from Cacofonix, the village bard. I laid low for a while, hiding, also hoping he'd go and give someone else a song.

Finally, Cacofonix went away, thank God, to serenade the village chief, Vitalstatistix.

'Here Dogmatix,' shouted Obelix. 'We're going now.' Obelix stood at the gate of the village with his good friend Asterix at his side. Barking contentedly I trundled to their feet.

We hiked far into the forest. 'Rrugh, rugh, ruugh!' I barked trying to signal that wild boar were near.

'Ah, Dogmatix, what is it?' Asterix questioned. 'Have you found something?'

I ran into a clearing and in front of us sat a whole family of wild boar.

On the way back Obelix kept muttering 'You never let us down, do you Dogmatix?' I ran ahead barking, to signal that we had returned.

Chris Reed (11)
Downview Primary School

A DAY IN THE LIFE OF A TELEVISION

At last, the fire alarm has stopped. It's deafening. Oh no, it's started again. Why did that stupid kid have to light a fire in the kitchen below the fire alarm? *Bang,* came the sound of the door slamming.

'George, why did you light a fire? I want an explanation now,' George's mum said angrily.
'What!' said George now running around the house in a mad panic.
'Get here now!'
'Okay, I'm coming,' George started running towards his mum.
'I want an explanation about the fire now! said George's mum getting more angry than ever.
'Well, um,' said George nervously, 'I accidentally tried to burn some paper in a bowl and some of the paper fell out and st . . .'
'Go and wait outside now!'

George started walking outside and his mum got the fire extinguisher and sprayed it at the fire and after about five minutes the fire went out. Then the fire engine came and firemen came running through the door and shouted 'Is everything OK?' and ran into the kitchen.

George's mum replied. 'Yes everything's fine.'
'Well, we heard your fire alarm going off so we came here.'
'Yeah, my son decided to light a fire in the kitchen.'

The firemen said bye and then walked out.

Gary Chandler (10)
Downview Primary School

WASTED

'Get off Barker,' I groaned, as I sat up from being asleep. He jumped off me into his basket, the street was busy to my surprise. I took the worn, grubby hat off my head and placed it on the ground, the cold, stony ground. I was waiting, waiting for a passer-by to drop some coins in.

'Please,' I beg, 'just a few.'
'Here, take this,' a kind civilian offered me, as he passed me a £5 note.
'Thank you, thank you very much.' I answered. I was really hungry, starving. I went into the shop opposite. All eyes turned to me as I walked in, (I felt horrible), all looking at my frayed and shabby clothes. I picked up a sandwich with my numb hands, paid for it, carefully pocketing the change and walked out back to my bed; my cold, moth-eaten bed under the leaky roof.

Barker welcomed me joyfully as I returned back to my normal spot; everyday, every week. I sat there for hours in the same uncomfortable spot, eating my sandwich and stroking Barker.

As the crowd of shoppers gradually faded away it started snowing, snowing cold powdery snow. The cold, gripping my toes and fingers, moved mind-numbingly up my limbs. Everything was fading, I wasn't focused or even thinking anymore. Even the future seemed remote . . .

Simon Belton (11)
Downview Primary School

A Day In The Life Of Hedwig (Harry Potter's Owl)

Why me, why couldn't I be just like a normal owl and only fly around when I want? For one thing it is rather boring flapping around delivering Harry's letters and for another I do get quite tired. My dear friend Dolly and I are thinking of redecorating the aviary, spruce it up, you know what I mean.

Here we go again, another letter to deliver. I'm going to retire one of these days. Not another letter for Sirius Black, what has Harry got about him. I am now too . . . tired . . . to . . . go . . . on, *phew,* finally I'm back.

Oh no, here comes Dumbledore, quick need to hide.
'Hmm, I need a reliable owl who will be able to make the journey.'
Good he chose Dolly, see you later, sweetheart.

Just as I thought the day could get no worse I noticed a pile of letters a mile high in the corner of the aviary. Thank goodness that there was only one for me to deliver and it only has to go to the dining room. How I wish I could have just one peck of that glorious food. I dropped the letter and flew, I just couldn't handle the temptation. I am so tired. Now what? Harry had just come in, he was muttering something about parents evening, no don't look now, he's got a letter in his hand.

Emily Lippitt (11)
Downview Primary School

A DAY IN THE LIFE OF . . . MY DOG

'Argh.' I woke up in the middle of the night, it was pitch black and all I could hear were owls and other wild animals. I walked down the stairs to find my dog biscuits in my bowl. I ate it fast as I was so hungry. I was just about to walk up the stairs to my owner's warm, cosy bed when I was disturbed by a rustle in the bushes.

Burning with curiosity, I walked through the hallway to find a horrified cat staring up at me as if to say, 'Don't chase me, please.'

Of course you can guess what I did. I chased her out of the cat flap, over the bush and straight into a brick wall. I gave up, I couldn't see her anymore, so I climbed back through the cat flap in pain and into the living room. In the morning my owners came down looking puzzled.

'Where's the cat?' They said to each other.

There I was sitting there on the mat saying to myself, 'She'll never come back now!'

Then one night, about a week later to my surprise, she came walking in as if she had nothing to be ashamed of. I thought, 'Well, I'll take that look off her face'.

I took a big leap, the cat maiowed and I barked. The fight ended, there I was standing outside in the freezing cold, when the cat was asleep in front of the fire in a mischievous kind of way. So not everything has a happy ending!

Carlie Davis (11)
Downview Primary School

A Day In The Life Of A Stalfos

'Wa ha ha ha' I grunted as I flipped myself out of the ground with my rusty, but strong sword and circular shield in hand. My rotting bones groaned as the door opened in front, and a small man, about seventeen years in age walked in. I saw that he had a huge sword in both hands and a great mirror shield on his back.

My brother lunged at the man and before I knew what I was doing, I too had lunged at him. I thought that this small man would be quite weak, but he was actually really strong!

He attacked me using some sort of magic fire that I thought only the Phantom Ganon could use. Stalfos can usually survive fire, but those sort almost killed me and did kill my brother! 'Graaaa' I shouted in my gruff voice. I threw myself dangerously at him and we were locked, sword on sword, in battle. Like a spring, we came apart and then I grabbed him by the shoulder, but his clothing ripped, and he disappeared in a cloud of metallic green and gold. My brother's bones lay scattered all over the floor. I will have revenge, for tomorrow is another day . . .

Christopher Ramsdale (11)
Downview Primary School

A Day In The Life Of A Wasp

Another action packed day. Left the nest early to start scavenging for food.

A lucky strike! A curled up sandwich with rich-smelling ham, just ready for turning, with any luck I'll even find a maggot, while busy feeding on this absorbing ham sandwich aware of the deafening noise around me.

A group of boys came over. Me, minding my own business, I started to wonder whether to move. Before I could even think the words in my brain they kicked my delicious sandwich with me on it over the other half of the pitch. I jumped off and started to wonder why they had done it.

They were just so jealous I had this mouth-watering sandwich and they didn't. I felt so angry I made some venom, flew over and decided I would like to eat some nice juicy flesh instead. So I stung them one by one, all three of them.

That will teach you a lesson not to take other people's things.

Molly Turnbull (11)
Downview Primary School

A Day In The Life Of A Cat

The alarm clock went off a bit earlier than usual. I stretched my spine and rolled over exposing my tummy to the open kitchen. I peered over to my food bowl . . . wait it's empty! Surely they couldn't have forgotten to feed me, their adorable, fluffy, obedient cat. They have! Well, it's lucky they left my cat flap open. I pushed my head towards the flap, it swung open, then flipped back behind me nearly catching my tail. I sniffed the air. Then I saw my prey - a helpless bird was squashed in the middle of the garden, I pounced, then I realised it was already dead. I turned my head and saw the most glittery, shiny, big spider's web. My feet started running towards it. I placed a paw on the web, but was surprised when my paw went straight through it, breaking the beautiful web. I then got annoyed and threw myself onto the shrivelled up web but it got stuck to my paws. As I rolled over it came with me, catching me like a net. Then I decided to take a mouthful of the dead bird.

Suddenly I heard my owner calling me, so I rushed inside, trying to dodge the feathers on my way. It was no good, a feather got stuck to my paw. My owner gasped in horror, it looks like it's back to the garage for me.

Becky Balshaw (10)
Downview Primary School

RING, RING

The mistress of the house came bustling into the room carrying a tea tray. For a moment I thought I saw her consider using me to phone the doctor again but I must have been mistaken because a second later she called, 'Jenny, more camomile tea, Elizabeth wants more camomile tea!' in a strident voice. I knew what that was about. I had been present when it had started.

Elizabeth, the mistress's daughter, had come over with scarlet fever. Mistress had used me to call the doctor and everyone had fussed over Beth without knowing what was wrong with her. The doctor had announced that she had scarlet fever and everyone had fussed over her even more.

Jenny came into the room carrying a steaming mug of camomile tea. As she handed it to Mistress she murmured in a low voice, 'How is she?'
The mistress replied in an even lower voice, 'Not much better I'm afraid. Even the doctor sounded pessimistic when I contacted him this morning. I'm telling you, if she isn't any better by next week my thumbs will definitely be down for the worst!'

Mistress took the tea tray up to Elizabeth and I watched Jenny go back into the kitchen. I was proud to be of importance in this crisis. Those poor people in the picture on the wall. All that happens to them in a day is that when visitors come they get gawped at.

Rayhun Aminian
Downview Primary School

A Day In The Life Of A Spider

'Aha, oh no, not another screaming fit, why does it happen near me? Here we go again, out of the window. Scurry, scurry, scurry, look I found a corner for safety. Why is that lady waving a white flag at me? I give up, it said in big bold letters, I am not that blind. Why is this world scared, this seems strange. Here comes the tissue, can you mind my legs?

I have planted a web in the corner of a warm relaxing room. It is good for catching my tea and gives a good view of everything. The children stomped in.
'Why can't I have it?'
'You always want my things.'
'Get off!'
'Ahh!'
'Go away.'
'Mum!'
'Shut up you two, I am fed up with this.'

How does that mother cope with these brats arguing all the time? When my eggs hatch my children won't behave like these, otherwise I will eat them.

A wasp flew in and made an annoying buzz. I will put a stop to this rubbing my legs together waiting for the juicy bug to fly towards me. My tummy is rumbling. Got you, I wrapped it up in my newly fresh silk. Here comes a vacuum, *broom, broom.*

This vacuum is going to get me, I'll have to make a run for it and leave my catch behind.

Run, run, run, my little legs were really sore. I need to get to safety now.

Natalie Gillies (11)
Downview Primary School

A DAY IN THE LIFE OF A PHARAOH

I was on my way to the pyramid which, when I died I would be placed inside. The route we took had been strewn with flowers to celebrate the completion.

As I travelled through a small village cheering rose from the crowd that had gathered to watch their brilliant, modest, stylish queen (e.g. me) proceed to her pyramid.

'Hyroglphia,' called my servant. I lifted my head.

'The pyramid awaits your inspection,' she smiled. I looked at a giant monument covered with rubies and diamonds.

'It's perfect.' I smiled broadly. Another cheer rose.

I suddenly remembered I had to choose who would come with me when I go to the afterlife.

OK, I need my make-up, servants, jewellery, my entire wardrobe and my kitten Abi. That's about it!

'Becky,' I called from the other side of the chariot. A brown haired girl appeared, she smiled.

'Yes, Hyro?' Becky and I were more like sisters than pharaoh and maid. I showed her the list, she nodded in approval as she read it.

'Why am I not on the list Hyro?' she queried. This was the best part I thought to myself.

'If you are friends with a pharaoh you will be useful in the afterlife.'

'Are you saying I am no use to you and I'm not your friend?' gasped Becky.

'No, I'm saying you will rule when I die and to never be friends with a pharaoh!' I laughed.

Anna Champion (11)
Downview Primary School

A Day In The Life Of Santa Claus

'Christmas Eve, Christmas Eve, haaaa!' Santa Claus sighed.
'Dear, your iced tea and frozen fish are ready.'
'I'm busy love!'
'Doing what?' Mrs Claus asked curiously.
'Errr, feeding the monkeys?'
'*What monkeys?*'

The only reason I didn't want to have the iced tea and frozen fish is because they really are well and truly frozen! The last time I had frozen fish my teeth fell out and I had to have false ones.

Am I so silly? Monkeys! Mrs Claus knows full well, we don't own monkeys. Should of said reindeer, I am feeding the reindeer.

'Hi, Santa how are you?'
'Oh you know Bob, cool!'
'Well, you might not be after this Santa,'
'Why Bob?'
'Emmm, well you know the pooping penguins, the elves have been so rushed off their feet that we have forgotten to make them.'
'What!'
Santa could of cried at this terrible news.

'Santa, Santa, I heard about the pooping penguins and I had an idea!' cried Spot the dog.
'Go on.'
'Well you could not give the pooping penguins to the kids but . . .' Spot was cut short by Santa.
'What if the kids want those pooping penguins they will get them.'
'No, instead they can have a . . . a . . . oh what was it again . . . a . . . a . . . show! With Tweenies and Teletubbies. It will be great.'
'Wow, what a good idea,' exclaimed Santa.

Boxing Day

'Hey, hey it's time to come and play with the Tweenies, yeah!'
Then Santa heard one little child say, 'Wow, this is better than any toy
in the world. And that pleased Santa so much.

Kelly Gunstone (10)
Estcots CP School

A Day In The Life Of The Earth

'I think I fancy a little nap, give myself a morning rest . . .' muttered the Earth dozing off . . .

Suddenly the Earth awoke with a start. She peered around space and things looked a little different. No, wait, they felt different too! The pain in Earth's side was gone!

'Oh my! The hole in my ozone layer is gone! Goodness that feels better. Oh, and I can hardly believe it! My body feels light and clear; no pollution! No factory fumes either! How different things are!'

Earth went on like this for a little while, gleefully happy, noting all of the little changes.

'Hmmm, since things seem so much better, let's have a look at what those humans are doing . . .'

At first Earth could not believe her eyes. There was no crying! No guns! No sadness, war, arguments, anger or fighting! There was only peace, happiness, trust and love.

'Oh,' cried Earth, 'What lovely people! They are so kind and gentle! The animals look healthy and happy, and there is no deforestation! What a perfect world . . . perfect world . . . perfect world . . .'

With a jolt Earth's eyes flickered open. The pain in her side was back, her body felt heavy and polluted and the sound of war and anger floated into space.

Her heart felt a spasm of pain; and a tear trickled from her eye.

'I only hope that one day my dream of a perfect world will come true. One day those humans will learn, but when? I can only hope.'

Rachel Day (10)
Estcots CP School

A DAY IN THE LIFE OF AN INVENTOR

'I've done it! I've finally invented the super power automatic *Mach 2* lawn mower.'

George Block gazed up at the astonishing black bulk of machinery complete with its own scarlet lights. After three years of inventing it was finished.
'Well, here it goes.' He reached forward to switch it on. The whole machine seemed to come alive and start whirring. The lights began to flash. He slipped round to the control and programmed it to go and cut Mrs O'Mally's lawn. He slid open the giant double doors and pressed 'Go'.

That lunch time George switched on the TV, the newsreader popped up. George was just on the brink of changing the channel when he noticed his lawnmower in the corner of the screen.

'We can now see some live coverage of this terrible monster in action,' the reader announced. The screen showed his invention had just rambled down a street and was heading for Brackleby Lake like an elephant that had just seen a mouse.

Without thinking, George dropped his cheese and pickle sandwich, rushed to his electric blue sports car and sped off to Brackleby.

As he arrived at the town he saw it speeding towards the lake. He took a giant leap and pelted after it just in time to whack the 'stop' button. He breathed a sigh of relief.

An hour later he was apologising to the mayor.

'Sorry, about all that, but I have another idea for a walking washing machine.'

'No!' came the reply.

Christopher Morrell (11)
Groombridge St Thomas Primary School

A DAY IN THE LIFE OF BONNIE THE CAT

No, not the vet's! I'm not going, there is no way you're going to get me in that basket. Ouch. Where am I? Bang. Fooled again. They always get me with the towel.

I'm off for my annual check-up at the vet's but this year I'm having an injection, help!

Well here we are, the most dreaded place in the animal kingdom - the vet's.

'Bonnie, please come through to Mr Baker's room, thank you,' the voice called. They placed me on the examination table. Shock, horror. I've never had to endure such pain in all my life, and to think my owner had said it wouldn't hurt!

'Bring her back next year for a booster injection.' I couldn't believe my ears, come back to have another injection? I leapt at the vet's face, claws out and screamed, 'Meeooww!'

'Aaahh,' the vet cried, astonished at my sudden change of mood.

'Calm down Bonnie,' my owner said soothingly reaching out gingerly to pat my brown fur. I decided to calm down and slid slowly to the floor leaving the vet's jacket in shreds.

'Out, get out of here, I never want to see you or your cat again.'

As I lay in the garden that night after a treacherous ride home I watched the golden ball of wool my owner referred to as the sun disappearing behind the trees. I wondered what I could do to the next vet I go to. I purred to myself and flopped over in the daisies and fell into a deep and well-earned sleep.

Sarah Vardon (11)
Groombridge St Thomas Primary School

A DAY IN THE LIFE OF AN EAGLE

The orange ball of fire gradually rose above the fantastically white chalk cliffs. It was a new day and time to go on one of my early hunting trips for I needed some breakfast. I spread out my spectacular wings and took flight.

While flying over the pebbly terrain below I spotted a small young deer drinking from a tiny sparkling stream which I had never noticed before on my past flights. I dived and felt the rushing of the wind against my feathers. My first attack was a complete success. I rose up into the brilliant blue sky with a scent of victory about me. This was a great day for me, the catch of the young deer meant two days supply of food for me without having to go out and hunt again.

Now I was in need of a cool refreshing drink to quench my thirst. But first I needed to drop off my heavy burden of food so I flew down to my nest of strong twigs and soft furry moss and dropped the delicious food down into the nest. I set off to the waterhole. All the animals drink from it and it is often crowded and busy because everyone wants a drink. I ventured to the edge of the water and paddled my feet into the cool inviting shallows. When the shot rang out my head hadn't even lifted from the waterhole.

Nick James (11)
Groombridge St Thomas Primary School

A DAY IN THE LIFE OF CARROT

Carrot was strolling through the streets kicking a rock. He couldn't feel his feet because he was so cold. People looked round in disgust. Carrot was in a group with other lonely children. Carrot was his nickname, because he had orange hair. They all had nicknames: Scramble, Ratatattat, Fishface and Kipper. All of them had creased and holey clothing. They cuddled up together. They were all frightened except Carrot. One day Carrot was going looking for food, when a man came up to him and said 'Do you want a home and some food?'

'I have to go now. Sorry,' Carrot said and walked away, but then, secretly followed the man home. He went back to his gang. Then in the morning he went back and saw a sign on the door welcoming homeless children. Carrot went up to the door of it, because all his friends were in there. He wanted to go in too.

Thomas came to the door and said, 'I'm afraid there're no beds left. You'll have to sleep outside.'

In the morning Thomas went looking for Carrot and found him in the middle of the road. Then Thomas said, 'I will care for all the children. They are still as important as grown-ups.'

Madeleine Feltham
Groombridge St Thomas Primary School

A DAY IN A LIFE OF THOMAS BARNADO

Thomas Barnado lived in the Victorian times. He was called Doctor Thomas Barnado because he was a doctor. He was still training to be a doctor when he came across a group of boys in the street. They were all bunched up together shivering in a dark cold corner. Then Thomas said to himself, 'I must help these children.'

So he bought a big house in the middle of the town. It has white clean beds and lovely fresh food. He helped every boy and girl in the house.

Then one night a little boy called Carrot knocked on the door and asked if he could stay the night. Thomas said, 'You'll have to sleep on the streets.'
So he did. In the morning it was a nice sunny day. Thomas looked for Carrot all over town. Then eventually he found Carrot, but it wasn't all good news. Carrot was in the middle of the road dead and Thomas said he would care about every child that asked him to.

All the children were very special to Thomas Barnado but Carrot was the special one. Barnado felt so sorry for Carrot that he didn't eat or sleep for a day.

Zoe Neilson (8)
Groombridge St Thomas Primary School

A Day In The Life As A Motorist

It was the day of the grand race Everyone was nervous, including me. We mounted our bikes. Number one was me, Magraph, two was Chater, three was McNamara and four was Seal. I waited for the green light to flash. We were off to a crashing start, *Crash*! Number two (Chater) crashed into four (Seal).

'So it's between Magraph and McNamara now,' I heard the commentator shout.
'But what's this? Seal is getting back on his bike and he's off!'
'He's good but I'm better.' I muttered to myself. I wasn't listening to the commentator but I wished I had.

When I was near the finish line the bottom stand fell down. A rhino's head stuck out of the bottom stand. There was a scream of terror as everyone made for the exit. Everyone except me. I just rode off towards the finish line.

I finished the race first and I rode towards the rhino who chased me as I was the only one there.
'It must have escaped from the zoo,' I said to myself. I knew the way to the zoo so my plan was to ride into the zoo and into the rhino's cage and escape quickly by locking the rhino in its cage. So I rode off in the direction of the zoo.

It wasn't long before the rhino was in a rampage. I rode as fast as I could towards the zoo. The rhino was occasionally distracted, but it soon went back on the track. It was knocking anything that got in the way out of the way. It ran over ten cars, four vans and five Land Rovers. Finally, we got to the zoo. I went into the rhino's cage, the rhino came in with me so I quickly rode out and locked the cage door.

Huw McNamara & Ryan Seal (9)
Groombridge St Thomas Primary School

A Day In The Life Of Van Gogh

Van Gogh was the most tragic artist who ever lived. Nothing ever seemed to go right for him, he was not very happy. He never even smiled in his own self portraits. Van Gogh was born in Holland in 1853 and died in France in 1890.

Van Gogh did not decide to become a painter till he was grown up. Van Gogh always tried his best at anything he did. So he went to different art schools to learn everything he could about drawing and painting. When he was quite young, he drew poor people and in one of his paintings there were only a few potatoes for dinner. The colours in Van Gogh's early paintings are very dark and sad because he wanted to say to everyone that poor people live a hard life.

One day he saw some very colourful paintings. He liked the brightness in the work. Soon Van Gogh's painting became really bright. Because Van Gogh was always sending and receiving letters he got to know his postman. In 1886 Vincent moved to Paris.

Jessica Spicer (9)
Groombridge St Thomas Primary School

A DAY IN THE LIFE OF AN ELEPHANT

It was a lovely day and we went to have a wash. My friends and I played in the water until our parents called us out. After a while we had something to eat. I didn't eat much. We eat grass, foliage, small branches, twigs and fruit. My friend's uncle died because he lost all of his teeth and could not feed himself, so he died of starvation. Our ears are used as fans to create a stream of air over our bodies. Our tusks are elongated incisor teeth that continue to grow throughout our lifetime. People think that because we are the largest and most powerful of all living land mammals, we are also the most gentle, living in peaceful family units. Our trunks protect our skin against insect bites with a dust bath. We live together in family units but adult bulls are solitary. Our call is a throaty rumbling which we do constantly to communicate or loud trumpeting when we are angry. We are entirely vegetarian. We live for about 70 years. The thing I like about being an elephant is that you have fun and you get to go for walks and play in the water. A day in the life of an elephant is worth a lifetime of any other creature.

Emma Pickford (11)
Harcourt Primary School

DOLPHINS

In the cold Pacific ocean there was once the land of the dolphins. They jumped and leapt out of the water; they were the most amazing creatures of the sea. The water was still and dull but when the dolphins came, the sea became alive and wild. The dolphins are like gently leaping waves against each rock.

Dolphins can swim under water right to the bottom of the sea. Dolphins swim through the water swishing their tails up and down to propel themselves forward. Dolphins are the best animals in the deep blue sea. At sunset they will dance and play on the waves like people. I would watch the dolphins all day and even all night. They are like real ballerinas.
At home my mum says, 'Been watching them dolphins again?'
You see my mum doesn't understand about the dolphins. They are lovely things but she doesn't share my fascination. That night I had a dream about me swimming with them. It was fantastic and I told Mum. She said, 'One day you will get to do it for real.'

I went to the ocean, then I went home and started my life as a dolphin watcher.

Ashley West (10)
Harcourt Primary School

DOLPHINS

In a country not far from here, a dolphin who lives in the deep blue sea is happy. She jumps through the air like she is at shows. Sometimes she comes out of the deep blue sea to shows, but not all the time. The deep blue sea is a peaceful place to relax in. The waves splash like the rain falling from the sky. The birds fly around, singing in the sky. Dolphins push through the water with their tails. She does tricks in the water. In the last two days she has been taken out of the deep blue sea by people from Sea World to make her do more tricks and more difficult tricks. It is so amazing to see her jumping in the deep blue sea with her friends. When she was taken out of the water, they wouldn't let her go back to her friends. This lady walked by Sea World and she heard the two men talking, one was saying, 'Take her back,' and one was saying, 'Keep her.' The lady found a phone and rang some other people and said, that they wouldn't let her go back into the sea. So they came down and got her and put her back in the deep blue sea to swim with her friends, then they went home and the dolphin was happy ever after.

Jessica Campbell (10)
Harcourt Primary School

A DAY IN THE LIFE OF BIBI THE CAT!

Bibi lives in a house at 26 Paraker Way. She is so lazy. The only time she actually gets up is if there's food or if she needs the toilet. When she sleeps she always snores. She always sits in the sun and is very boring. When you stroke her she just turns her head. She sits on the window sill nearly all day and sits on the table as well. She messes it up. She is always scrounging. She is very old. She is fourteen. That is very, very old for a cat. She is quite rude as well and when you call her she just turns away. She nearly eats all the food we give her a day. When she sits on my lap she sticks her paws in my legs. Bibi wakes up and goes for her breakfast. Then she goes and lays in the bright sun. Then she goes to the toilet. She eats again, goes back to sleep. She gets up and lays on the chair with nothing left for us to sit on. Then she has something to eat, goes in my room and sleeps. I love her but she is so lazy and quiet that you wouldn't know if she was there.

So you see, a day in the life of Bibi the cat is boring, because all she does is *sleep and eat!*

Jasmin Cowdroy (10)
Harcourt Primary School

A Day In The Life Of Creepy The Caterpillar

Creepy the caterpillar was walking along on a nice hot colourful day in the summer. Suddenly this great big dark shadow appeared from nowhere. Creepy was unaware of this. A big brown bird swooped at the caterpillar, but just missed. Creepy was running as fast as his sixteen legs would carry him. He tried to get home but the bird swooped again and yet still missed.

He ran up a tree and into a cosy place which happened to be a birds' nest. Creepy didn't know that. He felt something warm. He lifted his head to see a big brown bird with her eggs. She was not very happy. Creepy was on his way out of the nest and on the way home again being chased by the bird.

He ran and ran until he reached home. He told everyone at home.

Amy Thurling (10)
Harcourt Primary School

A Day In The Life Of Harry The Mouse

Every day Harry the mouse wakes up in a cage full of straw. A wheel and a drinking bottle hanging from the side of his cage and food on a platform. Harry is a fluffy ball with fat, chubby legs and beady swift-moving eyes. He starts his day by making an annoying little squeak that echoes in my ears. He does this to make me get up and fill up his bowl with his breakfast. After eating his breakfast he would go and have a quick run on his wheel and take a sip of fresh cool water from his bottle. After this he would just stand and stare at the walls. After this busy work I'd let him out of his cage. Usually he just curls up in a ball and looks like some round fluff. He usually after this just goes to sleep.

After waking, he just sits there and waits for me to come home. As soon as the door makes a little creak his ears prick up like thorns and he climbs his ladder and hides, but he just gets bored and drops off the ladder, asleep.

Calum Muir (9)
Harcourt Primary School

A DAY IN THE LIFE OF SPOT THE DOG

One morning Spot woke up, he ate his breakfast, then he ran round to his friend's house next door. There, he and his friend Jake chased their tails and went and chased the cats. When they got bored with that, Spot went to a gap in the fence. He barked to Jake to follow him. Spot jumped through the gap in the fence, Jake followed him. They crossed the road safely.

Next they ran across a meadow. They were really enjoying themselves. Suddenly they saw a river ahead of them. Spot dived in and splashed about, Jake followed him. After a lot of splashing they finally reached the other side. Here Spot realised he felt hungry, so did Jake.

They found a rabbit, killed it and ate it. Next they came to a lake and again they dived in and swam across. On the other side Spot realised that he was getting slightly homesick, so he turned round and went back the way he had come.

He swam across the lake, Jake was close behind him. Again they felt hungry so they caught a rabbit for dinner, ate it and swam back across the river. Finally they ran across the meadow for it was getting dark, and crossed the road. Here they went back to their homes. Spot was very happy to be back home in his cosy basket. He had enjoyed the adventure, but he liked staying at home the most.

Rachael Martin (10)
Harcourt Primary School

A Day In The Life Of An Owl

I woke up in the night. I did not feel well. The day began. I went to clean my teeth. When I looked in the mirror, I had feathers and a beak. I didn't feel scared. I tried to fly but I couldn't, I tried again. Up I went and out of the window. I flew and flew. I saw a rabbit and dived down to get it. I missed. I tried again, I got it in my claws. I flew to a nearby tree and ate some. It was lovely. I ate more and more until it was all gone. In the tree there was a hole big enough for me to get in. It was very warm as it was a cold winter day. I flew out and collected grass, leaves and feathers and made a bed to sleep in for the daytime. Owls don't go out in the light. I was awakened by a bang. I looked out and there was a man with a gun and a net. I got out of the hole and flew away as far as I could away from the people. It was getting light, there was a tingling feeling in my wings. They were turning back to skin. I landed on the ground before I fell down I had to walk home. I was over six miles away from home. I went back in a lorry. Mum and Dad were asleep. I was too sleepy to stay awake. I soon dropped off to sleep.

Daniel Bailey (10)
Harcourt Primary School

A DAY IN THE LIFE OF HENRY VIII

'Where is my crown!' I roared. I am so angry. My wife Catherine of Aragon has given birth to a daughter called Mary, when I wanted a son. 'Where is my crown!' One of my servants was coming. Just then my wife came in holding Mary in her arms. Catherine was wearing a burgundy dress with a gold shawl.

About eleven o'clock, we rode to the tower of London where we were going to execute the countess of Salisbury. Then on came the Countess. Catherine could not let Mary see so she covered her eyes. Then *chop!* Off came her head.

That evening I had a feast of pork chops, beef, turkey, peas, sweetcorn and carrots. For dessert I had mint choc chip and chocolate ice cream. Strawberry, toffee, fudge and chocolate sauces. For drinks, brandy, scotch, wine and my favourite beer. One of my servants put Mary to bed while Catherine and I talked. Then by ten o'clock I went to bed in my royal bed.

The next morning I had an English breakfast; sausages, egg, bacon. By eleven o'clock I got in my carriage with my wife and daughter to go to York for the day. By evening we had a massive feast again. My servant took Mary to bed and I talked to Catherine. By ten o'clock I went to bed.

Holly Fitton (10)
Iwade CP School

A DOLPHIN

Today I've been swimming. I was jumping from side to side, up and down. It's good fun and funny. When you are under the sea you can see fish, it's brilliant, fascinating. I can do lots of things underwater. I eat fish and all kinds of things.

I enjoy being a dolphin. Oh, I am twenty-six years old. I've got lots of friends, people who I meet are very kind. They like me so much they can't come away from me. I'm blue and I never let my friends down. My name is Georgina Louise Fairhurst. My mum, Annette, my dad, Leslie, sister, Jessy, brother, Paul. 'Oh no! Look,' I said to my friends, 'someone is killing the other dolphins. Come on, we've got to help them. What's wrong?'
'We're not going to help them, they might kill us,' said my friends.
I said, 'I'll go myself.' So I went and freed the other dolphins. They said I was a hero. I said thank you and we all became friends, so I've got more friends than I thought. My old friends said I was excellent!

I became popular. My mum, she had a baby dolphin. She called it Chris. We were so happy together and enjoyed everything.

Georgina Fairhurst (9)
Iwade CP School

A DAY IN THE LIFE OF ERIC LAWSON

It was my first match of a lifetime and Celtic was in the Scottish league. Our first match was against Rangers, but first we had to stand still for two minutes because there was a plane crash with Rangers supporters in. Celtic kicked off. I got the ball. I dribbled it past everyone and I struck the ball in the top corner. It was a great goal by Eric Lawson. Rangers kicked off again - Celtic were playing very well but Rangers were passing the ball like a real team so we could not tackle them. Then the Rangers player struck the ball, but our fantastic keeper, Daniel Smith, punched it over the cross bar. Rangers took a corner - it was a great corner, but not that good because Daniel Smith jumped up and caught it. Daniel Smith kicked it out, Eric Lawson crossed it to Jamie Smith. Jamie Smith took the ball round the keeper and tapped it into the net and it was a great goal. Celtic were 2-0 up. Rangers kicked off again. Eric Lawson tackled Paul Teague and took it round everyone and scored. Celtic were 3-0 up. There were three minutes extra time. I tackled Robert Varrier. Eric Lawson hit the ball from the centre and the ball went over the keeper and into the net. The final score was 4-0 to Celtic.

Paris Reeves (10)
Iwade CP School

A Day In The Life Of Roly

I had a dream. In my dream I was Roly out of 101 Dalmatians and this is what happened. I was born on a stormy night. My mum was Purdy and my dad was Pongo. Miss De Ville wanted us for our coats but our parents wouldn't let us die. We were ten weeks old and they came for us, Horrace and Jasper, they worked for De Ville. Our parents had gone for a walk and Nanny was looking after us. Jasper whacked Nanny around the head and Horrace came for us. When we got in the van there were lots of other puppies. They took us to a big house outside of London. Horrace and Jasper were watching TV, then De Ville came storming in.

'Kill them tonight,' she said.

'Woof, woof,' I shouted at De Ville.

'I want my coat from your friend, or you're dead.' De Ville stormed back out.

'We should get out of here,' I whispered to the others. 'Come on, we're going.' I told them so we all set off.

'Come on Horrace, we've got some killing to do,' said Jasper.

But by the time they said that, we had found our parents and were on our way home. What we didn't know was that we were being followed by De Ville herself. In an hour's time she had found us and was just about to kill us when I woke up in my bed, but what happened in the end?

Katie Whiffen (10)
Iwade CP School

A Day In The Life Of Mameluke

I'm a Mameluke. I'm a man in the days of the Celts. I'm a fighter that rides a horse and throws knives. The Scarens, my people have joined with near tribes to conquer the Egyptians. The Mongels and Celts were eager to join us for they are also on a quest to destroy the Egyptians. We are awaiting orders from Joan of Arc, a French General. She ordered us to destroy an Egyptian cathedral. She sent us a monk and her royal guards to help us on our quest. We set off on our adventure. On the way we fought an army of longbowmen. We defeated them. We ended up at their gate, but two watchtowers surrounded them. We sent over our bombard cannons, one of the people holding it died, but the rest were kept in tip-top condition. Me and my fellow Mamelukes were ordered to depart from the others. I was put in charge. We ran to a panel of ground that was out of range from the watchtowers. 'Attack,' I called. We knocked it down. I sent a Mameluke to tell the others I'd found a way in. The rest of us entered their city with caution. We found a stable but destroyed it. I told another Mameluke to tell the others to find another way in. Orders from Joan. We stood our ground near the cathedral. The others had found another way in and were already attacking the cathedral. So I called 'Attack.' The cathedral crumbled to pulp and we returned to our city. I was classed as a hero from that day on.

Terry Brookman (10)
Iwade CP School

A Day In The Life Of A Ghost

'Hello, I'm Heidi, I was killed in a road accident last year. I am now eleven. It gets quite lonely up here but at least I have you to talk to. Right, We're gonna have some fun. Didn't you guess no one can see me. I'm invisible. Off we go. This is the place I was killed 7209 highway, the flowers are a bit rotten now, yuck! Oh look, Mummy's left me something in the middle of the lot but it is not rotten, it says

'You are my little sunshine! My little sunshine! You make me happy when skies are grey, I never noticed how much I love you, so please don't take my sunshine away.'

That brings a tear to my eye that does. I'll tell you what, shall we go and visit Mummy? Oh all right, we'll go at night but there is no point, she can't see me! We'll go anyway because I love her. Wow! Look at the house, I have not seen this in ages, it's all glittery and new. Ah! My mum's crying, don't cry Mum, I love you, don't cry. Oh! There's my cat Maisie. Oh! Oh no! What's wrong? It's dead. Oh, let's play a few tricks, Mum's crying over the cat. Let's rattle the pans, turn on the television, flush the toilet! I'll write a letter, this is what I'll write.

Dear Mummy, I'll always love you, from Heidi XXXXX

That will make sure I'm always in her heart. I am going to heaven now. Bye, bye. Remember me!'

Alissa Solecki (10)
Iwade CP School

GERI: PURE

'It's 7 o'clock and I'm dead tired! Last night I did a live performance at Wembley and as you can hear from my voice I'm not feeling too well.

As a test of my strength as a pop star I've got to do another live performance tonight, but this time it's at a concert hall in Leeds. I really don't think I'll be able to do it. I don't want to let my fans down and if I do I'll never forgive myself, but then you can just say to yourself everyone has days off.

I've really got to start preparing for tonight. I don't know what songs I'm singing and to make things even worse which is virtually impossible, my clothes and make-up designer has been taken ill, and my hired make-up designer is totally rubbish! Now I've got to choose my own clothes and believe you me, I've got no idea about it.

It's 8 o'clock and my concert starts in an hour. At the moment, I'm travelling to Leeds in my new concert bus. I still don't feel well, my voice is a little better, but I can't get to all the right vocals, so I've got to sing the songs with reasonably low vocals. At the moment, I'm going to be singing, 'It's Raining Men', 'Lift Me Up', and loads more!

It's five to nine and I'm going on stage any minute now . . .

Kayleigh Grant (10)
Iwade CP School

A DAY IN THE LIFE OF TOM THE TIGER

One day I swapped my life with Tom the tiger. When I got to where Tom lived I slept for a while.

I awoke from my sleep and I hunted for some food. Then I ate the food that I had found. I had found quite a bit. Then I licked my cub's fur. Then I had a nap. When I awoke from my sleep I played. I played hide and seek with my cubs and my friend called Rachel. I hunted for some deer to eat for lunch. I bit into the deer I had found, it seemed a lot of food. After I had eaten I played roll with my best friend called Hannah because we were next-door neighbours. After we had played we went to sleep. When I had awoke, my aunt came round. She brought some meat for the cubs, and some more meat for me. Then we walked in the jungle. After we had walked in the jungle we talked. Then my aunt went and we went to sleep. When I awoke I was in my own house and doing my homework.

Megan Crocombe (8)
Joy Lane Junior School

A DAY IN THE LIFE OF SWIMMY THE GOLDFISH

Chapter One - The Foreign Goldfish

In a pool, in a Whitstable front garden, a mother goldfish was laying an egg. When the egg was out, the mother waited for it to hatch. In the Arctic, a tern was flying south to the United Kingdom to check out the heat. It happened to fly straight to the pool where the goldfish was and her baby egg. The tern flew to the pool and looked in. She saw a goldfish egg and didn't know what it was so she grabbed it to show her friends in the Arctic. Then she realised the incredible heat and flew back to the Arctic. She showed it to her friends, as she did, it hatched.
'What are you going to call it?' asked Slippy the seal and Panta the Penguin.
'I think I will call it Swimmy!' cried the tern in delight.

Chapter Two - A New Mate

Swimmy was eight months old when the tern who was working as his mother died. She was hit by a dolphin by accident and drowned. Swimmy had found out that he could look after himself quite well, so he didn't really need a guardian. He was getting used to his new home. His gold body was turning white because of how long he had stayed in the Arctic.

When Swimmy was two years old he had started going to the bottom of the sea to check out the different types of fish. He had had a nasty encounter with an octopus. He had escaped a shower of ink. He swam to the surface and a seal was staring at him.
'Hello,' it said. 'My name is Slippy, what's yours?'
'Swimmy,' replied Swimmy.
'I've been watching you and you are quite impressive. Would you like to be my friend?'
'Okay,' said Swimmy.
'I was born in the Atlantic Sea,' Slippy explained to Swimmy.
'Hello,' said a squeaky voice. It was a penguin.
'Look, Panta the penguin's here!' cried Slippy. 'He swam from the Antarctica across the Atlantic Sea to the Arctic.'
'Cool!' said Swimmy, and swam away.

Chapter Three - Tricking Sharp

Slippy had an enemy called Sharp. He was a swordfish. Slippy knew he couldn't beat Sharp on his own, so when Swimmy was three years old he asked Swimmy for assistance.

'All right,' said Swimmy. He agreed these as the plans:

1. Slippy jumps in the water and Sharp comes pelting at him.
2. Swimmy jumps in the water and grabs Sharp's tail.
3. Sharp stops swimming and Slippy ties Sharp's nose to his tail with his tail.

They did it, and then untied Sharp. He swam away and never came back. 'That was funny,' laughed Slippy. 'Thanks for your help!' Swimmy nodded his head and laughed too.

Chapter Four - A Happy Ending In The Arctic

Swimmy is now seven years old and Slippy is nine. Panta thinks he should go on a diet. He's been eating too much salmon, and he should get back onto things like cod and tuna and mackerel. A young fish got lost and Swimmy showed it the way to Greenland, where it wanted to be. Swimmy knew that he would have to go south because of summer coming up, like he had done seven years before. In the summer it was also his birthday, so he was quite sad not to be with his friends on his birthday. But, he was eight, and he swam back to the Arctic where his friends greeted him once more. He soon had a girlfriend when he was ten. They got married and then the babies came. Thousands. Swimmy lived happily with his wife in the Arctic.

The End - or maybe not . . .

Chapter ? - Hidden Chapter

'Gosh! I've been thinking about my whole life in one day!' said Swimmy the goldfish. He thought about Slippy, Panta, Sharp and his fake mother tern. He went and laid down on his ice bed, and sunk down into a dream that you have just heard.

Ronnie Simmonds (8)
Joy Lane Junior School

A DAY IN THE LIFE OF GWINNIE THE CAT

Gwinnie the cat has her breakfast, goes outside to play. Comes back in, sleeps on my bed, jumps off when my sister comes in. Sleeps on the window sill, goes outside, jumps over the fence, walks off and comes back at tea time. And that is a day of Gwinnie the cat.

Alys Scott (9)
Joy Lane Junior School

A Day In The Life Of Dody The Dog

When Dody the dog wakes up he has some food, then goes and sits in his basket. He goes for a walk, he plays in the garden. Then he sits in the living room, then has lunch. He sits in his basket, fights with the dog next door, watches telly, then he goes and sleeps in his basket. He wakes up and goes swimming in the sea. Comes back for dinner, then sits in his basket and sleeps by the fire. Then he goes upstairs and sleeps on the bed.

Carys Powell-Smith (8)
Joy Lane Junior School

A DAY IN THE LIFE OF RACHEL STEVENS

One night I wished to be Rachel Stevens but then my dad called and said it was bedtime. Then I had a dream that I was Rachel Stevens. I was in a concert, I was singing with the rest of the band. We were singing Don't Stop Movin.' After we signed loads of autographs. Then we went to the hotel that we were staying in. But then it was all over and it was the morning. I saw I was still Rachel Stevens.

When I went to school everyone was thinking I was a new girl at the school, but when I spoke they knew it was me. Then I sang in front of the school. They all thought I sounded really good. Then it was quiet reading, but instead they had to ask me questions. Somebody asked me 'How did you get like this?'
I answered, 'I don't know, I just woke up and I was like this.'

It was home time and I went down the town and everybody wanted my autograph. I saw the band and Rachel was missing. Then they saw me and we sang Don't Stop Movin'. Then I went home and there on the table was a huge dinner. I asked my mum and dad why it was so big.
They answered 'We're having Rachel from S Club 7 for dinner. Look, here she is.'
It was actually me. They had said that because they hadn't looked at me when I got in. They had only a small part of the dinner and I had loads of it.

Rebekah Crocombe (8)
Joy Lane Junior School

A Day In The Life Of A Sorcerer

Hello, my name is Buc, I'm a sorcerer and I live in the Sorcerer's Academy. I am a student sorcerer, this is my last year before I graduate as a professional sorcerer.

The date is 24/5/305, today I'm going to try to do a new spell for my final exam, but first I need to get some potions and lotions and a new assistant while I'm there.

The potions and lotions and assistant shop, called 'Sorcerers R Us' was on the edge of the enchanted woods. I met my friend Slash the knight on my way.
He said, 'Get on my pet dragon and we'll give you a lift!'
With a puff of smoke we sped to the city of Speed on the edge of the wood. I decided what I would need, volcano rock, suntan lotion, flipstone, rainbow crystals and my new assistant, an owl.

My spell will make lava sprout up out of the ground and spread and fill the beds of the evil Black Priests. First I was supposed to put the volcanic rock in the cauldron then the rainbow crystals and finally the flipstone mixed with the suntan lotion, but I did it in the reverse order. Instead of lava I got *ice!* The ice froze the Black Priests so Owl and I quickly teleported them to the North Pole.

Even though the spell was wrong, I passed my exam with flying colours because I rid Speed of the horrid Black Priests forever.

Tomes Linehan (11)
Knockhall CP School

A Day In The Life Of A Baby Shark

Hello, I'm a shark and I'm looking for my mum. It is so cold in the sea. I am sad because I'm all alone. Mum thinks I'm big enough to look after myself. Well, perhaps I am. She's going to meet me in Australia, I've got to make my own way there.

I'm feeling hungry, better start looking for food. I can smell blood, I'll follow the smell. I find the remains of a seal. I circle it first, sniff it, look to see if there are any more sharks about, circle it once more then attack. I feel better after eating.

I'm very cold, I want my mum. How am I going to find Australia? What's that up there? It's got dark. Is it my mum? No, it's too big. I'm scared, it's enormous, will it hurt me? I'll take a peep, it's a ship. Mum has told me about these. It might go to Australia. I'll follow it.

I followed it for hours, stopping for food on the way. There was a sign saying Australia ahead - danger Great Whites.

Suddenly, I heard a familiar noise. It sounded like my mum. *It is my mum.* She was pleased to see me and proud that I'd made it on my own.

We swam towards a beautiful rock where I told Mum all about my adventure.

Jamie Jones (11)
Knockhall CP School

A DAY IN THE LIFE OF AN ARACHNID

Hello, nice day today isn't it? Ah, sorry, I just went blurting out without introducing myself. I am an arachnid. Can you guess what that is? I'll give you a clue. I have eight legs. My prey is locust and crickets. Crickets and locusts are my favourite and I also eat other insects.

I live in a tank and it's peaceful here. Yes, finally a chance to escape. Food time. Right, here's what my plan is. I am going to go when he opens the lid. I'm going to pounce out and run. Ready, steady, go! Yes, I'm free. Jump onto the fridge and then the cabinet and the floor. I'm going to make it, he's gaining. Out of the door. Oh, there she is, the missus. Whenever she sees me she says, 'Get that thing away from me, ahhh . . .' He's gaining, *no*, he's got me. Help, help, give me freedom, someone call the cops.

Back in this tank again. Better get a drink and a snack too. Wow! Look at that one. I'll have him. I pounce, my fangs dig in his chubby body and I suck the blood out, then chew. Lovely. By the way did you guess what I am? I am a tarantula.

Jonathon Blackwell (11)
Knockhall CP School

A Day In The Life Of A Giraffe

I love being a giraffe, but sometimes it can get a bit boring. I don't know a lot yet because I'm only two months old. I've got a mum, dad, sister and brother. I'm not as old as them so my neck isn't as long, and I can't see as far as them. I can be funny sometimes because I haven't quite got the hang of galloping yet.

I live in a safari park and people come and visit all the time. Mum, they're taking a picture, quick, pose. We love getting our picture taken, because we are so beautiful and we are so good at posing. There is one problem though, it seems so quiet when the humans go home.

One good thing about living here is they give you lots of food. The best tree I like to eat leaves off is the Acacia tree, they are so yummy. Mmm, I wonder if it's time to eat yet, my tummy is really rumbling and it's making me feel sick.

I get fed up with just standing here, it can make me really grumpy. I wish there was something like a ball to play with, the seals have got a ball. It's so unfair. I know when my food is coming because I have got a brilliant sense of smell and outstanding good eyesight.

Joanna Hares (11)
Knockhall CP School

A Day In The Life Of A Needle

Always the same old routine, I get up in the morning when I'm shaken about. It's been the same for the last few weeks, up at ten by Karen, she's the person who first picks a needle and goes into her room. I haven't been chosen yet but today is my big chance. Yesterday, her best needle snapped on the denim, so hopefully, it's my turn. I'm bored of staying in the box. Here she comes now, please, please pick me. *Yes!* I've been picked. I hope it's not a fancy new sewing machine, all they do is go up, down, up, down, all day long.

Damn, brand new electric machine, worst of all sewing machines (as the rumour goes) just my luck. Oh luckily, I'm going through red velvet, my favourite, in with the thread, that really tickles, tastes like someone spilt coffee over it, now I'm being stuck to the machine, here it comes. *Wow!* This is fun, the complete opposite of the rumours, like the roller coaster I was put on in someone's purse, spooky or what, oh, it's finished. Oh no, please not the denim, please, *please* not the dreaded denim, please, have mercy, have mercy!

Oh no, goodbye cruel world, my life has ended, I have no chance of survival, here it comes. *Aaarh!* The pain, can't take it, my nib's snapped.

What, it's stopped, where am I? Is this Heaven? I must be faint, I will be being remoulded soon, my life is over, I can hear the furnace, here it comes.

Liam Harvey (11)
Knockhall CP School

A DAY IN THE LIFE OF A SNAIL

Beep, beep. The alarm rung. Yes, today's the day I leave the tree. I live in the middle of the forest and I live with my mum who is one year old and my brother who is one week old. My dad went to France on vacation and got eaten by a French man. Me, I am five weeks old and I have never been further than an inch away from home.

'See ya later, Mum,' I said.
'See you later son,' Mum said.
So I wandered off in search of a friend. After a while I found someone I had already met before. It was Sluggy. 'Sluggy, old pal,' I said.
'All right old mate?' said Sluggy.
So me and my mate Sluggy went off to look for food.

Eventually at 6:00pm we found somewhere to eat and we had lettuce and radishes, the lot and after we had finished we were stuffed and we slithered back to my house where we spent the night.

During the night I got woken up several times because we had hedgehogs trying to break in. There were two of them but seeing as Sluggy was sleeping on the sofa, once they eventually got in, Sluggy was more than enough to please them both.

Richard Medhurst (11)
Knockhall CP School

A DAY IN THE LIFE OF AN ELEPHANT

One tropical day it was weary and a busy day in India. I'm an elephant called Foxy, not an ordinary elephant. I am a clever animal who never forgets what the turtle tells him and always remembers the adventures he's had too and loves to eat peanuts.

Andy also lives in India with the clever elephant. He is not quite the same as he has the most terrible memory anyone has ever heard of and always says 'really' when he has heard a joke before and acts really bad when he is out with the clever elephant. It takes Andy the turtle three hours to walk over the bridge. Andy is seventy years old and used to be a teacher that taught science for five years and was paid £20,000 a year and was quite a rich teacher indeed.

Clever Foxy is seventy-five years old and used to be a carrier for the Indian people and was fed 250 peanuts a day and bananas and Foxy was very happy when he was fed.

He was offered three million for Foxy when he was working for them.

They suddenly saw a boy go to school and thought they should go to school also to learn lots of things like reading. So they went to school. They were there for two years. When the headmaster said they could be class teachers, Andy and clever Foxy were teachers with a high wage.

Andrew Fox (11)
Knockhall CP School

A Day In The Life Of A Cat

Hello, I am called Tara. I am a black cat. I have blue eyes. I hate dogs because they stink. I sit and watch the cars go past. I don't know who my parents are. I am eleven years old. Do you know who I am? I don't talk, I miaow.

I am a tabby cat. It's Monday morning. I am having a bath. Then I watch the cars go past with my friends. I go in when my owner calls to have my lunch. I go and play with my friends called Kel, Kerry, Rebecca, Will, Ni, Liam and Sunny. Then I go in and go to sleep. Monday night, I have a bath which takes a long time if you do it right. I watch the cars go past, that takes about an hour. Then I get called to eat my dinner. Then me, Kel, Kerry, Ni, Liam, Rebecca, Will and Sunny go to a disco and have fun. Kerry is going out with Kel, Rebecca is going out with Will, Ni is going out with Liam, I am going out with Sunny. Kerry, Rebecca and Ni are my best friends. Liam and Kel are my brothers. I have a sister called Keely.

I think it's time to go and get some of my cat food. Then I might go to sleep in my bed with my brothers and my sister, or I can sleep in a nice warm bed. I mean goodbye when I say miaow, goodbye.

Tara O'Connor (11)
Knockhall CP School

A Day In The Life Of A Lion

Oh here comes that snoopy zoo keeper who is coming to let us out. Look outside, it's a perfect day. I am going to snooze under the trees. Hooray, we are out. Where is that zoo keeper? I'm hungry. I hope she gets here soon.

Here comes the person who owns the zoo. He has not been round here for ages. The keepers are opening the gates. The children already start to scream as soon as they get through the gates. Look some of the adults are taking photos. Smile or make funny faces.

Look, here comes the keeper. It's time for breakfast. The keeper is going to say a speech all about us. Here goes:
'These animals have come from Africa. They have been imported here because the people over there were killing them for fur coats.'
Yab, yab, the same speech every day.

The kids are coming with their ice cream. Please don't drop it on my head today. Here comes the keeper again. She's got our water. It looks like lunch time. The keeper's gone back and got our lunch. I hope it's deer, the lamb was horrible.

While no one is about, I'll tell you a bit about myself. I have a golden kind of fur. I hate lamb but I love deer. I have big black eyes and a long tail. I love children and I hate people.

I am having another snooze under the trees for a couple of hours. Sleep, sleep. I just woke up, it's 4 o'clock. It's time we went in to play inside. The keeper is coming, let us in for our dinner, then we can play.

Joanne Hull (11)
Knockhall CP School

A Day In The Life Of A Bench

Here goes another day in the freezing cold weather. I know that I'm going to be busy today. I tell myself, all the children are playing on the ice, so their mums and dads will want somewhere to sit.

When the day began, all I was doing was standing there waiting for someone to sit on me. Then all of a sudden, this really posh family came and sat down. They were drinking tea, and I thought to myself, wouldn't it be great if I could have some of that and that made me feel sad because I wished I had a family and something hot inside me.

Soon after this, an old woman came along and sat on me. For some reason she started to talk to me. She said, 'I wish I was a bench and then I would live an easy life.'
I thought for a moment and felt pleased because she respected me.

Then from the distance, I saw the same boys that spread the graffiti all over my bench yesterday. I tried to warn the lady but of course she could not hear me. It was too late, the boys had hurt the lady and had spread the graffiti all over me again. The problem is that the boys just think I'm a lump of wood and have no feelings.

It is near the end of the day now, I start to feel tired and I hope tomorrow will be a much better day.

Leanne Hoskins (11)
Knockhall CP School

A Day In The Life Of The Millennium Dome!

There goes the boat that's passed me three times today and there's all the business people going to work, all happy and cheery. There goes the bus that takes people round London and here comes the first load of people to come inside me, but I haven't opened yet, there's still five minutes to go.

People start flowing in when the tolls open. The largest amount of people I've had inside me is 10,000, but I've got quite a lot today and it's only ten past nine.

I'm as long as ten double decker buses and as tall as Canary Wharf. When people arrive, I'm a bit nervous because if they don't like me I don't know what they'd do to me, but I'm also happy and excited.

I always hate twelve o'clock because it's time for the show and they bounce on my belly and it tickles me.

It's lovely and peaceful watching boats flowing down the river Thames and watching the London Eye turn slowly, full of people looking at me.

It's closing time now, all the business people are going home. I get all upset and emotional. I always get lonely when they go home. I hope they come back tomorrow.

Jamie Mackenzie (11)
Knockhall CP School

A DAY IN THE LIFE OF MY HAIR

Hello, I am part of you, do you know what part I am? I am your brown long, light-coloured hair on your head that blows in your face every day when you run.

Remember on Monday morning when you brushed me with your yellow brush, do you know how much you hurt me? You wouldn't like it if I pulled your eyelash, would you? Remember on Monday lunch when you washed me and you never got all the soap out, I was all horrible, it got all sticky with water in it.

Remember at dinner time when you let your best friend pull my hair around? Why don't you let me have my hair dyed like your friend did, you know Jenny's hair is my best friend. I like her hair, I think you should get me a new colour. Oh! By the way, I think you should take me to the chemist to get me some powder for the nits in my hair. They are starting to itch. I'm thinking of having my hair cut short, but I think I will miss it.

I hope I get a good night's sleep because you are always crushing me so I hardly get to go to sleep. So I will go now, bye.

Rebecca Elliott (10)
Knockhall CP School

A Day In The Life Of An Elephant

Oh, it's great being an elephant, but sometimes I wonder what if . . . Ah, there's my call for breakfast. I wonder what the menu is today, palm leaves or a special treat. That was the best breakfast I've had since I was born (two years ago).

Now it's off for a wash and brush my teeth. Right, there is my twig, now let's brush those teeth, and for the wash. Right, now I've done my teeth, wash and breakfast, so let's go and play with the others in the sand dip.

I absolutely love the sand dip. It is so much fun and you can take all of the family and mates and it doesn't cost one palm leaf. I don't know what I would do without it. I think it's time to go and stand at the edge of the track for some pictures to be taken of me, well you couldn't miss me anyway because I have a long fringe which is shaped like a triangle and my hair is as long as my fringe. Click, click, click, right that's my photo session over, now I'm going to see the family. Right, just a little bit until I get to the tree near the lake where my parents live. We were chatting for ages about the family and what has happened. Now I better be off, it's time for bed. See you later.

Crystal Kolsek (11)
Knockhall CP School

A Day In The Life Of The London Eye

Oh no! This side is too heavy which is making it hard to keep moving around. Hello, my name is the London Eye and I live in Greenwich right near the river Thames, so that means I get very cold in the winter because there is always a cold breeze coming from the river. My best friend is the Millennium Dome and he lives right next door to me and I talk to him all day long.

As well as talking to the Dome I watch and laugh at the people going to work at Canary Wharf. The only thing wrong with my job is that I'm a little bit scared of heights, but don't tell anyone because they will think I am stupid because what I do for my job and they will all laugh at me.

I like my job because I can see all kinds of people and what they are doing, and I see happy people, nervous, scared, worried and even angry people because they have to go to work.

When people come on me for a ride I feel very happy but sometimes I feel nervous because it looks like some people are going to be sick over me (and I don't want sick over me because it is disgusting). But when they get off I feel sad and lonely because I like seeing people being happy and having fun, and it makes me feel happy and pleased because I am making other people happy. See you later.

Lucy Wenham (11)
Knockhall CP School

A Day In The Life Of A Tree

Oh no! Here comes that woodpecker banging on my side. I try to move my branches but I'm too old and stiff. There goes Mr Banabe off to work. I wish I could go to work. There goes Miss Pennyfor, she's going to the gym to meet her friends and get fit. I've got no friends and I can't move let alone jump or run.

I wonder what the day is today, oh yes, Saturday. Oh no! Today is going to be a nightmare. There's no school for the children. I've got two hours to prepare, I cannot do much but it rained a lot last night so I'll, oh no, I can hear them. Here they come. I should not be scared. But they are horrible little things. Please say they haven't got it, yes, they've got it. Children in my day used to be so nice and not play with the dreaded *football*. I hate being used as a goalpost.

Ouch, please stop that, it hurts. I've got a river next to me and, *splash,* whenever they miss, *splash*, which is usually often, I get soaked, or *ouch*, get hit or *snap*, they break my branches or *owo* straight in my stomach, that hurt a lot. Now after two hours of that I need a long drink.

All the little flowers play all day, moving about, what's going on? A lorry's planting a tree next to me, yes they are, now I've got a friend.

Chantelle Smith (11)
Knockhall CP School

A DAY IN THE LIFE OF A SPIDER

'Wake up,' said Ant. 'It's 8:00am, time for breakfast.'
So I got up and climbed out of the muddy hole which was meant to be his home.
'Muddy hole, oh no! That must mean that it's raining.'
So Ant and I scurried over to an overhanging leaf. 'Oh no!' I shouted, 'My web is being destroyed by two children!'

Meanwhile, Ant was fighting with a worm and shouted to me, 'Come and help me with this chunky worm I've found.'
'No, I need to build a new web.' Luckily it was starting to brighten up. I looked around and saw that everyone had woken up and I could smell the pollution starting to gather up in the air, and the sound of car engines. I quickly ran to a different area and started to build a new web with brand new silk. I built it by a tree so that the children couldn't destroy it. I stuck it on one end of a twig and a leaf and another. I started to run around in circles and then started to run the other way until it was finished. Then a giant fly came buzzing in and hit the web and stuck so I quickly ran out and tied it all up in silk and dragged it home. I heard children playing and said to myself, 'It must be ten past three, school must have finished.'

James Parker (11)
Knockhall CP School

A Day In The Life Of A Hawk

I perched well-balanced on a large dead branch above the treetops. A breeze ruffled my feathers as I checked for any signs of prey. Instantly my sharp beady eyes caught sight of a small fieldmouse. At that same moment I soared off my branch and an undercurrent hit me which immediately took me high up above a patchwork blanket of fields and woods. However I wasn't looking at that as I was focusing on my prey. I tried to concentrate and seeing my chance made a spectacular dive.

Ignoring the wind rushing past I kept my eyes on the mouse. Suddenly it saw me and tried to take cover, but it was too late and I had it in my talons in seconds. I then took the mouse in my beak and swallowed it whole. But the mouse was hardly enough to fill me and off I went to find another meal.

After about an hour of hovering in the air I spotted my first real meal of the day. I made another dive, but the rabbit had seen me and had taken cover in a burrow.

The sun was setting and turning the sky red and pink as I sat on my branch with my head tucked under my wing, dreaming of the nice fat rabbit that I am going to catch tomorrow.

Rebecca Boys (11)
Marden Primary School

A DAY IN THE LIFE OF HERCULE POIROT

My day starts with Westminster bells chiming in the distance. Oh how pleasant. Thinking thoughtfully about the crime whilst slurping down the rest of my coffee, I think about the suspects but really I've got nowhere.

Walking down Oxford Street I look in the windows of the chic department stores - oh quelle richesse. The scene of the crime was at the front of the National Westminster Bank where a business man was murdered by a dagger. I greeted the inspector with a friendly 'bonjour'. I was surprised to find I was invited to Harrods but with great relief I did not have to pay the bill! After a truly wonderful lunch I go back to Oxford Street to question staff at the National Westminster Bank. No luck.

Feeling rather thirsty I go to a side street cafe to buy a bottle of mineral water before I catch a taxi back to my hotel.

I am very cross as I still haven't found any clues or even a witness. I think I'm an old man but still 'every cloud has a silver lining' doesn't it? Combing my black moustache I go to bed - my mind on the crime, so I take a sleeping pill. That's better, my day ends at last with zzzzzz!

Elizabeth Adam (11)
Marden Primary School

A DAY IN THE LIFE OF MY AUNTIE NICOLA

Auntie Nicola is a diving instructor. She travels all around the world looking for a good coral reef. So far she has been to Thailand, Australia and the Cayman Islands. Every day you get to go down into the ocean. She likes places where it is sunny and has clear blue skies. She comes back once a week from her boat to stock up on supplies.

In the morning she has to get up and get all the tanks full of air. This all happens between 6 o'clock and 7 o'clock. At about half past seven all her students wake up and get dressed. Then she talks to them about the place they are going to dive at. At 8 o'clock they go into the ocean depths. She uses signals to communicate. All divers have to go in groups of at least two in case they get separated from the rest. In a normal day she would see about 60 types of fish, 5 types of sharks and rays and hundreds of different types of coral. It is quite a difficult life keeping all the students calm and quiet because if you hold your breath at all it can cause a serious lung injury. If you come up fast and it is not treated your lungs could burst. So if anyone does she has to put them in the decompression chamber. This is just a normal day in the life of Auntie Nicola. It's great to be a diving instructor.

Ben Sampson (11)
Mereworth CP School

A DAY IN THE LIFE OF A 50P

Hello, I'm a 50p. At the moment I'm living in a Winnie The Pooh money box. There are lots of other coins and a five pound note. I can hear footsteps. Someone's reaching under the bed. Ah! We've been tipped upside down. She opened it from the bottom and picked . . . me! I get shoved in her pocket. Very dirty and bouncy.

I've been pushed through a slot and exchanged for a drink. That's not fair! Some of the coins are getting squashed. Hey! Who's that? I've been picked up by the 'claw' and pushed through the change slot.

I've been picked up in a greasy hand. Ouch! Where am I? Oh, I'm on the floor. I don't know where on the floor I am. Ow! Everybody keeps treading on me. I've been spotted and picked up in a clean hand smelling of fairy liquid.
'Here's your pocket money dear,' said the lady holding me. I was handed over to a little girl.
'I'm going to buy some sweeties Mummy, can I?'
'Oh okay then, but be quick,' said Mummy.

Great! I'm in a strange box now that jerks out every now and then and a coin gets taken. Ah! Now it's my turn. I'm going into a black purse. I'm suffocating.

Ten minutes later. 'Here's your money for doing the washing up Sophie,' said a lady.
'Thanks Mum,' replied Sophie.
Hm, somehow I recognise that voice.

Here I am back in a Winnie The Pooh money box again. That's a day in the life of me, just a 50p.

Amelia Leader (11)
Mereworth CP School

A DAY IN THE LIFE OF ME, A TOOTH!

I was minding my own business when suddenly a huge finger grabbed me and wobbled me about. Jenny *knows* that makes me even more loose. I did my best at breakfast but she was eating Cornflakes and everyone *knows* they're really crispy and anyone with a wobbly tooth would *know* not to eat them. At lunch she had an apple. What are you trying to do to me?

Anyway, the next thing I know, I've got a rope around my waist! You'll never guess what happened next; she tied the other end of the rope to a door and her brother Benny slammed it so hard I flew out of my socket and fell on the floor with a *bump!*

That night she stuffed me under a pillow and crushed me with her head. 'Ouch!' I screamed. Her snores drive me up the wall. Anyway, she stopped snoring after a while; peace and quiet at last! Yet nothing ever goes my way. A bright light filled the room. You may be wondering how I saw her under a pillow. Well, I had been pushed out of the bed by Jenny's hand, which was not the most delightful feeling. Anyway, the fairy spotted me on the floor and carefully picked me up, leaving £1 under the pillow. We zoomed up to the heavens and she stuck me on her tooth building. That's where I am today. I guess it's not that bad! Is it?

Naomi Cresswell (10)
Mereworth CP School

A Day In The Life Of A Nit

'Ah, it's morning. Oh hi, my name is Itch. My life is easy. I just jump to and from different people's hair, but I have one big problem. I'm allergic to shampoo! I'm going to tell you a really good story about when I was living on a little girl who hated nits but she hardly ever washed her hair, until one day it happened. She washed her hair!

I'd never been on anyone who had washed their hair. I was just crawling around when suddenly high pressured water sprayed me. I jumped for my small life and clung onto a piece of hair, then a massive hand came down and swooshed around! I lost three of my friends Scratch, Annoying and Irritating. I watched as they swilled around the plughole and got sucked down.

'Abandon person,' everyone shouted.

Luckily the little girl's mum was there. Everyone jumped on. I was saved but then I started to sneeze. Everyone laughed.

'Ha, he's allergic to shampoo!'

Lawrence Puckett (11)
Mereworth CP School

A Day In The Life Of Me

Hi, I'm a snail. Hm, let's have a look at my daily routine.
Daily routine: 1 - eat, 2 - sleep, 3 - eat, 4 - eat, 5 - bury myself in the ground, 6 - crawl along the garden, 7 - eat, 8 - sleep.
Also, we snails have our own fact file about us:
Name - snail, Registration - 2034000523, Breed - common garden snail, Size - 7.7,4.2cm.

Today has been a hard day, but the weather was great! The rain was chucking it down all morning! Also luckily for me it started to cool down in the afternoon, making the climate very damp.

I went over to the old rockery to see a worm who is called Worm. He kept bumping into the walls though. After that I slimed my way over to the pond. I got there eventually. I ate some of the water plants. There was a bird in the tree nearby! I hid, it spotted me! The large crested robin dived down and grabbed my solid shell. I struggled and the robin dropped me! I tumbled to the ground. Luckily I fell safely onto a compost heap. I slowly crawled off. There was a lovely smell. I wondered what it was. Slowly I moved towards a large deep pit in the ground. It had a fizzy liquid in it. I slowly moved towards it. Inside it was the remains of snails and slugs.

A snail, a slowly dying snail said to me slowly, 'Run, get away as fast as you can.'
I moved away from the garden as fast as I could. I was safe. Now time to sleep.

Christopher Hall (11)
Mereworth CP School

A Day In The Life As A Coin

I lay there in the Arsenal money box waiting for the chosen one, the leader Jack. Wait, here he comes, he has chosen me, the 5p coin. I wave to my friends the £50 note and the 1p coin. Maybe one day we may bump into one another, maybe in a till or a pocket. He takes me to a small, quiet shop in the local village. He reaches into his pocket and he gets me out the nice shiny 5p coin. He has just traded me for five penny sweets. Why? I lay there in a till that looks like it should belong in the iron age. No, it's the army of non-shiny coins, they have been known to hurt shiny coins. What? The hand's coming in, he gets me and I am left in an old man's pocket that smells like oat meal. Wait one minute, it's my best mate the £50 note. I asked him how long he had been out of the money box, and what had he been spent on, obviously something far superior to the five penny sweets which I was traded for. He replied that he had been used to buy a PlayStation game and had been exchanged on more than one occasion, before ending up in the same pocket as me. It proved to me that even though we were separated for a while that is it great to re-find a friend.

Robert Astley (11)
Mereworth CP School

A Day In The Life Of A Burger

Hi, I'm Benny the Burger and I'm sunbathing in this grill. Wait a minute, what's that, it's a big pink thing with five other long things sticking out. Hey, what's that on top of me, it's square and yellow.

'The name's Cheese, Chunky Cheese,' said the yellow square, 'and you're in a cheese burger which is about to be eaten,' Chunky said. 'What?'

Crunchhh! Ahhh!

'Where am I?'
'You're in the human body,' said a voice.
'Who are you?'
'I'm Bob the blood cell,' replied Bob, 'and you're going to be digested,' he said again.
'What? Ahh!'

Hey, what's that sign over there, it says 'stomach'. What is that up ahead? It's extremely big, it's going to crush me.

What, I'm still alive but I'm in a river and it looks like one under the ground. Ahhh, I remember it's a place called the sewers. What is that big pink thing again and it's lifting me up. It said 'This will be good for the cows, a nice meal.'

I'm in a wooden box. Hey, don't beat me up.
'Mooo!' said the thing.

What, I'm back on the grill and it wasn't a dream. They must have killed it for the meal. Oh well!

Michael Weaver (11)
Mereworth CP School

A DAY IN THE LIFE OF A PONY CALLED PEPPER

Hi, I'm Pepper and this is the day in the week I hate; *Saturday,* lesson time.

Andrea is my owner and she's a boring old scum bag, doesn't do anything but count the money she gets for lessons. I think the money should be donated for more food in my bucket.

It's around 7.30 and the dogs are barking so that means that Andrea's here.

'Stand up Pepper, stand up.' This is so amusing watching Andrea getting in a fliss. Emily's now tacking me up and I've been as good as gold!

My first lesson was with Jade. She loans Murray (my pony mate) at least Jade's a good rider and after a lot of pleading from Jade, Andrea gave in and said we could do some jumping.

Then a bit of a drama happened, Hannah was riding me, Jade on Murray and Emily on Polo, Andrea firstly asked Hannah to push me into a canter and as usual I gave a little buck but then did a smooth canter all the way round. Next it was Murray's turn, he stood in the middle of the arena like a plum pudding eating the grass so Andrea told Emily to have a go. Polo went into a full gallop all the way round, jumped over the area fence, galloped up the road nearly bumping into Sandy on Baby. Baby side stepped into the road making a car swerve and crash. After that big fluster we went into the field and had dinner.

Hannah Hook (11)
Mereworth CP School

A DAY IN THE LIFE OF A PONY CALLED BABY

Crunch, crunch! Hi, my name is Baby and I have just recently moved into a new home, and I have a lovely owner called Sandy. I love my life because I do whatever I want, well sometimes. Today we're going on a hack and Sandy is going to be riding me. She's not that good but she's only a learner. I'm just about to finish my food then we are going to go.

I'm going with Polo and Sandy's friend is riding him. I really like Polo and I think he likes me. Well, we're off now and this is gonna be good.

Now we're just about to go up a hill and then canter down it. Then me and Polo are going to go off into the wood and then it happened there, it was Sandy telling me off and telling me to stop, so I did. But Polo didn't and Hannah was still shouting at him when suddenly he stopped and it went all quiet, then we took them back.

We told our mum about what happened, then fed and brushed them. Me and Hannah then had dinner and went to bed.

Sandy Coles (11)
Mereworth CP School

A Day In The Life Of A Flea

Hi folks! I'm Little Joe. I love my exquisite job. I am the skilful, not yet swatted flea - that you guys hate so much.

Today I'm on Bob the Labrador. But he's going to the vet's at noon, so I'm forced to move home. I've packed my mini bags and when he's in the vet's I'll get a lift outa here.

It's noon and we're down at the vet's. This place gives me the creeps. It's too clean. It's like a laboratory undergoing a serious operation, deadly. Sick pets wander hopelessly around looking dazed. The receptionist is a dragon. She looks like if you ask her how she was, she would fire you. I'll start looking for a new home straight away.

I've got quite a selection. A scruffy, matted coat, no he's having a flea treatment. A poodle, why not? It might be fun. One long run up . . . one colossal jump . . . one new home. Wow! Well done Joe, you've got a fancy new home. It's all powdered and . . . achoo . . . sorry. Well I'll make myself at home.

My tent's up, looking great. Sweep the lawn, spick and span. Overall conclusion, perfect.

Oh no, the squatter. Run, run . . . run! Ahhh, black.

Don't worry, I survived. Just teasing you there. Oh, so you do care. Thanks, I care about you too. No, look behind you, a three-headed monster drinking blood. Oh, just your mom. Hey, not my fault.

What a long day!

Sarah Burns (11)
Mereworth CP School

A DAY IN THE LIFE OF AN ANT

It's a hard life being an ant especially having to keep a strict schedule; get up, get water and then, with my colony, dig and last but not least, go to bed.

One day I was just minding my own business when a voluminous monster lifted me up, it shook me vigorously and I fell like rain onto the hard concrete, then it ran off. I slowly dragged my foot and myself to the colony. I got back and banged it up. I had to get the water but as soon as I got out I saw another monster. I crawled on top of it, she started to run, I had to grab on. I heard the wind gust past. I couldn't hold on, I let go and swung. I was now on another monster. I stayed on it for one minute then I flew off again. I landed on the floor. I tried to get up but I was stuck, behind me was some pink, sticky stuff. Another ant passed me.

'Help!' I shouted. It walked over, it pulled me out and took me back to the colony.

Now you've just heard a tiny bit of an ant's life. As I say, it's a hard life for an ant.

Jodie Ernst (11)
Mereworth CP School

A Day In The Life Of A Shark

Hi, I'm Sharkster the shark and I'm just about to go and catch my morning breakfast. Hang on a minute, a dolphin just swam past. Let me tell you something sharks hate - dolphins, they get on your nerves.

Forget breakfast, let me teach you some things that a real shark does. Firstly let's go to the place where all the fish hang out. Right, we're here. The secret is that you have to be quiet. I'll just sneak over to that lump of coral on the other side and then I'll jump out and surprise them. Ready . . . steady . . . go!

I should have jumped out faster, they must have known that we were coming.

Let's forget about that, let me give you the facts about sharks. Lots of people are scared of them because they think that sharks rip them up and then eat them, which is not true for all sharks. If you like being a shark think again. Lots of people are hunting them down just for fins. It's also very lonely and boring because lots of people are scared of us. I hope you have enjoyed being with me and hope you have made up your mind, thank you.

Tom Clark (11)
Mereworth CP School

A DAY IN THE LIFE OF A LAMPPOST

Hi, I'm a lamppost and I'm going to tell you about my boring day. Well, at about 5.00am I have to turn off my light and some cars start to go past and sometimes when it rains people zoom past and *splash* all the water onto me and I get all cold and wet. Sometimes dogs go past and they make the floor wet by lifting up their back leg. Luckily there is a girl lamp post so I always talk to her. But it's too bad, she has already got a boyfriend. His name is Paper Chain.

Sometimes I get jealous because he always blows kisses to her and they ignore me. The bad thing about being a lamp post is you don't move around, you have to stay in the same place all the time.

Whenever a silly person is walking with their head turned they always bang into me and it hurts. Sometimes people at night come and steal money out of the shop and from children. I can also hear everyone's private talks. I get really annoyed when my light goes out and I can't see anything. That is how my life goes on; go away dog, get lost you little mutt. Bye.

Damian Rollinson (11)
Mereworth CP School

A DAY IN THE LIFE OF A FROG

Yawwwn, another day of catching flies. Most frogs love them, but I hate the stuff. They make me sick to my stomach. I mean, frogs for generations have enjoyed many a happy day guzzling down flies.

My own mother used to guzzle down at least a hundred a day. Just because I'm a frog I'm expected to love to eat those little flying beetles. I suppose it's because I can't bear to eat things that fly. Their constant buzzing is just so horrible, it makes me hop away and hide.

Of course, I have to find other food. So I hop into some unsuspecting person's house, leap into their larder and stuff my little face with chocolate biscuits. After that I waddle back to the lake and take a long drink of cold water before lying on the reeds and going to sleep.

Sam O'Leary (11)
Mereworth CP School

A DAY IN THE LIFE OF A £2 COIN

Just my luck, at the moment I am stuck to a damp, dribbly piece of bubblegum. It smells just like an apple but it's definitely not an apple. My last owner dropped me and I was picked up by a baby who stuck me in its mouth. I was covered in dribble. Then the nerve of it, I was taken away and put in a pocket where I was taken to the washer - never again! First I was spun about getting wet, yet again, and then I got chucked on a line to dry. I was blown by the wind. But I met a 50p coin, he was chatting about how he went to France and met a Franc. I fell asleep and when I woke up I was stuck to the gum, it's a mystery.

Tom Cannon (11)
Mereworth CP School

A DAY IN THE LIFE OF A RAINDROP

Ahhhmm, oh it's you. Someone told me you were coming, let's just get on with it.

Hi, the name's Drop, Raindrop. I don't come from around town. I travel you see, that's what raindrops do. If it wasn't for us there wouldn't be any plants at all. How? You ask. Well, let me fill you in with my daily schedule.

At the moment I'm in the sea - a salty smelly place, it's so boring. All I do in there is get swallowed by fish and come out the other end, not my piece of cake!

Then evaporation, I love this part. The sun's bright rays, or whatever you want to call them, suck me and my mates up into the huge clouds - there's a great view from up there. Then we travel in them at about three miles an hour. We arrive at these cliffy mountains and it's so tiring doing all this travelling, so we drop, that's where I get my name from. This part is the wet part, rain. Now we just relax. When we land we start to trickle down and form a stream but not all of us survive you know, some land and some form puddles and that is horrible, but you still evaporate but it's really crowded, I should know!

Eventually I trickle my way through some really cool places - London, France, Spain, Italy, Canada. It's great, but we all have to do our share.

Hannah Talbutt (11)
Mereworth CP School

A DAY IN THE LIFE OF THE WICKED WITCH

Hi, I'm Henrietta and unfairly, I have been christened the 'Wicked Witch', you might have heard of me. When I'm using that name I'm quite famous. Anyway, I'm going to tell you about where this nickname came from.

I was happily polishing my gingerbread house when these two children came pushing through the long grass at the edge of my garden, they looked terrified.

'Come in dearies, I don't bite!' I said. I beckoned them inside and began to follow them in. At that moment, my evil sister decided to play a trick on me. As she was a wicked witch she had done a spell which made it so that she took over my body and I zoomed into a glass ball. Unluckily for me and the children (I later found out that their names were Hansel and Gretal) I could not reverse the spell from my new position. The only thing I could do was see out and what I saw next would ruin my future social life.

My sister suddenly turned vile. She locked the boy up and made the girl a slave. She made her chop away while she started a fire. She was going to eat them! I tried to do something, but in a flash of light the girl had run across the room, pushed my sister into the fire, freed her brother and they were off.

My sister used a spell to get out of the fire. She shook her fist at them but they were away.

So I've been framed.

Emily West (10)
Mereworth CP School

A DAY IN THE LIFE OF A TOOTH

So there I was, chewing away on a pen lid when a long, wriggly finger decided to pop-in and say 'Hi!' Well, you could imagine my horror when it started pushing its weight around, wobbling me about in the middle of class! Fingers nowadays, you'd think they're royalty the way we treat them. Biting their nails, letting them push us about. Anyway, there I was being pushed about. I hope he knows I'm not giving up with a fight, I thought to myself. It was a brutal battle, blood flying everywhere, but in the end the finger won. I said my farewells and out I plopped, into a . . . what is it?

A place with lots of books. Oh wait, I heard tongue talk about it. A tray, that's it, a tray. Then along came the finger again. He picked me up and sealed me in an envelope. So that brings you here. Now where I am at the moment? Little bursts of light come and go and the occasional eye now and then but apart from that it's nothing special. Oh wait a minute, we're on the move. I've found a little hole. I can see seats, a driver. I'm on a bag pocket. It's (yawn) too dark to see anything. Goodnight!

Sshh, be quiet. It's night-time and I've been stuffed under a pillow. What's that twinkling noise? Oh my God! It's the tooth fairy. She flew me up into the big mouth in the sky.

James Kailanathan (11)
Mereworth CP School

A Day In The Life Of A Killer Whale

Every day of my chaotic life is a fight for survival, avoiding the destructive human rubbish that pollutes the sea, known to us as home.

I swim around opening my huge mouth when necessary to swallow a school of fish or two.

Suddenly, an engine starts to roar, rocketing closer as the minutes pass by. I send an echo monitoring through the ocean and warning all of the whales it's coming across.

I dive but my tail shoots, uncontrollably, out of the water. I pray they didn't see me. I look back to see where they are. Only a few metres away. They couldn't have missed me. A gun shot and a harpoon comes plunging past me. Close but not close enough. An ear piercing echo alerts me of something bad. I glance to my right. Cassie, my killer whale sister, is pierced by a ruthless harpoon. She sinks downward. She is dead. We know we must carry on, for our lives. We reach the bottom and propel ourselves forward. The sound of the engine grows louder, They must be over our heads now. We wait for the killers to pass over us, then we turn to mourn next to Cassie. Unfortunately we weep almost every day because someone is hunted down and killed. My life is too awful to be true, but I know I must cope for my family's sake.

Why do men do this? Every time something becomes extinct, a part of this planet goes with it.

Could we be next?

Matthew Kiddie (11)
Mereworth CP School

A Day In The Life Of A Cat

Hi, I've just got out of bed and I'm called Kate the cat. It is 7 o'clock in the morning. I got up and went down the stairs. My parents were asleep. I cried and cried but no one came to let me outside to get my food. I'm inside and feeling very sad because I'm hungry. I'm called Kate. I'm sneaky and I look great.

Cats have a play and then lunch, which can be birds, then sleep in a tree. They are good jumpers and climbers. If they have a wife, they would go and look after her then look after the babies and take them to play with the cat ball.

We go the grass and play until we get tired, We go to sleep in the basket.

The next day at 8 o'clock, dad was up first. We went off into the garden to have breakfast, then we have a game of hide and seek. No one could find me though. It was 5.50pm when we went to the swings.

We climbed on to the swings and them jumped off, then we went to eat birds but I'm not very tall and I missed the birds. Dad got one and we ate it, then we went to bed and slept.

Stuart McLachlan
Mereworth CP School

MOHAMMED ALI

Ring! Ring! Ring! I stretched my long, powerful arms and grabbed the new telephone.

'Hello, this is Mohammed Ali,' I answered sleepily.
'This is the USA Army. We would like you to join us to fight against Vietnam because we have been under attack. I will give you two hours to give me an answer,' said the man sternly.

I gave it a hard thought with my wife. I told her that I didn't believe in killing innocent people. Two hours later I told the Army what I believed in.

'I don't believe in killing innocent people, so I am not going to help you,' I told them proudly.

'That means we have no other choice but take you to court!' shouted the man. I explained this information to my wife and she was terrified at the thought of me going to jail. I was ready for it but I wasn't going to go to jail without a fight. I couldn't sleep that night thinking that I would be in court in eighteen hours . . .

The thing that makes me feel proud even if I go to jail, is that I stood up to what I believe in. The time went too quickly and before I knew it I was in court.

'What do you plead Mohammed Ali?' asked the judge.
'Not guilty,' I answered nervously.

Three hours later, the judge was ready to announce the conclusion.

'We find the defendant guilty!'

Mohammed Hadi
North Heath CP School

A Day In The Life Of The Sea

He woke up really early and stretched his arms, his hands lapped back down onto the covers of his great blue bed. He recognised one of his really great friends, the Manatee. He and Manatee splashed around for a few hours before Manatee rushed off for his breakfast. All alone, he wandered around looking for something to do.

He peered up and stared at the gleaming sun. 'I wonder?' he thought. He jumped with great force and leapt out to touch the sun with his blue watery fingers. It was no use, he flattened back down to the surface of his great big home.

He swam down into a dark and weary place. Suddenly the sun peered out from a cloud and its great bony fingers lit up the whole of the ocean. He looked down and saw the lovely rainbow colours of the Great Barrier Reef! 'Wow!' he thought with open-mouth disbelief. 'I never knew this place was this amazing!'

He swam along the Great Barrier Reef for what he thought was hours. He watched it glitter and sparkle as the sun shone to light up the ocean.

Suddenly Manatee appeared. He and Manatee both swam along watching every colour change and dazzle them both. As quick as a flash Manatee sped of as if danger was coming. Then as if from nowhere a killer whale appeared. He hid in the Barrier Reef until the whale had gone. It was time for bed.

'Goodnight!' he whispered.

Claire Haley
North Heath CP School

A DAY IN THE LIFE OF KATE WINSLET

I woke up and found myself thinking about the new film I have just acted in called 'Titanic'. In Titanic, a girl called Rose (me) falls in love with a gorgeous boy called Jack (Leonardo DiCaprio.) Jack is a romantic young boy who won the tickets aboard Titanic. The film ends with a sad ending though, because Jack dies.

Anyway, enough of that. I got up and clambered out of bed and went to eat breakfast. I wondered what the cook had prepared for me that morning. Mmm . . . the smell was wafting through the many corridors of that lovely British hotel.

I'd only just eaten an enormous pile of scrummy pancakes - and the cook was filling me up another plate with bacon and eggs on it! I loved it there and all of the people that came with it. They were all so nice and friendly and welcoming - I didn't want to go home!

I wondered what I'd do that day - probably just lounge around. It's so tiring being an actress - not! Well I suppose it's a bit tiring sometimes, but there's a treat at the end . . . a free hotel! I love being an actress, I wouldn't want to change it in anyway at all.

Whoops, I almost forgot to tell you (something crucial!) I'm having a baby. I'm really excited. If it's a boy I'll call it Lucifer and if it's a girl - I don't know!

Well that's enough from me, Kate Winslet, on June the nineteenth 2000.

Danielle Harding
North Heath CP School

A DAY IN THE LIFE OF MONET

I woke up to the busy streets of London. I was ready to explore with my blank canvas and paints with my beautiful wife Cammile. Away from my father trying to paint my life like a picture.

I left Cammile to explore the shops whilst I went to find the picturesque scenery for me to exaggerate on my parchment. I watched from a great height at the people scurrying around like ants. I started a cartoon sketch on my parchment as I always do, and slowly bought out my new paints, ready to start painting.

I met Cammile for lunch under a huge willow tree by the river; its leaves brushed my face and the willow painted sunny images on me, I felt extremely contented with my life.

Cammile and I walked back to the house we had rented, and she went to see what we could get for dinner at the stalls outside and I painted, brushing slowly at my sketch.

Before I knew it the sun had gone down. Cammile lay asleep in the bed next to me and my dinner lay cold. I drew the red velvet curtains on the cherry red sunset, watching it go to bed under the mountains, and I fell into a dreamy sleep.

Rachel Ven
North Heath CP School

A DAY IN THE LIFE OF JK ROWLING

I groaned and rolled over, and focused my eyes upon the digital clock. It was only nine-fifteen. I closed my eyes again and willed myself back to sleep.

Suddenly my eyes sprang open. 'Oh no!' I moaned, jumping up from the comfort of my goose feather duvet. I had to be at the filming studio by ten-thirty, that only left . . an hour and fifteen minutes!

Hurriedly, I showered and pulled on some new jeans and a jumper, as well as other accessories. I rushed my breakfast and was soon at the studio.

'Hi Joanne,' the filming crew were always friendly to me. 'Right through there, you know what to do.'

I wandered into a large glass room with a transparent panel in front of me. I slipped on some headphones and stared through the panel where I could see the characters Harry Potter and Ron Weasly.

It was two o'clock by the time we'd finished. We only filmed two scenes but I was happy.

I couldn't believe that my book was actually being made into a real film!

I got a lift home and ordered my favourite takeaway meal. My children were at my mum and dad's house for the day and night.

After some television I settled down to bed and snuggled down drowsily to a deep slumber.

Gail Lowden
North Heath CP School

A Day In The Life Of The Sun

I woke up really early today and stretched my bony fingers out far to tickle the lazy people fast asleep in their beds, then Mars circled round and I woke up the little Martians who were tucked snugly under little rocks.

As the day wore on and the planets passed me, each wanting a little of my warmth and staring at me enviously, I forgot all about looking down on the world and checking the plants were growing.

Who should come along? The rain cloud blabbing on about rules and if I didn't look after the world he'll come and rain, it was really close as I hate seeing little earthlings put on their sad faces.

Suddenly as I was just getting ready to relax and let the clouds take over, along came Pluto talking absolute rubbish, demanding his share of light and angrily wanting to know why he was always last. So at the end of the day I was quite relieved when all the planets had passed so I could put on my night-clothes and clamber into my bed of stars waiting to see if every planets' moon came out so tomorrow it will happen all over again.

Laura Smith
North Heath CP School

A DAY IN THE LIFE OF AN OAK TREE

Wake up early morning, stretch out my weak brown branches. It's winter now and my leaves are falling off. All the time, day and night, I feel a slight pain because a leaf will fall off one of my branches.

People are coming, slowly plodding along the stony path with saws and chainsaws. Every day one of my friends are killed for their amazing oak wood.

The ice cold frost laying against my chocolate-brown bark making me feel slightly chilly. The morning breeze swaying my oak branches as they reach for the golden sun. More leaves drop to the solid ground.

It's lunch now, so my leaves feed through the precious food that keeps me alive every day.

The men, chopping trees down at my sides, killing my life long friends. This is not what I want but it happens every day.

The sun starts to set and woodcutters disappear. I'm left to eat my last meal alone. So, slowly my leaves feed through my food. The last meal is over and I'm glad that no disturbance has come to me in this adventurous day.

As I start to close my barky eyes, I think that today was a day to enjoy because I lived it. As the day ends, I slowly drift off into a deep, deep sleep.

Rikki Partridge (11)
North Heath CP School

A Day In The Life Of A Victorian Servant

The Victorian era inspired me because; today we take everything for granted - whereas in the Victorian era they would work through extreme conditions to achieve the smallest thing. If we hadn't studied the Victorians at school, I'd have continued to take my luxury life for granted . . .

I posted off my month's wages to father today (£3, 3 shillings) that is their money for food this month. Father's work money pays the rent. I have heard nothing of them for months now, and I wish that I could write to them, but my letters have to be read by the mistress before they can go.

My old room was much more comfortable than this one. A tall girl with orangey hair came today, and she now has my old room - I have the cramped attic room next to the boiler.

Cookie dug me in the ribs to wake me up this morning; it was four o'clock in the morning! She wanted me to help her to cook the breakfast for the mistress and her family. They are a handful, six children that I have to look after in a twenty-four hour day. The baby twins, Melissa and Dillan are sweet children and are hardly any bother. Terrance, Lloyd and Sydney are the bothers of the whole family, they know every trick that was ever invented.

Melissa wants her bottle, I'd better go and end this entry here.

Lottie Brown.

Katie Felton
North Heath CP School

A DAY IN THE LIFE OF DAVID GRANT

I had an early operation on a Spaniel dog, it had swallowed a small round ball earlier on this morning. I love taking care of animals whatever they are. Yesterday I looked at a lizard, it was very dehydrated.

Being on TV, I make people aware of how they should treat their animals, the way they would treat a relative or any human really! I also wrote a book about the animals we have rescued.

Later that day after the Spaniel operation, I saw a lop-eared rabbit called Pip-Kin. It had matted fur around the bottom of her back. I told the owner to keep brushing the rabbit about once a week (some people are so lazy!)

After I saw the rabbit I had my break at last! I only had twenty minutes to have a cup of tea when I had an urgent case. A dog had been found lying on the side of the road. It had a broken leg and one side of its face was bruised.

I had to do a serious operation, it took about two hours. I put a splint in its leg and I looked at its face, the bruising would get better in time.

My last patient was a tortoise called Shelly. It was nothing to worry about, she only needed her nail clipped.

After a long, hard day at work I went home, put my feet up and relaxed.

Katherine Hilliard
North Heath CP School

A Day In The Life Of Stuart Pearce

I have chosen a footballer called Stuart Pearce. He has played for many football clubs, and he inspires me to never give up on what I want to achieve.

This is a day in the life of Stuart Pearce. He is woken by his very small alarm clock, which he tries to make as quiet as he can so he doesn't wake his wife. Silently Stuart gets up and gets changed into his football training kit. He has a quick breakfast and is out of the house by 7.00am. Stuart drives for twenty minutes to get to West Ham's training ground.

Yawning widely, he grabbed his boots and put them on. He liked to get to training really early. That way he could have a little sleep for half an hour.

After a few hours of hard training Stuart feels ready for the match against Manchester United later that day. After another drive home he finds his wife and young daughter eating their lunch. Stuart was sweaty and tired so he got a towel and had a shower. He got changed and had a big lunch. It was time to get ready for his match. His wife wished him luck, and he set off.

When the match was nearly over, the score was still 0-0. In the last minute of the game, Stuart is fouled, and it's a penalty. He is really nervous when he steps up. He shoots and scores making him the happiest man in the whole world.

Jake Mulcahy
North Heath CP School

A Day In The Life Of Tammy Girl

I wake up as the county mall opens. The manager of my shop is striding towards me. Then she comes to my eyelid, (which she calls the security guard) and she opens it with a key. When she gets inside she checks that both the upper and the lower floors are tidy and in place.

When the manager has finished, she comes down the stairs to the lower floor and she opens up my heart (the safe for the money), which I couldn't live without. Don't worry it is hidden! She takes out some money and she places it in both tills. (The upper floor and lower floor tills) for change.

At around 8.45 my staff are beginning to arrive, they talk amongst themselves and sort out my insides. (The clothes and products). They are chatting amongst themselves about what they did the night before. One of my girls called Sally had even been at a disco from ten till five in the morning. She had bags under her eyes and was practically asleep. When my manager saw her, she became very angry and sent Sally home to get some sleep.

The store is opened at 9.00 and many people are crowding into me like white blood cells helping me to live, we had a new design come in last week and it is selling like crazy.

It is 5.30 and I have closed, it is nice and peaceful though my staff are chatting and giggling as they finish up.

It has been a busy but refreshing day. Tomorrow I get restocked! The staff and manager clean up, then when they are finished, the staff leave and the manager closes me up.

I'm left in peace to sleep.

Zoe McMillan (11)
North Heath CP School

MICHAEL JORDAN

It was championship winning day and I was ready, today was a very important day as it was my last ever game. I had a gut feeling that we were going to win, I could just sense today was going to be good.

As I walked down to my limousine, I was swarmed with media, babbling all these different questions, but I just blocked them out and blanked them; I had to concentrate as today I would have to play the game of my life . . .

I arrived at the United Centre and gazed at it, picturing what would happen inside.

1st Quarter . . .

It was steamy, loud, and I was on fire. I had scored eight of my last nine shots and by half-time I had thirty-two points. The four-day lay off had not affected us as Scottie Pippen, and the rest of the team were putting on a show with dazzling dunks and cohesive teamwork. Soon though we started slacking and Utah were gradually clawing their way back with intensity, and a barrage of successive shots; and by the end of the third quarter we were back on our heels.

4th Quarter . . .

I was cold, we were down, it was clutch time. The first five minutes, I was rolling smoothly, but we were still swapping points. We needed to find an offensive momentum turner.

It never came.

Until the last second. It was silent, Bill Russell was in front of me. I went in came back for three . . .

Tom Raymen
North Heath CP School

A Day In The Life Of Anne Frank

I woke up this morning and father pulled down the blackout screen. I took a look out of the window and all I could see were buildings crumpled down on the ground and smoke all around in the far distance. The only thing that was missing was the people; the streets were deserted.

Yesterday it was our big Jewish celebration. All the food we were reserving, we ate. It was great! It would have been better if we were at home, but at least we had it here in the Annex.

At the moment, I am eating my broad beans, (it's all we've got except the porridge, but I don't like it either. My mother has just got up and later we are all going to try out our new tin bath (that we got yesterday), one at a time.

It is now my turn to try out the tin bath. It is really small and I can't believe how cold it is. I think I'll just have a quick wash then I'll get out and carry on with my studying. Yesterday my father and I worked on maths for the umpteenth time and today we will work on short hand.

We have had to go to the attic as all the soldiers are searching this area for Jews. If they find us here hiding in the attic, they all send us straight to a concentration camp to be gassed, we don't want that to happen

Georgina Warren (11)
North Heath CP School

A Day In The Life Of . . . A School

It is very important to go to school because you learn to read, write and learn other subjects. Most of the time, I like going to school but there are days when I just don't feel like waking up!

The morning bell rings at quarter to nine. We all line up, to go into class. Teachers come to collect their class and then we go in. We hang our coats and bags up and if you have a pack lunch, we place it in the trolley.

We then get our Numeracy books out, and our teacher tells us what to do. When it is time to go for assembly, the juniors get their chairs and line up in order and walk into assembly smartly. Someone goes to get Mrs Wylie to start the assembly. We begin by saying our prayers and also pray for the sick people. We finish our assembly at nine thirty.

Soon after that our teachers take us into class and we carry on with numeracy. By now most of us have had enough of work and are happy and excited to go to play! We have twenty minutes of play and we make the most of it.

After play we start our literacy lesson. We have two groups. While one group reads to the teacher, the other group does literacy work. However, there are a few students who try to get out of it by wasting their time! They also disturb others who want to work and learn. They walk around asking for sharpeners or rubbers. When parents were invited to a literacy lesson, my dad found it very strange to see people walking around not listening to the teacher!

At twelve o'clock the bell rings for the infants to go to lunch. While they are having food, the juniors play outside and have lots of fun, until Mrs Wylie comes to call us in.

During play time girls skip and boys play their own games. Work is all forgotten. At this moment we are only interested in playing! Before we know it, the whistle has gone and play time is over.

We go into class and do silent reading for fifteen minutes. The teacher does the registration again while we are reading. It is very quiet in the classroom, you can even hear the birds sing.

The last subject of the day finished at quarter past three. After that we pack away, and get our belongings together, ready to go home.

Everyone is busy. Sometimes it is noisy and our teacher gets annoyed! Lastly, we end the day by saying our prayers and go home at half past three.

Although I'm glad to go home, I learnt a lot at school and enjoyed being with my friends.

Sarah Britto (10)
St John Fisher RC School, Erith

A Day In The Life Of A Cook

Today when I woke up, it was 7.40am. 7.40! I was late by fifteen minutes. Quickly, I jumped out of bed and leaped into the bath. After I had both washed and brushed my teeth, I was delayed by ten more minutes, so I had to miss breakfast. Before going to work, I quickly had to pop in to the corner shop to buy a birthday card for my wife. After getting the card, I jumped back into my car and drove off. 'Phew, on my way to work at last.' I sighed. When I approached the restaurant I work in, I could see my fury-filled boss through the doors of the entrance.

'You're late!' my boss was screaming at me.

'Sorry sir.' I tried to explain.

'Hmm, well just don't let it happen again,' my boss begged me.

'Yes sir!'

It was 8.27pm when customers started to come.

'I'll have a pizza for my children and . . . '

'No dad, I want a burger,' said one of the customer's children.

'Okay, I'll have a burger with the pizzas,' said the customer.

'That'll be £7.94 please,' I said.

'Okay. Two pizzas and hey son, what type of burger do you want?'

'A cheeseburger please' said the boy.

'Okay two pizzas and a cheeseburger coming up,' I shouted. When I finally gave the customer his food, other customers came in.

'Wow, the business is going up like never before! We haven't had this many people for as long as I can remember!' my boss said one day.

At the end of the day, I was about to close the shop, when my boss said to me, 'Your work will not go unrewarded. I will give you double wages, you work like a professional.'

'Thank you sir, I really appreciate what you're doing.' I was suddenly speechless. The thing is, I didn't really think about it until I was on my way home. '£500.00 a week. I never dreamt of that happening. It must be my lucky day for sure.' I was so excited that I nearly sped past a police officer!

'Watch it! I could give you a ticket for that!'

'Sorry sir,' I said.

When I got home, I surprised my wife with the card and said 'Hey Jane, Happy Birthday and guess what?'

'What, what is it?' She desperately wanted to know.

'I got a raise at work! Soon I'll be able to take you wherever you want to go' I replied.

Timothy Osibo (10)
St John Fisher RC School, Erith

A Day In The Life Of A Teacher

Once upon a time, there was a teacher who lived in 13 Timothy House, her name was Ms Ladale.

One early morning her alarm woke her up at 7.30am. She looked at the calendar, it was Tuesday, so she said PE day. In a flash she took a shower, put on her trousers and her top and ate her breakfast and went to school.

When she got to school, she called out the register, after she talked to her class about thugs. A few minutes later, it was time for assembly, today was sharing assembly and we were talking about a good neighbour. She had chosen the people she wanted to read. Assembly went well.

In maths, she taught her class how to find half of a number, a third of a number and so on.

In English, she taught her class, how to read a story about Rina and the Moon.

In RE, she told the class to draw a picture of how they wanted the school to look like.

When it was lunch time, she ate her lunch.

After lunch, it was time for PE. In PE, she played a couple of games with her class and played some music.

After PE, it was home time. When she got home, she was not hungry so she took a nap.

Adeola Omosanya (9)
St John Fisher RC School, Erith

A DAY IN THE LIFE OF A DOLPHIN

I am Laura and I am going to be a dolphin for a day.

We dolphins sometimes stay with our packs. In packs there are males and females and young ones. Females go off with each other and males do the same.

Most days we jump up from the water, to see if there are hunters about and see if it is safe for us to swim to the east.

We are the best swimmers, we can get a gold medal for swimming.

We love swimming, we have to go really fast when there are sharks, was it last week, yes it was, when one of my friends was eaten by one and we have to hide from them all the time now.

When we females give birth to our babies, we have it underwater, as always it is hard because sharks are attacking us at the same time. When it's time for eating, we go hunting, when there are large shoals of fish, we dolphins get together to form a school of dolphins. Then we make whistling sounds to confuse the fish so that we can trap them and they can't escape. We mainly hunt during the day.

We dolphins are very sociable animals and we are always there to help each other out. Some of my friends got caught in some fishermen's nets, it was very sad because they died. Some of my friends even perform and do tricks and acrobatic tricks in front of humans. Who are humans? We get fed lots and lots of fish if we do this, it might be fun.

If I'm lucky, I will live to be 50 years old but it's such fun living with my family and friends.

It was fun being a dolphin for a day but now I am back being an ordinary school girl.

Laura Faithorn (10)
St John Fisher RC School, Erith

A Day In The Life Of . . . A Gym Club

One golden Sunday morning Crossways Gym Club was opened by Anthony Fells for anyone aged three to twenty.

That same day a girl called Sarah Rita Simons came from another gym club called Heathrow because she thought it was rubbish and she heard about this new club and she was going to try it out.

Two hours later they had to warm up and then when she got onto the beam, she had to do her sequence, and could do a pike somersault on beam and she did her somersault on beam but she fell off.

She had learnt something at Heathrow, which was if you fall off or manage to fail anything, get straight back up and do it again.

So she got back up and did it again and she landed on it this time.

She thought it was good so she thought she would stay.

One hour later they had a break and Sarah had a sandwich, a drink, a bag of crisps and a chocolate.

When they had to go back down, they went on vault and Sarah could do a Tsukahara and she fell over, then she said to herself, don't give up, get up and do it again.

After she did it the second time, she was awarded the first senior gymnast in the club. She was so happy that she was never going to leave this gym.

The following thirty minutes, they went on bars and Sarah could do two giants back away and she said to herself, 'Come on Sarah you can do it, I can do it.'

So she got on the bar and did it.

Then nine o'clock struck, it was time to go home.

In the car, Sarah decided to phone her friend from Heathrow to come and join her at the new club on Saturday. Anyway back at the gym, it was all calm, still and dark.

All of a sudden the music started to play but nobody knew who was there, people were thinking too hard, that sweat was running out of their heads. 'I have got it, it could be Lindsey or Jack.'

'But they're dead!'

Then the tramp started going bong bong! Nobody knew who it was but it was the 24th of December (Christmas Eve). After 10 minutes, Anthony came back because he forgot his glasses and everyone shouted 'Happy Christmas Eve' and Anthony jumped out of his skin.

The moral is: Have faith in yourself.

Jaleesa Bernard-Thomas (10)
St John Fisher RC School, Erith

A Day In The Life Of Robin Hood

It was the 18th of August 1424. I was sitting in the usual tree deep into the forest of Sherwood, talking to Little John. I don't know why we call him Little John, because he is 10 times the size of us!

At 10 o'clock, we got bored, so we decided to take a trip to Doncaster, which is just about two miles away from Sherwood.

Once we were out of the forest, it was a straight road to Doncaster but I stopped when I heard cries behind me. I ran to see where I thought it was coming from.

It was a tax collector, taking money from a poor old woman. I took out my bow and arrow and shot an arrow right in his back, then he collapsed to the floor in a crumble. I gave back the money he took from Friar Tuck, another friend of mine, to share the money with all the poor. Then I went back on course to Doncaster.

Half eleven was the time I arrived back in Doncaster.

Five minutes later, I saw a crook I did not like: The King, Sir Rodger of Doncaster.

'Hello, have you done anything good today?' I said meanly.

'Yes, I took money from the poor, no, make that my tax collector, took money off the poor! Ha, ha!' he explained.

'No you didn't, he's dead! And you will be too!'

I took out my bow and arrow and shot him in the heart.

Tom Powell (10)
St Mary Star Of The Sea RC Primary School, St Leonards-on-Sea

A Day In The Life Of A Horse

I just woke up and I'm famished! I hope Rachael gets here soon. Here she comes. 'Hi Timber' I rub my nose against her to show her I'm starving. So she goes into the feeding room, I love my feeding time especially when I get Polos. I'm the first to be fed um . . . I'm finished.

Then I get my hay and Rachael tells me I have to do a lovely canter or I might have to retire. Then she went out to see Tess so I started to think. I have to do a heavenly canter so I don't retire.

I thought long and hard about it. It was nine o'clock, the first ride but I wasn't on that one, so I decided to eat the rest of my hay. I'm still not full so I lent over to Bruno's stable, he's out on a ride, so I stretch my neck over the stable door. I started eating Bruno's hay. It was really nice oh no! Rachael saw me! She sighed and walked away. It was eleven o'clock and it was my ride and a little girl called Rhianna came running up to me. She stroked me kindly, I had a trot then canter. Fantastic, I heard Rachael scream with delight.

Rhianna Andrews (9)
St Mary Star Of The Sea RC Primary School, St Leonards-on-Sea

A DAY IN THE LIFE OF ELLEN MACARTHUR

11th February

The wind had dropped right off near the end and I sailed the last few miles gently upwind surrounded by the waiting spectators and my support team. I felt very excited, upwind in light air is the one point of sail in which Kingfisher struggled without the Genoa and it really dragged these last few miles out.

I was enjoying what was a final fabulous parade, walking round the decks taking photos of the Kingfisher bathed in floodlights from the hovering helicopters. There was an enormous crowd and a real sense of anticipation for this arrival. As soon as I crossed the line, the red flares were waved and the fireworks lit the sky above the French port in celebration.

My support team charged on board and after officially 94 days, 4 hours, 24 minutes and 40 seconds, I was no longer alone, but with the awesome support I've generated from all around the world. Crossing that line was one of the most extraordinary solo race performances ever. I've got so used to my competition ability in this fleet that it's very easy to forget that I'm the first woman to complete a circumnavigation in under a hundred days and the youngest competitor to complete the race. I feel very proud.

Matthew Suggitt (10)
St Mary Star Of The Sea RC Primary School, St Leonards-on-Sea

A Day In The Life Of John Logie Baird

Wake up, grab breakfast and off to the inventing room. Mother gave me a phone call this morning to say how good the television was becoming. I called a few workers together to discuss something important.

'Well I say old chaps, this is our lucky day, we've got some brilliant news. Our televisions are going to sell like dust being blown by the wind. We're going to make big money' I told them proudly.

'Higher the price' an old friend called.
'£50.00'
'£60.00'
'£70.00'
And soon the whole room was filled with loads of noise.

'No, no, no! Leave the price and let's just get to work improving our fantastic invention.'

Everything was silent as we walked back to our thinking desks. I thought about the way the television was. Small, black, white and silent. We could bring in a bit more colour. I started planning out how to make it appear, while everyone else sat back in their chairs twiddling their thumbs probably thinking.

I called everyone together 'Anyone got any ideas?'

'Make it taller and wider'

'Give it sound'

'Brilliant and I've been thinking we could also give colour.' I continued after them. That night I continued planning the new television set. It wasn't long after that I phoned my father to tell him how we were to improve it. It was that second I looked back at living in Hastings and a big smile came over my face for that was where I invented television.

Kate Longmire (10)
St Mary Star Of The Sea RC Primary School, St Leonards-on-Sea

A DAY IN THE LIFE OF MICK FOYLE

Mick Foyle has been through 15 years of pain and suffering in the World Wrestling Federation. He has been retired once and fired twice, it must be terrible to be in a World Wrestling Federation match when your career, your one and only, your pride and joy is on the line. It must really hurt inside when you fail, when you loose that opportunity to be the one when little kids look up to you and say that they want to be just like you when they grow up. To have youngsters who actually believe and feel the destruction and pain, whilst you fall to the floor, when your time is up. As your golden opportunity turns to dust and having one of your three kids tranquillised by a sledgehammer and following sudden death. It must be hard to live by waking up and looking at your lovely children and knowing that one isn't there. It must be tough having over 2,000,000,000 fans and mostly all of them remind you of your missing child. Sometimes it makes you cry and sometimes you just say no to yourself, that you're not going to shed any amount of tears, do you just want to give up? Why do you think you want to sell your soul to the devil himself? Thank you.

Dominic Porter (9)
St Mary Star Of The Sea RC Primary School, St Leonards-on-Sea

A DAY IN THE LIFE OF PIP

On Saturday we usually go out as I always need a walk for my exercise, everyone seemed not to notice me. Then I heard it, the name of the most famous me 'Pip.' I ran to fetch my lead and collar. Mark put it on me. We were going to the woods. In the car, I stood up and looked out of the window. A cliffside, I barked out loud, then all of a sudden, we were flying out of the road and out, down, down, down, we came under the clouds.

Boom! We all had landed and I was the only one here alive. I jumped out of the broken window, it was all sandy and there was no sound.

I barked and still there was silence. The echo of my own voice. All I knew was what had happened, I was out on my own. It began to rain, so I ran under a tree, I put my head into my paws and watched the rain come to a halt. I was so scared, I cried and cried, I awoke. It had all been a dream.

Linda O'Sullivan (10)
St Mary Star Of The Sea RC Primary School, St Leonards-on-Sea

THE DAY AND THE LIFE OF MERLIN

Hello, I am the great wizard Merlin, I am 100 years old and I live in a place called Tintagel. I cook up spells and at the moment, I am making an invisible spell. Now what book is it in, oh yes it is there page 109. Ingredients; the dark knight's heart, the golden apple and the flame from the blue feather dragon, crack bang, where is everything. Now the whole world is invisible. I need to get all them ingredients. I need to pack my bag. In goes the magic carpet and the map.

The golden apple tree is on the top of the tallest mountain in the world and here I am, it is too tall to walk up so I will fly up, grab an apple and fly to the dragon's cave. I unrolled the magic carpet, I went flying up and up and up. I grabbed an apple, crash I have landed in a tree near the dragon's cave. I got a stick and put it in the ground near the dragon's mouth, I tickled the dragon, fire came out his mouth and set fire to the stick, I grabbed the stick and ran all the way to the dark nights. I challenge you to choose your weapon. 'Magic' I said, 'get me this man's heart,' I got his heart, I ran home and put them in my big pot, bang, crash. I ran outside, everything was back to normal.

Stuart Parnell (10)
St Mary Star Of The Sea RC Primary School, St Leonards-on-Sea

A Day In The Life Of Lady Brassey

I got up early today, the boat was swaying vigorously. During the night a storm had brewed. I didn't want to get up in the wind and rain but I had to because we were going to land on a Polynesian island.

We have just noticed that we can't land, because the sailing directions tell us that the inhabitants are 'hostile' and Sir Belcher mentions that some of them tried to cut off his boats.

From what I can see from the deck, the island is beautiful, with luxuriant vegetation of many kinds. I can see blue smoke curling from the treetops. This island is beautiful, but I still can't help thinking about how life must be back in Hastings and Catsfield. Still, I have Tom my husband, the children, and the black pugs and other pets with me, so I am certainly never lonely.

I have a list of people who will stay on the boat, for the whole journey, they total 11, including the commander, the surgeon, the captain, and a crew of 32, counting the nurse, the ladies maid, and the stewardess. Other than dogs, I have found lots of other exotic animals en-route. I love animals, and Tom says that I am a great horsewoman.

The day is almost over, I can see the sun setting behind the tall palm trees, the blue smoke is standing out next to the brilliant yellow sun.

Sophie Kelley (10)
St Mary Star Of The Sea RC Primary School, St Leonards-on-Sea

A DAY IN THE LIFE OF DENISE LEWIS

'Wake up! Wake up!'

'Muummm, I can wake up myself.' Here we go, today the press are coming here to interview me. 'I think you should have a bath before the press get here honey.'
'OK mum, don't worry about it!'

One hour later.

'Oh no, mum where is my pink hair pin?'

Ding dong!

'Mum get the door please!'

Ding dong!

'Mummm . . . I have to do everything around here, hello you must be . . .'

'Tony Five Hand, how do you do?'

'Come in, make yourself at home.'

'So are you ever going to move out?'

'Yes, I'm moving to London, my friend lives there.'

'What about your boyfriend - ever going to get married?'

'Uum, I'm not sure?' Ring, ring!

'I better get that.'

'Hello, who's calling?'

'Denise, it's Dan, are you free? It's important!'

'Well, the press are here, I'll meet you at FY's bye!'

'I must be going. People to see. You know how it is.'

'Thank you for coming!'

2 o'clock at FY's.

'Thanks for coming,' he said, 'By the way will . . . will . . . you marry me?'

'Dan, of course I will.'

Two years later, they tied the knot.

Georgina Buck (10)
St Mary Star Of The Sea RC Primary School, St Leonards-on-Sea

A Day In The Life Of A Dog In The Street

One day it was raining, it was cold and windy, a dog was in a bin looking for food but he saw an old tin. He was an old dog, he is 100 years old in dog's years. He is big and has been lost for 5 years. The dog ran to this little box to go to sleep in it, when he went to sleep, a car went so fast, it ran over the box. The dog ran out as fast as he could and made it. The dog jumped on an old bed and a van came down the hill, it was a dog catcher. It saw the dog and it got out the net and ran after the dog. The man caught the dog and went to put him in the van. When he opened the door all of the dogs ran out of it and the dog bit the man's bum.

The dog went running back to the old bed and lay down. People were coming down to the shop, the dog ran to them, he saw that they had food. When he got there, the people said go away fat dog and the people walked away from him. The dog was sad because he saw people hitting stuff. He saw people and they were the people who looked after him when he was a puppy and lived happily ever after and did not get lost again.

Nicholas Webb (9)
St Mary Star Of The Sea RC Primary School, St Leonards-on-Sea

A Day In The Life Of A Manatee

One bright sunny morning I was playing with my friend Sundance until a human came into the water and started following me. I was swimming gracefully across the river. The human was shouting, 'His weight is 1100lb.' A little person grabbed a plant and threw it in the water. I ran away with it. After I had eaten the plant I tried to go to sleep but the moonlight was shining on me and then there was bursting colour in the sky.

I sat on a rock and made ripples with my flipper until I fell asleep. Then Sundance woke me up by splashing me, she was showing off in front of the humans. I gracefully swam to the other side of the river, I grabbed a plant with my snout and gobbled it up. I lay on my back and scratched my belly with my flipper. I sat on a rock and relaxed for hours and hours until I fell fast asleep. Sundance swam gracefully to the other side of the river to get some tasty plants and then she sat on a rock and relaxed for hours and hours, then she fell fast asleep.

Jodie O'Rourke (9)
St Mary Star Of The Sea RC Primary School, St Leonards-on-Sea

A DAY IN THE LIFE OF HHH (TRIPLE H)

As usual I woke up early, to train to get myself really fit so I can be at my best. First, I have to run around the streets of Greenwich, Connecticut for about one hour and by that time I would have run five to six miles.

I would slowly jog back to the Smackdown Hotel and meet my wife, Stephany McMahon Heilmsly who then gives me my breakfast, it's a scramble egg sandwich. You see I've got to train extra, extra hard because tonight I have to face three more people in the main event of Wrestlemania 16. I have got to face The Rock with Vince McMahon, the Big Show with Shane McMahon and finally Cactus Jack with Linda McMahon. There is a McMahon in every corner. As the hours have gone by, there is only one hour left.

I go to my locker room and get changed for the match, then I just go out for a ten minute run around. A person takes my weight and height, after that he gives it to the ring announcer so he has all his information. When I make my entrance to the ring I hold my WWF title, finally I hear my music and I make my entrance with Stephany, then the Big Show with Shane, Rock with Vince and finally Cactus Jack with Linda.

At this time I have feelings running through my head. I'm always thinking 'I will win this'. I think it will be a very hard night, a very, very hard night.

Jacob Kirimli (9)
St Mary Star Of The Sea RC Primary School, St Leonards-on-Sea

A Day In The Life Of Free Willy

Today is the day that we film our brand new movie. You remember Free Willy One and Two, well we are now doing a Free Willy Three. I'm really excited because I get to meet two new killer whales. One of them is called Nickee, I'll let you into a secret, Nickee and me, in the story really like each other, and in the end we have a baby, the baby is the other new killer whale.

I was well trained by a boy called Jessy. There is a new boy, his father kills us killer whales and sells us to the Japanese. Randolf's new helper tricks Jessy to use binoculars that have some kind of eye shadow, then the driver takes a photo of the crew, then Randolf says that Jessy looks like a racoon with black eyes.

When we started filming, I thought something was going to go wrong. Nothing did go wrong, in fact everyone needed soaking during the middle of filming the movie. The worst part is where I get shot in the tail, luckily Jessy removes the spear. Jessy gives me and Nickee lots of juicy oranges. The new boy feels a bit sorry for me and my family because he had gone on a little rubber dingy. The boy rubs his wet fingers against the side. Jessy and the new boy dive into the water. I then start swimming with them. The day was great and we all enjoyed filming it.

Charlotte Moon (9)
St Mary Star Of The Sea RC Primary School, St Leonards-on-Sea

THE DAY IN THE LIFE OF . . .

The army of ants scuttled along the concrete path onto the green grass. The large army lived in the Smiths' back garden. They were searching for food, suddenly they moved nearer to the picnic. The Smiths were having a picnic on their garden grass.

The army moved forward onto the mat, where the Smiths food was, and hurried toward the giant chicken sandwiches, and pulled them apart to carry away. It took thirty ants to take half the sandwiches, they left the rest because they had found something else, they had found a sausage! After twenty more ants had come, they lifted it up to carry away.

Suddenly, out of nowhere something blocked the sun from their view and it landed right on the sausage! The ants scurried away to the bushes while a giant stick continued to hit the ground.

Unharmed, the ants ran back out to the grass and waited. Soon after a white, snowy sort of mixture scattered down. The ants started to become confused and quickly noticed that if they stepped on it they died!

The number of ants decreased so the remainder of the ants retreated back to the base, they had to dodge giant feet and a football. They ran for their lives and jumped into the hole where their nest was. They had food for the night, but less ants. That was the day in the life of an army of ants!

Alice Starkey (11)
St Philip Howard Catholic Primary School, Herne Bay

A Day In The Life Of A Mouse

'Stupid cat,' he mumbled as he squeezed the chunk of bread through the hole behind the washing machine which was only 4cm tall and 3cm wide. Just the right size for him as he was a mouse.

As a mouse he had a very large family, 237 to be exact, so his parents had not given him a name, so he was known as him, he or it.

As he set off for his home (a hole by the fireplace), his heart was still beating loudly after his close call with the cat earlier.

After safely eating his bread he set off to the strawberry patch in the garden for his lunch.

Just as he turned the corner into the hall, there was a loud shriek as a human dropped eight Tesco's bags, narrowly missing him but he still managed to get covered in a mixture of Surf washing powder and Heinz Tomato Ketchup.

Suddenly Twinkles, the ginger Cheshire cat whose face looked as though it had been hit with a frying pan, came streaking into the room, pounced, missed and smack right into the wall!

In the confusion he slipped out to the kitchen, out of the open door then, 'snap', a mousetrap. The end of a three month life of the one they called him, he or it.

Max Wood (11)
St Philip Howard Catholic Primary School, Herne Bay

A Day In The Life Of A Blood Cell

'Wheeee!' A blood cell gets catapulted out of the heart. It is a new blood cell called Adz. He has never been all the way round the body before so this is his first day. As a blood cell he knows to just let the blood carry him around the body, but he doesn't know what it is like in the different organs.

'I wonder where I'm going first?' says Adz to himself, zooming down the arteries. He zooms for about half an hour, then another blood cell comes up to him.
'Hi!' says the other blood cell.
'Hi!' says Adz. 'Do you know the first organ I will be going in?'
'Yes,' replied the other blood cell. 'The lungs.' And with that the other blood cell speeds off.

It is very windy in the lungs. The blood gets pushed around everywhere. Adz feels quite dizzy when he gets out.

He goes to the liver next. It is quite normal to go through except that it is very dark and it takes longer to pass through.

When Adz arrives at the bladder, he gets a nasty shock. 'This place absolutely stinks!' he said and he gets out as quickly as possible.

Finally, Adz gets back to the heart. What a great first day!

Adam Povall (10)
St Philip Howard Catholic Primary School, Herne Bay

A Day In The Life Of Tiger Woods

I had just been experimented on and my brain was swapped with Tiger Woods' brain because he was the other volunteer.

The machine was an invention by a scientist, who, after what occurred, thought it had not worked but I knew something had because I felt I was in a different body. I didn't tell him because I wanted to see what it would be like in this body.

After an hour, they told me I was entered in a tournament, 'The Grand PGA Nations' Cup'. When I reached the tournament I started to play golf, practising for the first round.

I did well in the first round and the good thing was that I was doing it all by myself with a little help from the body of Tiger Woods. In the second round I scored second best in points, because Lee Westwood scored the most points.

In the third round it was neck 'n' neck between Westwood and I. On the eighteenth hole it was very close, I just pipped it by scoring a birdie whilst Lee Westwood took four shots to sink his ball. I had won the tournament, The Grand Professional Golfing Association Nations' Cup.

I was handed the cup by a veteran international golfer soon to retire, Jack Nicklaus, with £50,500 as an extra prize.

I left the tournament, wondering when I would ever return to my natural state and where my proper body was and my proper life.

Bradley Harrad (11)
St Philip Howard Catholic Primary School, Herne Bay

A Day In The Life Of A Stallion

I am a free spirit of the countryside. I am a great example of my breed. You may think it is a great life for a horse like me, but in fact, it's very hard, as you're about to find out . . .

Yesterday morning, I awoke very proud of myself. I would soon be a father to my wife's foal. I was so happy. I told my wife I'd be back soon, and went for my morning stretch. I galloped through sunny hills and shady glades, and soon circled round to return to my wife.

When I returned I found my wife with our new little stallion! I was thrilled! But no sooner had I set eyes on my son, I heard *bang! Bang!* It was a group of hunters. I edged my wife and foal on. The last thing I wanted was for them to be shot. When they were clear from the poachers I got ready to gallop but *bang! Bang!* A bullet hit my back left leg. I quickly limped away.

My wife walked over to me and licked my wounded leg. She tried to get it out, but failed. Then my foal came over, pawed the wound and managed to dislodge the bullet! My wife then licked and treated the wound and I was soon feeling better, all thanks to my little foal and my wife.

So you see, it's not easy, and believe it or not, it's just another day for a wild stallion.

Joanne Goldsmith (11)
St Philip Howard Catholic Primary School, Herne Bay

A Day In The Life Of A FBI Agent

I got up in the morning hoping I wasn't still on the Sid Vincent case, he is one of the biggest criminals in America. I had my breakfast, then got ready to go down to the station.

I got there for nine o'clock when my shift started, it finished at nine o'clock at night. I was looking to see how many thieves there were today. Woah there's so many. I went over to the boss and said, 'Hey, hey, boss have we got Sid yet?'
'No, but he has robbed another bank.'
'I've got to go, just stay on the Sid Vincent case.'

I went straight out to the car to go and get my lunch, but on the way I saw some joy riders and I pulled up straight in front of them risking my life, but luckily they stopped just in front. I got them out of their car and put them in my car and took them straight down to the station. It was afternoon now, and I had a tip-off from one of my informants about Sid Vincent - he was planning another robbery!

We sneaked into their base but it was too late, they had already gone, they must have known we were on their trail. Then I said, 'My shift is over I'm going home. I'll get Sid tomorrow.'

C J Bithell (11)
St Philip Howard Catholic Primary School, Herne Bay

A DAY IN THE LIFE OF NELLY FURTARDO

I woke up today full of beans. I was so excited, I was going to record my first album today, called my name of course, Nelly Furtardo. I better get ready for today - let's see; I have my bag, my lippy, my back-up lippy and my purse.

I told Jeffrey to call the desk and tell them I will be on my way. I arrived at the recording studio at about 11.30am. When I got there Jay invited me in so I went in.

I took my stand and started to sing, 'I am like a bird . . .' Then the recording producer Jay distracted me by saying, 'Beautiful, beautiful.'

All of a sudden I froze. Jay asked me what the matter was. I replied, 'I can't remember the words.'

Jay shouted at me and told me I should know them all by now! I asked my manager if she had the words and she did, I was so happy. Then the DJ (Jay) called the manager's assistant to ask Top of the Pops if I could have a smash hits performance, but they said they would call him back later, so I started to sing again. Then there was a phone call and they said I could have a performance. So at the end of the day, I had an album and an opportunity for the big time!

Faye Fish (11)
St Philip Howard Catholic Primary School, Herne Bay

A Day In The Life Of Mike Tyson

On Tuesday the 9th May, I woke up with the sun shining in my eyes. I walked into the kitchen, got an egg and cracked it and then drunk it. I got my tracksuit on and went for a jog to the shop that was over a mile away.

When I finally got there I got some carrots, some fruit and some eggs because I needed to get some food in for the big match tonight, Lennox Lewis vs me. I left the shop and jogged home. When I got in I had my food, sat down and had a rest.

After a while I finished resting, got into the car and drove to the boxing arena where I was to fight Lennox Lewis. At first I was practising with the punch bag, then I started skipping for about ten minutes. After that I stopped and put my lucky boxing shorts on and started walking into the ring.

When I finally got to the ring I saw Lennox standing there looking at me. The next thing I knew the referee shouted, 'Fight!'

Lennox came storming in, he jabbed me twice with his left, he then went for a hook but I ducked and jabbed him with my left and by surprise I jabbed him with my right hand. He fell down and the referee said, '1, 2, 3, 4, 5, 6, he's getting up, 7, 8, 9, he's fallen down . . . 10! The winner is Mike Tyson!'

Tom Chidgey (11)
St Philip Howard Catholic Primary School, Herne Bay

A Day In The Life Of Whoopi Goldberg

I woke up at the crack of dawn desperate for some breakfast. 'Arrgh,' I said yawning. I got up, then walked out to the kitchen and rung the bell to get the maid to make me some breakfast.

It was then I remembered about having a shoot for my new film, 'Fine Day'. Ring, ring, ring went the phone. Then in the middle of a mouthful of Alpen I jumped up and answered the phone.
'Morning,' I said happily.
'Morning Whoopi,' said Charlie. 'Still OK for this morning's shoot of the new film?'
'I certainly am, 4 o'clock at Chapel Road,' I laughed.
'That's it,' Charlie said cheerfully.

At that moment I put the phone down and went to get dressed. I got Kingsley the butler to get the Porsche out and drive to Chapel Road. When I got there I put my make-up on, and changed into my screen clothes.

'3, 2, 1, action,' shouted the director.
Hours and hours had passed, stopping and starting again. I've had enough, I thought but I must carry on.

At last it was time to go home, so I called Kingsley on my cellphone to come and pick me up. I was home within forty minutes. Then I got into my silk pyjamas and went to bed.

I felt so exhausted but I also felt as if I had done a good day's work.

Dominique Ifill (10)
St Philip Howard Catholic Primary School, Herne Bay

A DAY IN THE LIFE OF MY DAD

I woke up and realised I was my dad! I knew I couldn't get out of it so I got dressed and went to open the arcade. I did not know what I was doing but I did my best.

About ten o'clock an idiotic woman came to me and said a machine was broken. The woman does not know anything - all it needed was an extra ten pence coin. I was doing OK!

After a couple of hours my uncle told me to empty the machines but I never know which key was which. I was gutted, Uncle Mick had to do it. He looked at me strangely.

Then I had to serve ice cream which was quite hard. I never knew it was so hard being a grown up.

It was time to get supplies of ice cream but I realised I could not drive. I got in anyway. I got stopped by the police as well and my dad's going to be mad at me!

I thought I'd better tell them but my mum, she did not believe me.

I was thinking, 'Where is my dad? I wonder if he's me. Oh no my life is ruined.' That evening I was back to normal. I asked my dad if he was me. He thought I was crazy and I'm grounded for two weeks.

Matthew Khoury (10)
St Philip Howard Catholic Primary School, Herne Bay

A Day In The Life Of Vicky

'Miaow, hello.' Do I get fed around here or what? It's as if I don't exist, just because I'm small doesn't mean I'm not a living thing! Oh look here someone comes at last, yep, getting closer. Hey where are you going? 'Miaow feed me!' (She just walked off without even looking at me). See what I mean about not getting fed?

Here comes my keeper, Fiona, she'll feed me. No! Don't pick me up. 'Miaow feed me!' Yes hello to you too. 'Miaow get off!' I don't want to kiss you, stop kissing me. Hurray, she is going to feed me, at last!

All that food is going to make me fat, so I best go outside and chase some birds for some exercise. Ah, there's one! If I remember from what my mum taught me - it goes: Stop, look, bend, focus and pounce. Nearly got it!

Now time for some exploring. 'Hello Vicky.' Oh there's my owner, every second she is either picking me up and kissing me or annoying me. 'Miaow go away!' I love her and everything but why can't she just leave me alone?

I think I'll explore in the house today for a change. Let's see, I'll find a nice cosy place where I can't get disturbed or pestered.

Finally I've found a place at last, now I can get to sleep. One packet of Whiskers, two packets, three packets, four packets, cat heaven!

Fiona Flaherty (11)
St Philip Howard Catholic Primary School, Herne Bay

A DAY IN THE LIFE OF PHILIP SLANG

Howdy ya all! Welcome to America. I'm Philip Slang. It's the 20th of July 2169 and I am going into space with Buzz Aldrin XIII and Neil Armstrong VIII. It's 200 years exactly since the first moon landing. At the moment we are being strapped into comfortable seats. They are in such a position that I felt like I am at the dentist.

Click! We are done. Speaker: 'Booster rockets on, in 5, 4, 3, 2, 1, all systems go, good luck team, over and out.'
We are warping up at maximum speed, I can feel it. Oh, hold on a minute. 'What's that noise?' Neil asks.
'It's our fuel tanks falling to Earth' was the reply.
We watched them fall to Earth. Twelve minutes later we had successfully landed on the moon. The door opens. We made it. Neil got out first. 'This is one small step for my ancestor, one huge leap for mankind.'

Buzz and I get out of the New Eagle and look back to Earth. It is strange here, no sound, no cars, no birds, no nothing. The atmosphere is so different. We can't quite see the Great Wall of China, but we can see the International Space Station. Our air tanks are running low. It's time to go. We rejoin Colin on Apollo 11 and go home.

I enjoyed the tribute but I'm glad it was only a day!

Matthew Quantrill (11)
St Philip Howard Catholic Primary School, Herne Bay

A DAY IN THE LIFE OF A BOOK

I have just arrived at Safeways and someone has already bought me, the new Harry Potter book just out. It is called 'Harry Potter Saves The Day'. After travelling around I was put on a kind of shelf, next thing I knew the surface I was on started to move. A person picked me up and then a bright laser shone on me, I was put in a bag and a little boy carried me in it. We got on a bus to my new owner's house.

As the bus pulled away I fell off the seat, and fell out of the bag, my new owner didn't realise and got off without me. An old lady got on the bus and picked me up and put me on the window ledge. I travelled around London for a bit. First the bus drove to London Bridge, then the Tower of London, on to Trafalgar Square, then next to Big Ben. Finally I got back to the bus depot where the driver fills with petrol and cleans the bus.

The bus driver took me into the office and put me on the desk. A man came out of the back door of the offices and said, 'I've been looking for you.' He picked me up and made a phone call. Next thing I knew the little boy ran into the office and picked me up and said, 'My Harry Potter book.' It was time for me to go home.

Ben Lassman (11)
St Philip Howard Catholic Primary School, Herne Bay

A Day In The Life Of Tiddler

Hi, I'm Tiddler. I'm a bit of an old cat but I'm still lively. First thing in the morning when I get up out of my house, no sorry my shed I have a stretch, yawn and waddle down the path for my breakfast.

In the shed I live with a hedgehog, it's brown, spiky and very loud. When it eats it grunts like a pig. At the back of the shed there are squirrels, and speaking of them it's nearly midday and it's time for some fun. I'm scared of them because of their teeth, but it doesn't stop me from chasing them!

It's just past midday and I'm getting bored chasing them, so I'm going back to sleep.

I can't get back to sleep because my back is itchy, and all this fur is making me hot. I know what I'll do, I'll go and cool myself down by rolling on the grass.

This is fun, hey, what is that black thing behind me? Oh it's only my tail, I'm always chasing it. Look there's a bug on my tail, the only problem is that I can't reach it, I'll flick it off. I'm going back to bed now, I'm exhausted!

It's night now, my owners should be home so I will go and see them, ye they're in. Now I can get fed!

This was another one of my exciting days, *not!*

Charlotte Binnersley (11)
St Philip Howard Catholic Primary School, Herne Bay

A Day In The Life Of A Car

'Here we go again,' I said as we zoomed down the A1, always the same on a Tuesday morning, always going to the swimming pool. Usually I don't mind, it's just because it is raining and I'm getting my lovely red bonnet wet.

I don't think my owner cares as long as they don't get wet which I think is stupid because they are just going to get wet anyway.

Oh no, guess what? We have broken-down and even worse we have broken-down right in the middle of a very busy road but luckily for us we are right next to a garage.

'Registration number, please,' the man asks my owner.
I hear my owner answer, 'H903 CAL.'
Then I heard something that makes my luck even worse, I have to stay in this horrible garage for five hours.

After what seemed like 200 days my owner came and got me. What a day! Some people think that my life is simple but if you think that then you may think again because it is not.

Kellie King (11)
St Philip Howard Catholic Primary School, Herne Bay

A Day In The Life Of A Tree

Today I was standing at the bottom of the garden, like I have done for the past nineteen years.

The sun was out. There was no one awake, all there was were birds singing. The kids were awake at 9 o'clock. The kids had come out to play on me. I don't mind it that much, but it does hurt a bit.

There was a bird on my branch, it was only a little bird. It looked like one that I had seen at the beginning of the year.

There was a cat going round and round in circles, finding somewhere to climb up me, and she did. Her claws really hurt me. She didn't get the bird because I put my leaves over the bird. I've got an old nest in my branches, it belongs to a family of blue tits.

At about 3 o'clock the dad of the house came out with the handsaw. He had it because my branches were getting too big. After he cut my branches off he painted the ends with wood paint so they wouldn't go bad.

I've got my blossom coming through, that means my apples are coming as well.

It was getting late when something started happening. I was returning to my body, because when I woke up I saw my body on my bed and I was in the tree in the back garden.

Sara Murphy (11)
St Philip Howard Catholic Primary School, Herne Bay

A Day In The Life Of A Rabbit

Sprinting across the race track I could see the finish line from where I was. 'I'm going to make it' I thought to myself. 'And then I'll be champion once again.' I'd been wanting to win the sports day cup for the under 10s for a whole year. I cross the finish line, however in a very strange condition. I finished as a rabbit! 'This' I thought 'should be fun.' I could skip school, I'll go and see Mum.
'Ahh' was the reply to this.

The very next day I was taken to the hospital but they said that they had no idea when it would wear off. 'In the meantime,' said their best doctor 'let him run around in your garden.'

Now here is where Mum made me mad . . . I could only eat vegetables! So after I had a very healthy lunch I had a quick sleep but kept my ears open for any foxes or my dogs. After that little nap I ran around in the fields, when all of a sudden *bang!* 'Weee, woah, woah, woah.' It was my dad out hunting with my dogs.
I shouted out, 'It's me Jonno, hold your fire,' and 'stop it!' But the shouts were drowned out by the shots. There was nothing for it but to run and soon I spotted a tree. I dived behind it, but as I dived a well aimed shot blew off my fluffy tail and as it came off, my size changed, my ears shortened and my fur shrank and I was human again.

'Jonno,' said my dad, 'what are you doing here?'
'Oh' I replied, 'I was just er . . . helping you catch that rabbit but it got away.'
'Oh well,' replied my dad 'better luck next time.'

That night at tea we had fish fingers and chips. 'Hey!' I shouted. 'Where's the vegetables?'

Jonno Ross (9)
St Ronan's School, Hawkhurst

A Day In The Life Of Bruce Gurcens

Bruce Gurcens is a scared and timid little boy who gets bullied all the time. I know this because I am his teacher, Miss Holden. He is the cleverest person in the class so I'm assuming that his friends call him 'Teacher's Pet'. Talking about friends, he only has one friend, Sherly Berks.

She is always trying to stop the school gang from bullying him. Although she means to be nice, she's only getting herself into more and more trouble.

In return for Sherly's kindness Bruce helps her with her homework so I think I should maybe start doing a few surprise tests! Today Bruce is walking with Sherly towards the gates but guess who's waiting for them . . . Tom, Jim and Marcus, the school bullying gang. They started to surround him, then suddenly the leader, Marcus said, 'Got yourself a girlfriend then Gurcens, you better have fun because she ain't gonna hang around long.'
'Oh do be quiet Marcus,' said Sherly sighing.
'How sweet,' said Marcus with a broad grin on his face and Tom and Jim started to giggle.
'The girl is sticking up for him.'
It was then that I decided to stop the fight. 'Go and see the headmaster.'
All three of them trudged along to the headmaster's office, and guess what? From that day on the three bullies (as they were called) never bullied anyone again.

Michelle Faure (9)
St Ronan's School, Hawkhurst

A Day In The Life Of A Troll

Let me describe trolls. Trolls are very strange because they can sit down and be as still as a rock for a hundred years. Trolls are very big and clumsy. Even a little boy can fool them. Sometimes you can build them up to such tempers that they explode. Most people do not know that there are several different types of troll.

Sea trolls live in sea and there they can search for a mate.

Water trolls live in big lakes and can disguise themselves as a floating root. A water troll can also turn into a glistening white horse. When a person touches the horse or rides it they will be under the troll's power.

The most frightening thing about trolls is that they eat people. Some people think that people who have gone missing in the woods at night might have been eaten by trolls.

Land trolls can live such a long time that sometimes they grow grass and trees on their heads and birds build their nests in the trees on top of their heads.

Trolls have advantages in that they are twenty times bigger than us. They hate the noise of church bells so they throw stones at them. That is why many strange stones are found lying around churches. Trolls turn to stone if they see sunlight and they can be killed by a troll sword which has a decorated hilt and can decapitate a troll in one blow.

Marcus Hall (11)
St Ronan's School, Hawkhurst

A Day In The Life Of A Horse

Horses are really good friends! If you have a horse, you will need to have a stable to use in winter. Horses also need a big field for grazing and eating the grass in, in the summer.

In the winter horses are still really nice even though it's probably harder work, because you have to clean out and put fresh hay in their stables. You would also have to make sure you brushed and put the horse's winter coat on.

The horses need to be ridden at least once a day. You must be very careful when they go out on frozen ground, for they may injure their legs. Horses often get scared by busy roads with cars on, they may buck or whine.

These animals are just as good in the summer but they will get very hot, very quickly, so they would be very happy to have a hose down with cold water.

Whatever the weather, horses always love their treats, carrots, Polos, and any description of mints are normally favourites.

So overall I think horses are great pets. Just one last thing, horses are very heavy and could easily break your toes. So just watch your feet!

Charlotte Peniston (9)
St Ronan's School, Hawkhurst

A Day In The Life Of A Chinchilla

Hello, I'm a chinchilla called Chilly. My fur is the softest in the world and I can bounce quite high. My owner came to give me some food. I was in a small cage. Yummy food, he has brought me my favourite, carrots.

'Morning Chilly, how are you?' he said. 'Would you like a runabout? As soon as he said runabout I ran to the edge of my cage and he let me out.

As soon as he had let me out I ran to the kitchen to get some more food, but I couldn't open the fridge, which had my favourite food inside. Then my owner came and opened the fridge for me and he got out sultanas and gave them to me and I ate them until they were gone. Next, my owner brushed my fur. The brush was getting old.

'I think we need to get you a new brush,' said my owner. So he went out to get me a new brush, but when he got back he had a new brush and a new cage, which was bigger and looked better. So he brushed me again and then he set up my new cage.

He gave me some more food later and moved everything into my new cage. My owner put cotton wool inside to make a comfy feel when I was sleeping. So I pottered around my new cage, I went through the tunnel which led to the top of my cage and then I sat down and slept.

Henry Garner (9)
St Ronan's School, Hawkhurst

A DAY IN THE LIFE OF A MODEL

This is one day described in a diary of a model. A bad day. I am an 18 year old model. Today lots happened. At 5am my mum woke me up because Eric, my fitness instructor, was coming. I got changed and I realised halfway through the lesson I am hopeless. What made the day even worse was my mother said she and my brother were going to America, without me!

After I got over the shock, I got in my limo and went to my company, Kelvin Klark. As my bad day was still going on, I got fired because I knocked over a few people on the ramp. Afterwards I went to my house, opened the door and I saw an invitation flutter to the ground. It was from Jason Sharp and I was invited to his barbecue.

I put on my best dress and told my limo chauffeur to drive me to Jason Sharp's mansion. Once I got there I saw loads of people, including Claudzee. Trisha (another model) and I couldn't believe it, Kalvin Klark! As I walked on I saw Jason and Kelvin talking. I said a friendly 'Hello' and started a conversation and I suddenly got rehired!

After the party I went home as happy as can be and my mum had rung. She said she got me a modelling job in LA! She told me to book a flight and go straight there. I packed my stuff and found out the earliest time was tonight.

I got to the airport and got on the plane. I said 'Goodbye' and the aeroplane left. *'Goodbye England! Hello Los Angeles!'*

That was the end of my day.

Rosie Mockett (10)
St Ronan's School, Hawkhurst

THE LIFE OF A CAMEL

Hi, my name is Sugar and if I can, I get my teeth into any sweet leaves. I wander around the desert with people on my back. I have two owners, Emma and Phoebe. I wish they could play with me, but when Emma rides me she whips me really hard. My feet are very flat so I cannot sink into the sand. Phoebe is so identical to her twin, Emma, but I can tell the difference because Emma whips me hard and Phoebe is gentle with me. Anyway, I like the desert but it is very hot. I like eating, sleeping and I love Phoebe.

My home is not really like a home, it is like a few blankets put on the sand. I was wandering around the desert one day and I suddenly felt a stud go into my foot. Oh no! How am I going to get this out? So I tried to get as far as I could without seeing Emma. Oh no! She saw me limping and she came up to me and brought out a pair of rusty old pliers. She said 'Poor little camelly wamelly,' and she prodded my foot. '*Haaaaaa, gulp*' as she pulled the coin out. It didn't hurt as much as when she whipped me when she rode me. Long before that a person came and pulled my tail very hard. I heard a sudden *snip*. He had pulled my beautiful fluffy tail off. I tried to go to sleep but that made it worse, it gave me nightmares. I have some camel friends, Thomas and Edward, they always show off about their fluffy tails. But I don't have one anymore. But I said to myself 'They are like whips that hit your bottom when you walk. *Who cares?'*

Charlotte Meyer (9)
St Ronan's School, Hawkhurst

A Day In The Life Of A Camel

Hello, my name is Humphrey the camel and I don't like my master because he makes me carry lots of his nasty luggage and he feeds me nasty, smelly cabbage *Yuk!* Today I have made my master very angry because I spat in his eye. So he kicked me and made me carry more luggage than ever.

While I was tethered up that day as a punishment, I had a nasty fright. A snake called Charlie, who was very well-feared in the neighbourhood, although one thing he lacked was brains. Because he didn't see an eagle called Hamish perched above him. Hamish swooped down on him and savagely slashed and pecked Charlie. Soon there was nothing left of him. *'Mmm'* said Hamish, 'that was very nice and tender,' and he flew off.

After all the excitement I decided to have a nice cooling wash, it was bliss. I stuck my head into the water trough. The water was rushing all over my face, washing between my ears. But I knew I should have a drink because I had a journey through the desert to a city two miles away.

As I set off I had no idea that my evil master was planning to take me away to the slaughterhouse and to buy a new camel instead. When we got there and I was awaiting my death, I caught sight of a rat called Marco.
'Help me!' I said to the rat. 'Help' I said, 'Help me run away!'
'OK, OK, stay cool' said Marco.
'I can't keep cool' I said, 'I want to run away but I am tethered up!'
'Don't worry' Marco said, 'I'll save you, just keep still and I will chew through those ropes for you.'
Just as he did, my master came down the stairs.
'Hey!' he said, 'don't run away.'
But it was too late. Marco jumped onto my back and we rode off into the desert.

Thomas Granger (9)
St Ronan's School, Hawkhurst

A Day In The Life Of A Dog Called Paws

It was early in the morning, about four or five o'clock. When my owner (whose name is Billy) shouted up the stairs,

'Paws, come on boy, good boy . . . come on I've got a *bone* for *you*.'

At those two words *bone* and *you*, I came belting down the stairs. The speed that I came down felt like Mach 100,000,000. I just imagined what it would be like in a real dog race.

'Oh he's so near the finish line, just taking a breather and he's off again. He's finished, he actually won the race.'

Just at that moment (when I was half-dreaming and half-awake) I crashed right smack into my owner, a boy called Billy. This hurt us both a lot. So after having my hour gnawing on the bone session. Billy took me out for a walk in the park.

I met my best dog friend in the park. He was called Oddball. His owner, Teddy, was also taking him for his fresh air morning walk too. His owner chatted to Billy for a bit. So Oddball and I went off to The Bush, got out our Jag XKR, went for a little drive, saved a female dog, had ten pints and then took our Jag XKR back to The Bush. We got back to our owners and said 'Goodbye.'

Then I let the day pass and then finally at long last, fell to sleep in front of the fire in my nice, new, warm basket.

Dominic Smith (11)
St Ronan's School, Hawkhurst

A Day In The Life Of Sleek

Hi, my name's Sleek. I'm an Arabian horse. I'm the best kept Arab stallion in the whole world.

I think on the schedule today. The first thing is a nice brush. I think my master might be a tiny bit angry with me because he turned me out and I had a good roll.

I've had my brush and I'm standing in the sun. My master, George, is doing something behind my stable. Oh, I know what he's doing, he's getting the hose ready. I must be having a warm bath.

I'm all shampoo-ey now and George is about to get at me with the hose again. It's actually really nice. Most sleeks in the world don't like it.
I know that from an old horse called Dusty, who had been travelling with his owner and he and George were friends, so they came to stay for a while.

Back to schedule then. I am now on the horse walker to dry off. After twenty minutes on the horse walker I get my strong, black, sturdy hooves rubbed to a shine, while George cleaned my tack. Soon we were ready to rumble. George clambers onto my back with a *thump*, nudges me with his spurs and we're off into the wilderness. Don't know where I am going, I've never been to the desert before but Dusty tells me it will be okay.

Ashley Welsh (9)
St Ronan's School, Hawkhurst

A Day In The Life Of Dreaming

Charlotte was getting bored in her English lesson. She was listening to a boring story so she started daydreaming about an Arabian desert. She started wandering through the desert when suddenly she saw an oasis in the middle of a rainforest. Well, she thought it was a rainforest, but when she got there it wasn't a rainforest or an oasis. it was some palm trees and a puddle. Charlotte was very confused about it because she thought that water went down into the sand and sunk. So she stood there for about ten minutes but it wouldn't sink, so she just forgot about it.

About an hour later Charlotte got really tired and, like a miracle, she saw a camel right in front of her and she was so thankful to whoever gave it to her. Charlotte got on and started walking. She was a bit wobbly to start with but then she got the hang of it. After that she saw a snake chasing a rat and she thought it was really weird.

The next thing after that she knew she was in her bed and dreaming. Charlotte was dreaming of having a puppy but then she felt a lick on the hand and she remembered that she had a dog of her own.

Emma Cobbold (9)
St Ronan's School, Hawkhurst

A DAY IN THE LIFE OF AN ARABIAN HORSE

Hello! My name is Minty. I have a kind and gentle owner called Charlotte. Every morning she gets up and brushes my mane and tail with a lovely gold comb. When we go riding, she always makes sure that my saddle and bridle are polished. We would then set off.

When we come out of the stables, we find that we are in the Sahara Desert. I swish my lovely white tail and trot off.

'How did we get here?' I wondered. I lift my head and smell the lovely smell of sand and coconuts. The sand is a lovely yellow colour and every now and then a streak of purple and green crosses the sandy desert. Then I smell something else. It's a watery smell and then I see an oasis with beautiful palm trees with ripe hairy coconuts.

Charlotte kicks my sides and I gallop off. When we come to the oasis, Charlotte gets off and runs to the see-through sparkling water and drinks gulp after gulp. I go to drink too.

When we have finished, Charlotte gets on my broad, white back and kicks my sides again. I gallop off back to the big brick and wooden stables. I was tucked up in my lovely sweet-smelling straw bed and Charlotte gave me some hay and carrots and some apples and water. Then I fell asleep and I heard Charlotte putting the big metal bolts in my stable door. As I dreamed, I thought what a long, exciting day it had been.

Phoebe Katis (8)
St Ronan's School, Hawkhurst

A Day In The Life Of A Desert Camel

Hello! My name is Shadow and I am a desert camel. I live in the Sahara desert. I go to the waterhole every week and have a lie down under the shade of the palm trees. Occasionally, there are a few sand dunes around my area but most of the time the weather is very hot.

One day I was wandering up the rocky mountain when my foot stepped on a foot trap. I was stuck! But then what did I hear? It was a human trying to capture me. He strapped some hard ropes around me and I was in great pain. But then realised that I was not crying because of the ropes, but because a bit of bone was stuck in the bottom of my foot. The man who was called Oliver, took the piece of bone out of my foot. I was very grateful.

I realised that Oliver was a very nice master. He opened his bag and got out a lovely juicy pineapple just for me. Oliver started to eat a coconut that was lying on the dusty sand. After that I couldn't tell what Oliver was doing, but I could just make out a kind of stick with a nib at the end (a pen) and a thin leaf (paper). Anyway, he put the leaf and the stick into his bag and asked me to follow him.

After a while, we had come to an oasis. I looked hard at the oasis and then I saw that the oasis was the same one I always go to. I met my three friends called Victory the falcon, Nibbles the camel and Willow the lizard. I had a talk about how I got my kind master. We had a quick drink and a rest and then we had to go.

It was nearly the end of our adventure. I smelled something funny. I saw that there was a multicoloured helicopter coming to pick us up. Luckily Oliver lives in Tunisia so I will love the environment there. We are going now. Bye!

Marco March (9)
St Ronan's School, Hawkhurst

A Day In The Life Of My Cat Rosie

Morning

One morning I would wake up at about seven o'clock. Wait for my mum (Elizabeth) to get up so that I could have breakfast. When I had had breakfast I would go and sit with my sister (Natalie). At about seven thirty I would go back to bed in my mum and dad's room. At about nine o'clock I would get up again, go into the garden, and go to the toilet. Then I would go and have a walk. At about nine thirty I would go back inside and eat some more of the breakfast I hadn't eaten. Then I would wait for my mum till nine forty.

After she had come home I would go back to bed till eleven o'clock. Then I would get up and go to the toilet again.

Lunchtime

At twelve o'clock I would go to my mum and yap for some food. Then I would wait for her to go out of the kitchen so that I could eat my food. Then I would have a drink of water and go and sit on the beanbag next to the fire till one thirty.

Afternoon

At two o'clock I would probably go an sit out on the sheet in the sun till two thirty. Then I would eat some more and go and sit on my mum till three o'clock. Then my dad would get up, and feed me some of his bacon from his breakfast. Then my sister would come home and go on the computer. I would sit on her lap for a bit then I would go and sit by the fire. Then at five I would go upstairs and go back to sleep. At about six fifteen I would be woken up to go and eat my dinner. After dinner I'd go out for a bit and come in at seven.

Then I'd go back to sleep. At ten I'd go out for a bit, come in at eleven and sleep by the fire.

Stephanie Estabrook (9)
St William Of Perth RC Primary School

A Day In The Life Of A Threatened King

Chapter 1 Cover!

'Your Royal Highness, there's an army on the horizon, you must take cover!' cried a squire desperately.

The sunrise, created by an orange-red ball of light, shone fantastically as the summer's morning began. As hundreds of armed soldiers marched confidently along the wide path, through the bloody forest. It got its name from many years gone by, from the greatest ruler ever, where his son was killed and where the blood of his murder still remains.

'Prepare the cannons!' announced King Pelenor VI. 'Arm our forces and let us be prepared for the evil that awaits us!'

'Yes my lord. But you must take cover. There are hundreds out there!' protested the young servant.

'I must fight for my subjects, I cannot call myself worthy if I don't.' stated King Pelenor.

'I shall take your place! I'm as strong, tall and skilful as you and nobody shall be able to see me under my armour.' suggested a sudden voice.

'It was the best knight in the court, Sir Nominous.'

'Very well. My overseer shall pick out my battle clothes.' agreed King Pelenor. 'Now go!'

Sir Nominous bowed and walked quickly out through the iron bolted doors, his strong paces echoing down the grand corridor. As soon as the footsteps were out of hearing distance, Pelenor summoned his bodyguards and only daughter, slipped a bag of gold in his cloak and crept down the winding staircase, through a wall by separating bricks and replacing them. He went under a tunnel and into a large room, where weapons and armour hung on the walls.

'All we have to do now is wait,' whispered the king.

Chapter 2 On The Battlefield

Back on the battlefield, screams and loud haunting cries surrounded the catastrophic area.

Many dead or groaning men lay upon the soft, red grass. Sir Nominous was fighting like a lion, putting all his strength in every blow. During one of his duels, Sir Nominous' sword snapped in two. As his opposition plunged his weapon towards him, Nominous grabbed his sword. As he fell he stabbed the opponent through the head. The blood trickled down his face like rain until there wasn't any left.

As the day went by and the sun started to set, a grey cloud appeared in the sky above. It started to rain lightly and soon the horn sounded to announce that the enemy were retreating. But as they left only a third remained alive.

We had won our battle!

Chapter 3 Survival And Rewards

Pelenor's troops walked joyfully towards the towering castle; some laughing with slight injuries, others hobbling on one leg and many staggering behind with horrific wounds.

King Pelenor, his daughter and two bodyguards had already returned to the hall, waiting for Sir Nominous' presence. The iron doors opened and there appeared a bloodstained Nominous.

'Ah, Sir Nominous, you have done me proud. For saving me and your terrific effort throughout this disastrous war, I hereby announce that you shall have this ring. It stands for bravery, love and justice,' proclaimed King Pelenor.

'Thank you my lord. I shall treasure this forever,' replied Sir Nominous gratefully.

From that day forth, Sir Nominous wore his ring in every battle and is now known as a famous, brave knight.

Megan Johnston (10)
St William Of Perth RC Primary School

A DAY IN THE LIFE OF PLUTO

The UFO

'Goodnight Matt,' whispered Mum.
'Mum I . . . I think I just saw a UFO.'
'Don't speak nonsense Matt,' said Mum, shutting the door.
So Matt went to sleep.
Suddenly light filled Matt's room.
'Arrgg! Mum, help!' Matt tried to shout but something was stopping him. Then a tube came out of nowhere and sucked him up. *Thud!* Matt had fallen into a dark chamber with ten other people. There were four other children who looked terrified. Two men, one who looked as if he was going to faint, the other angry. Then there was a toddler holding on to his mum and a teenager.

Going To Pluto

Bzzzmm! The UFO was leaving planet Earth at full speed.
'Hi! What's your name? My name's Phil,' said the man.
'My name's Matt,' said Matt.
'This is Liz and Chris,' he pointed at the lady and the toddler.
'These four are Becky, James, Ryan and Sam. I don't know his name, he hasn't spoken a word since he got here.'
'Eeerrk, eeerrk, eeerrk.' Two aliens came in the room with what looked like laser guns.
'Can you understand me? If you can, nod your heads.'
Everyone nodded.
'Good, the reason you can understand us is because of these mask-like things. We are taking you to our planet Pluto, to do experiments.
Suddenly Phil leapt at an alien but he crashed into an invisible wall.
Thump! The horrified man had fainted.
The aliens took off their masks.
'Arrgh!' screamed the children and Liz at the aliens' ugly bodies.
The aliens had purple faces with one big triangular eye, scary sharp teeth, a circular nose, three fingers with a horn thumb and weird clothes.
Then the aliens just vanished.
Thump! The UFO had landed on Pluto.

The Experiments

'Move! Move!' said the aliens with their laser guns aimed at everyone, especially Phil.

'Here are some suits for you. We've seen you on planet moon and we realised that you can't breathe on different planets. So we made these. They don't look the same as your suits but we think it'll still work.'

The suits looked a bit like wet suits.

Once they got out of the UFO there were lots of aliens around them. Most looked horrified, others were amazed and some were cheering. The aliens led them into a dome-like shaped house and into what looked like a big dungeon. They tied them with chains to the wall, so they couldn't escape through a window.

The next day four fierce-looking aliens came into the dungeons with laser guns and food. They gave food to everyone except the man that had fainted in the UFO. The aliens just untied him and told him to stand up and follow them. But what he did, was stand up and faint. So the aliens had to carry him to a big room with a lot of machines. They tied him to a big table by the hands and feet. Then an alien came in with a laser and a funny knife. He went up to the fainted man, looked at him for a while, wrote something in his notepad. He got his knife and stabbed it in his eyes, pulled it out and put it in a jar and studied it. Then he got his laser and took his jaws out with it and put them in a jar and studied that as well. Then he told the four aliens to feed the body to his pets.

Matt Vangool (10)
St William Of Perth RC Primary School

A DAY IN THE LIFE OF FLUFFY

It was Sunday morning; this was probably the best Sunday I would ever have because I was going to get my first ever pet. It was going to be a snow-white rabbit and I was going to call it Fluffy. I couldn't wait! First I got dressed, after that I went downstairs to have my breakfast. Once I'd had my breakfast I had just enough time to get my shoes and coat on and then walk to church. Church, I found, was always pretty boring. All you basically did was sit down and listen. I rushed home at the end and drove to the local pet shop with Mum to get Fluffy. We had Fluffy reserved so that no one would be able to buy him. But when we arrived the white rabbit was nowhere to be seen. I said that I would not go home without the rabbit. Mum eventually gave up and asked a shop assistant where Fluffy was, and he lead us to a small corner in the shop, away from all the other rabbits, in which Fluffy lay. We took Fluffy home and fed him, then we went to bed.

The next morning I found Fluffy in the middle of a fight with Razor. Razor is a huge street dog with extra long teeth. If Fluffy had rested for a millionth of a second he would be chopped up in neat little slices resting in Razor's tummy. Razor was scratched, bitten and angry all over. Fluffy didn't have a scratch. Fluffy attempted a dive under Razor's legs, and it worked. Fluffy shot right up and bit Razor's throat with an incredible force. A squeal of pain was ejected and Fluffy got out of the way just in time before Razor came crashing down to the ground. He staggered to his feet and slowly walked off through the bush, blood dripping in his path. He was never seen again. Fluffy hopped back to me and stroked my leg with his head.

An hour later I walked into the wood beside the motorway.
'Arhhh,' I shouted as I was whisked up by a rope and lay dangling by one leg, about five feet above the ground, swinging helplessly in mid-air.
'What should I do?' I asked myself. 'I know, I'll phone Mum on my mobile phone,' but when my hand dived into my pocket it found no mobile phone there. When I looked down I saw my mobile phone broken in the mud. Fluffy had now learnt his name off by heart, so I called 'Fluffy, Fluffy.'

My house was about thirty metres away so Fluffy could hear me. He pricked his ears and came shooting towards me like an arrow. I soon saw him coming towards me and he jumped incredibly high and landed perfectly into my outstretched hands.

'Good boy, good boy,' I praised him, 'now go and get me my covers and put them under me, then bite this rope so that I fall to the ground.'

And that's exactly what happened.

We strolled on further into the forest and then Fluffy spoke! 'I'm hungry.'

I stopped dead in my tracks, took him in my hands and ran home.

'Mum, Fluffy can speak!'

'No, never,' Mum threw back at me,

'Yes and we have to celebrate,' I exclaimed and all the party food you could ever imagine was lying on the table in heaps. I invited all my friends and because we didn't have enough seats we had to borrow one of the church's pews. Plus we won one million pounds for owning the first ever animal to talk.

Chris Jarvis (9)
St William Of Perth RC Primary School

A Day In The Life Of A Goldfish

I am a goldfish, and I live in a plastic tank with a yellow top. I am very happy here. I have a tankmate who keeps me company called Tom. I am Sarah.

I hear the family I live with coming downstairs. That means my breakfast. It's Sunday, that means a good clean out of my tank! Here she is speaking to us.
'Have you had a good night?'
She has just gone leaving our breakfast floating on the top. Two fish pellets. Quickly, smoothly I swim to the top. Two fish pellets are waiting for me. I feast on my breakfast. Next thing *crash!* I swim down and hide in the pond weed. Tom says it's the front door closing. It happens a lot! I think it's like an earthquake!

Now they have gone to church it is quite peaceful. We swim around our tank, exercising stiff fins, and generally enjoying ourselves.

Then later - crash stomp stomp. Oh no they're back.

Splash, help don't be caught. Help, help it's that awful net, they are trying to get us out of our tank to clean it out! Oh oh help I'll die, aagh, that was awful. They fished me out of my bowl and into a sinkful of water. They're putting fresh water, gravel and pond weed into our tank. Oh here is that horrid net again . . . and I am back in my tank again. Lovely and peaceful. I swim through the water weed and look down at the gravel underneath me, underneath me. Then plop, plop, plop, plop I would know what that means a mile away, feeding time. I swim quickly to the top and gobble down two pellets almost in one go. A little later it is beginning to get dark. I cannot see anything. I'll just settle down to sleep.
'And now folks the weather forecast for tonight and tomorrow.'
Oh no not him again, not that awful man on the telly! Just my luck.
'Miaow.'

First them, now the cat. Oh help, quick dive. Cover yourself up in the weed. Phew that was a close squeak. I'll either be deaf or torn to pieces today.

All quiet, the days aren't normally so hectic, because there's only the mother in the house. The kids are at school and the father's at work. Good night I'm going to sleep!

Imogen Robertson (10)
St William Of Perth RC Primary School

A DAY IN THE LIFE OF THE QUEEN

It was just a normal day at school when we started doing History. Then I thought about Queen Elizabeth II. So I asked my teacher 'Would it be possible to meet the Queen one day this week?'
But she just said 'You've got a day doing the cleaning!'
I tried to ask her why she keeps picking on me. When I was hoovering in the Historical room I saw pictures of King Henry VIII, King Richard II, Queen Victoria and then Queen Elizabeth II. Then, suddenly, I was swirling round and round, up and down. Then, I don't know, I think I was in Buckingham Palace. I look down at myself and I was in the body of Queen Elizabeth II. I was walking down the stairs and a handsome lad was scurrying around and said 'You should be resting for the big party, it is still on. I will get someone to come and keep you company. I think Prince William is around.'
A while later I heard a voice shout, 'Do not fear, Will is here! Hi, Grandmother, how are you? Anything strange or startling going on here?'
'Well, no not really, Willie!' I shouted 'but I went to see your father, Prince Charles, hopefully future king. Hopefully, not for a couple of years yet! You can't get rid of me that easily!'
I had to go and get my hair done by Mrs Bizz. I got it all curled, washed, cut and blow dried. Then my make-up had to be done and I had to be dressed by Miss Baba, because I had been invited to a party. The invitation said:
'Come to my party at 7.30pm at Crystal Palace tonight.
Yours faithfully, Tony Blair.'

Later on I was at the party. I was swirling around. Then I was back to me, me, me, me!

Aislinn Hanna (9)
St William Of Perth RC Primary School

A Day In The Life Of A Competition Winner

It was a lovely Sunday morning. I was watching 'Match of the Day'. They were speaking about a competition. To win the competition you have to draw your favourite football player. If you win you win a whole day at Old Trafford (home ground of Manchester United). You get to meet all of the Manchester United players and the manager as well. But that isn't all. You also get a tour of the stadium seeing the dressing rooms and the players' tunnel.

Almost straight away I got drawing my favourite player, David Beckham. I drew it to perfection and coloured every bit of it to absolute perfection. Later that day I ran round to the post-box and posted my entry. I waited and waited to see if I had won. Suddenly out of the blue a letter came through the letterbox. It was addressed to James Dance. On the corner of the envelope was a Manchester United badge. I ripped it open straight away. Inside was a letter from Sir Alex Ferguson and badge saying 'Visitor'.
'Yes!' I shouted excitedly. 'I've won! I've won!'
'What have you won?' Mum asked.
'A day at Old Trafford,' I answered. 'I won that competition I entered.'
I decided to read the letter and this is what it said:
'Dear James Dance, Congratulations on winning the competition. Your entry was no match against the others. We would like you to come up to Old Trafford on the 18th June. I will come and pick you up on the 17th June and you can sleep in the Old Trafford Hotel. Coming down to collect you with me will be David Beckham, your favourite player. When you arrive we will give you a Man Utd kit. See you soon.
Yours faithfully, Sir Alex Ferguson.

'I can't wait,' I said excitedly.
'At least I haven't got to drive up to Manchester,' Mum said.
'Can't I come?' my brother asked.
'No, you can't come,' I answered.
'Go on!' he pleaded.
'No no no and no,' I shouted.

On the day before I went I packed a bag of clothes ready to go. I slept in my clothes that night to make sure I wasn't late. That night I couldn't sleep because I was so excited. At 7.00am I jumped out of bed and ran downstairs, carrying my bag of clothes on my shoulder. At 9.00am sharpish Sir Alex and David Beckham would come and pick me up. At 9.00am on the dot the doorbell rang. I ran to the door and answered it. Unfortunately it was only the postman.

'Here's your letters,' he said. 'They wouldn't fit through the letterbox.'

Thanks,' I said.

'Who is it?' Mum asked.

'It's only the postman, I answered.

I was starting to worry that it had all been a dream. Suddenly a huge limousine pulled up outside our house. The driver got out and opened the back door of the car. Out stepped the figure of David Beckham and Alex Ferguson.

'Hi,' I said. 'Do you want to come in for a cuppa.'

'No, we'd better get going if you want to get there early,' Sir Alex told me.

'Hi,' I said to David Beckham, who was standing behind Alex.

'Hi,' he said back.

'Come on let's go,' said Alex.

'Okay, I'll get my bag,' I said.

'Bye,' I said to my mum.

'See you in a couple of days,' said my mum.

We left our house and started to make our way. Five and a half hours later we reached Old Trafford. We went straight to the hotel and then to my room.

'You have got an hour to spare,' Alex told me. 'Would you like to go for a swim in our swimming pool?'

The next morning I got up and got dressed. I ran down to the restaurant to have breakfast. I had a cooked breakfast and a drink of orange juice. The first thing I did was get a private tour of the whole stadium. Next I watched all the players training and even had a kick about with them. Last of all, I sat in the dugout and watched Man U versus Liverpool. Man U won the game 5-0. All too soon it was time to go home.

'Do I have to go?' I asked.
'I'm afraid so,' Alex answered.

It seemed a very long time to get home from Old Trafford. The few days I had been away had given me many happy memories. It was a time I will never forget.

James Dance (10)
St William Of Perth RC Primary School

A Day In The Life Of Sam

Sam wakes up to the sound of a cockerel crowing because he lives on a farm in the country. First he has cereal for his breakfast, then brushes his teeth. After that he goes out to feed the pigs on his farm. He thinks they smell disgusting and are dirty, but his father insists they are very clean animals and only smell sometimes.

With that task completed he is told to take a bath. He always protests and asks his father 'Why do I have to take a bath? You say pigs are clean animals.'
But he never gets an answer. Sam always asks this because he does not like taking baths. So he takes his bath. Once he has had his bath he gets changed into his school uniform.

His school is in the village and is about a twenty minute walk from his farm. Sam rides his bike there, so it only takes him ten minutes.

In school, year five, which is Sam's, are studying the Victorians in history. Sam enjoys history especially researching the village's past. His favourite lesson is art because he is very good at drawing.

Sam has many friends at school. At playtime they all play football and have lots of fun although, they sometimes have an argument about whether it was a goal or not. They usually get on together and sort out any differences amicably.

When Sam gets home he often plays on his PlayStation. His favourite game is FA 2001. Sam is allowed to play on the PlayStation for one hour.

After that he has his dinner, feeds the chickens and goes to bed.

Alexander Siamatas (10)
St William Of Perth RC Primary School

A Day In The Life Of A Footballer

If I was a footballer I would be like Roy Keane. He is my favourite footie player. And I want to be just like him when I grow up.

'Hi, I'm Roy Keane, and my team has got a match against Bayern Munich today, we're just training at the moment. Sir Alex says that Becks will be a sub with Luke Chadwick on the pitch, last time we played them we beat 'em two nil. Olé Gunnar Solskjaer scored the first goal and Sheringham scored as well. We have won the treble fourteen times. Anyway our match is on at one thirty. Kick off is at one forty five, I better get ready for the match.

'Sir Alex, I've got all of my things in my bag for the match.'
Sir Alex responded 'OK mate.'
Now all we'll have to do is wait until we get to the match.

And after, I said 'Might win the match.'
And it's four nil to Man Utd and the final whistle is about to be blown. All the goals were by Roy Keane and there goes the final whistle. The champs are celebrating in the changing room.

Danny Keane (10)
St William Of Perth RC Primary School

A DAY IN THE LIFE OF HELL

'I have to stop Hellmouth now, or the earth will be swallowed and whoever is not demon will suffer in *hell!*'

So I ran into the tomb with no fear, vampires grabbed onto me but I pushed them onto the floor. I stabbed them in the heart with my sharp, wooden stake and each one turned to dust. Then I ran through a dark, damp and old alleyway, I came out the other side and it was silent. Then I heard a roar followed by a flash of light, there was Hellmouth with its mouth wide open ready to swallow the world, so I ran towards him and kicked his mouth shut. He went to trip me up but I jumped and kicked him in the face. He had great big horns on his head and clawed hands and feet; he had spikes all over his body. Then he picked me up and chucked me across the room and I hit the wall with great pain. Then he started to open his mouth again, I ran towards him and punched him with all my might but nothing happened. He just kicked me across the room. I got up but it was too late. He was too powerful, so he swallowed the earth!

Torturing Hell

I woke up. 'Where am I?' I whispered.
'You are in Hell,' a man said to me.
He only had one eye and it looked as if someone had ripped it out and he didn't have a leg. He had ripped clothes.

Then I heard a scream. It was horrible. Everyone was screaming. I heard rips of bodies tearing open. The people, or should I say monsters, who were running it, were demons that looked like bulls, but on two feet and with axes. Everywhere I looked I saw people being tortured and stretched. The worst thing of all was people being put into a large box with spikes on the inner part of the door. They put lots of scorpions inside. A lot of the people were put on a large table; they got a knife and disembowelled them. Then I felt a cold shiver run up my back as a whip birched down my back.
'Get to work,' the creature clambered.

The Great Beast

That was the worst day of all time. This monster was going to fight anyone that was down in his or her work. That day everyone was queuing up to fight the monster. The first man that went into the arena was eaten whole. Nobody saw the monster unless they were fighting the beast. The second man got his arm bit off then his head. Then it was my turn. I ran out as I saw the monster. I had great fear. It had enormous horns and it was about one hundred metres high. It had hair all over its body and massive claws. He grabbed me in his claw and tried to crunch me, now I was losing blood fast. Then swords started to come out of the arena, with flames. I grabbed a sword and stabbed him in the foot. He screamed a mighty roar, so I grabbed five more and put two in the same foot and three in the other. By this time he was pouring with blood. I climbed up to a high platform then jumped on the monster and put a sword painfully through its head. It was choking loudly and the chokes were echoing loudly in the arena. I then pulled out a dagger and slammed it in his eye. He must have felt great pain, as his head exploded. I was still bleeding with pain as I fell to the ground, then I saw darkness.

The End Of Hell

I woke to people cheering, 'You are our hero, and you killed the mighty ruler of Hell. You are the new ruler. What is going to happen now?'
'Firstly there will be no Hell! There will be no suffering!' I said. 'The demons will be changed back to humans, we will work together to make this a better place.'

From that day on there was no hell.

James Mills (10)
St William Of Perth RC Primary School

A DAY IN THE LIFE OF MY MUM!

I might not be very interesting but when you hear this story, you will be very surprised!

One clear night, I sat under the stars and I saw a shooting star, I wished I was my mother, I didn't think it would come true so I fell asleep. In the morning my mum turned my CD player on and started dancing if I *was* myself I would have joined in but I wasn't me. I was my mum, so I said 'Turn that racket down, I'm trying to sleep!'
So my mum ran downstairs and had some Weetos for breakfast, she usually has toast but remember she's me and I'm her, but I still had to go to school, we had a test today. My mum and me still look the same but had each other's minds!

The next day I got all my sums right in my test because I was my mum! I liked being Mum but it got worse, I had to wash the dishes, make the dinner, iron the clothes because my mum just sat around watching the TV. I asked my mum if she wanted to switch back and she said 'No! No! No!'
She said she loved being a child because she never had to do any work. But to top it off I still had to do my homework.

That night, I looked up at the star and I saw a shooting star and I wished and wished to be myself again!

Morning came very quickly and I heard no singing and Mum was still in bed. Yes! I was myself again! And from that day on I was good to my mum because I knew how she felt because I had been my mum for a day.

Loren Syer-Willoughby (10)
St William Of Perth RC Primary School

A DAY IN THE LIFE OF . . .

One morning Midnight looked out of her bedroom window and smiled. She ran downstairs and made herself some snails on toast. Midnight was a witch! She had long dark hair, sparkly brown eyes and some freckles. Midnight was not like any other witch, because she didn't have a broomstick or a kitten.

When Midnight was dressed she ran down the spiral staircase to the cellar. There was only one spell that she could do, that was the money spell! Midnight ran over to the big book of spells, she flicked through the book, until she came to the page 1099. She read through the spell twice, then closed her eyes, muttered the spell and waved her arm in the air. When she opened her eyes she saw a pile of money! Midnight smiled happily, it was the second time the spell had turned out right. She ran back up the spiral staircase holding some money in her hand. She grabbed her bag and went outside. It was warm outside, Midnight strolled through the forest until she came to the town.

When Midnight got to the shops it was nearly lunchtime. She went into the pet store and bought a black furry kitten called Sooty. Then she went to the broomstick store and bought one about her size. Once she had done her shopping she went out to lunch at 'Wazzoy', a very popular eating place. Midnight ate so much that she was tired, so she decided to fly home. So she got on her broomstick, put Sooty inside her bag for safety and gave it a sharp tap and away she flew.

Midnight flew very high above the trees, and through the clouds. When she got home it was quite late, so she quickly made herself some snails and frogs' legs for supper. Sooty really enjoyed the frogs' legs too, but not the snails. They were a bit too crunchy for his little teeth.

She put her broomstick in the cupboard and Sooty curled up at the end of the bed. Midnight climbed into bed and closed her eyes. It had been a busy day!

Georgia Beesley (9)
St William Of Perth RC Primary School

A DAY IN THE LIFE OF THE LIONS

Hello, I am Johnny Wilkinson. Me and my friends, Joe Worsley and Lawrence Dalaglio are feeling a bit nervous, but we are OK. We have to take two Lions shirts and some smart clothes on our British Lions rugby tour of Australia. We have just arrived at the airport and have to walk to the plane.

We are on the plane and there's not much room for my legs because I'm England's kicker. We have been on the plane for ages and we have flown over France, Spain and now we are over India. It's really boring and there's nowhere to go except to the toilet.
'It's your captain speaking. We are running out of fuel quick.'
Aahh! Bang! Crash! 'I'm alright. Are you?'
'Yes, Joe is OK. Yes, Lawrence is OK. Crickey, that was close! We are lucky. There is another airport in the next town. Let's get a taxi.'
'Good Idea! Look we are just going through a town. There's the airport. Just drop us off here.' We went into the ticket hall and we explained what happened. They kindly let us on the next plane and the plane is a jumbo jet.

There is more room on this plane and it is longer. We have flown to the end of India. Now we are flying over the Indian ocean and we are about to land. We feel nervous after what happened last time, but I am a tough rugby player so I mustn't let it bother me.

Now we are just finding the rugby ground. I have found it. I am just putting my red Lions shirt on and I am leading the team onto the pitch. I am captain of the Lions Rugby Team and the crowd are going wild.

George Gillham (9)
Shorne CE Primary School

A Day In The Life Of My Auntie's Cat, Skippy

My auntie's cat called Skippy is a very sneaky cat, because my aunt lives just down the road from me and Skippy and I are good friends, so when I stop playing with him and go home, he follows me and sneaks in as well.

During the day while I am at school, he is waiting for me and he knows the time when I come home. He is probably thinking, 'I have to wait for a certain time and then she will come home so I can play with her and she will tickle my tummy, which I really like!' So when I leave home in the morning, Skippy's face is all sad and he is most likely thinking, 'Where are you going? We've only just started playing.' But when I get home, his face is all happy and he does little high-pitched miaows and purrs loudly.

When he sneaks into my house and you don't notice him, before you go out you must check he is not on my bed because he curls himself up into a little ball and goes to sleep amongst the toys on there.

If Skippy has sneaked in and my mum runs the vacuum cleaner over the carpet, Skippy runs like mad to the safety of being under my bed! I try to move him but he just does not budge, so I have to tempt him out with a piece of string.

I think Skippy's favourite things are to sleep, eat and get into mischief.

Kezia Brown (10)
Shorne CE Primary School

A Day In The Life Of Frank Spencer

This is a day in the life of Frank Spencer. A day spent at the seaside which for normal people would be lovely but for Frank - no, not for Frank Spencer.

It was a hot, gleaming summer's day when Frank suggested to his wife Betty that they go to the seaside. The decided to go by bus. While waiting at the bus stop at the end of their road, to Frank's horror the us came along. It was a big bus, it was a red bus, it was an open topped big red bus.
'Betty, I can't.'
'Can't what?' Betty replied.
'I can't get on that bus.'
'Oh Frank, why ever not?'
'Cause I can't Betty' he said wincing.
'Oh Frank don't be silly, hold my hand.'
Frank held Betty's hand and moved gingerly forward as the bus approached. The bus stopped with a 'shhhh'.
'Betty' Frank said nervously, 'are there any pigeons?'
'What on the bus? No silly of course there aren't any pigeons on the bus, why?'
'Well,' Frank whispered. 'When I was a boy a pigeon stole my beret from off my head when I went for a ride on a big, red, open topped bus. It swooped down and sat on my head and when I said 'Shoo, shoo you naughty little bird' it pecked at my beret and flew away with it in its mouth.'
'Oh Frank you poor thing' Betty said lovingly.
'I wouldn't mind but it was my Sunday one!' exclaimed Frank.
Eventually Betty convinced Frank to climb aboard the big, red open topped bus. They found two empty seats on the top deck right at the front. The bus moved off. Frank looked around in the sky just in case.
'Look Betty, I can see the sea.'
'Calm down Frank, you know what happens when you get excited.'
'Oh Betty, I haven't wet my trousers for ages.'
'That's what you said yesterday,' Betty said remembering as they got off the bus and stepped onto the hot sandy beach.

'Betty, shall we hire one of those little wooden houses on the sand?'

'Yes Frank but promise me you won't break this one,' Betty said sternly.

Betty And Frank slowly walked over to the chalet office where they hired a small chalet. Frank noticed a sign, which said *'All damage must be paid for'*.

When they had set out their deck chairs Frank took off his socks and shoes. Frank suddenly shouted 'Betty my feet are on fire!'

'Don't be silly Frank, it's only the hot sand.'

As they settled down in their deck chairs for a quiet afternoon, suddenly a pigeon swooped down and took Frank's beret from off his head and flew off with it.

'Oh Betty, it's happened again.'

Christian Purdy (9)
Shorne CE Primary School

A DAY IN THE LIFE OF THE SIMPSONS

On the 23rd of December 2001, when the two children were off school, the Simpson family went to Itchy and Scratchy land. This is four hours away from Springfield. The names of the family are Homer, who is Dad, Marge who is Mum, Bart who is the son, Lisa who is the daughter and Maggie who is the baby. Anyway, let's get on with the story.

On Sunday night the family were packing their bags apart from Maggie, of course, because she is only a baby! Lisa packed eight of her clothes, two books and four toys. Maggie brought a bottle, a dummy and a teddy. Bart packed ten stink bombs, a slingshot and a soldier set. Homer and Marge packed nappies, aftershave, shower gel, toothbrushes, a hairbrush, their clothes and toothpaste.

After a good night's sleep the family woke up excitedly, so they got themselves organised and got in the car. They drove two hundred miles and saw a beefy burger restaurant and they said *'Beefy Burgers!'*
'Can we stop here please?' Bart and Lisa shouted. At that point a lorry came whizzing towards them with dazzling lights.
'Agghhh!' Then all of a sudden it turned into the Beefy Burgers restaurant.
'Phew!' they whispered loudly wiping the sweat from their foreheads. They followed the lorry into the restaurant and they stuffed themselves with burgers. When they came out the children fell asleep in the car. It only took half an hour to go to the Itchy and Scratchy Land from the Beefy Burgers restaurant. Itchy and Scratchy Land is an amusement park. It is also a TV show. Not just any TV show but Bart and Lisa's favourite TV show.

The next day the children woke up at eight o'clock. Homer got up and shaved. Whilst he was shaving he cut himself with blood coming out.
'Ouch!' he shouted.
At that moment Marge got the hairbrush stuck in her hair.
'Oh' she sighed in a croaky voice and then it ended with the children fighting with Bart throwing soldiers, Lisa throwing books and Maggie throwing dummies.
'Be quiet!' shouted Homer.
'Your dad's right,' said Marge with the children tangled up.

An hour later they were in the hot sunshine in Itchy and Scratchy Land. The grown ups went to a love movie at two o'clock. It was also unsuitable for under eighteens. During that time the children were having a great time with Maggie in a deep toddler ball pond that made their day even better.

At six o'clock when the sun was setting, Homer and Marge came out of the cinema and there was a parade on and a scientist had designed an Itchy and Scratchy. The scientist had made the robots with lots of chemicals. In the parade an hour later an Itchy looked at the Simpson family suspiciously and came over to kill them so Bart broke into a camera shop and stole a camera and took a photo of it and then the Itchy fell to the ground with blood squirting out. Then out of nowhere, a million of these robots came to kill the Simpson family so Bart ran to the camera shop and stole all the cameras and said, 'Say cheese.'
He said it in French for a joke.
'Say fromage,' said Homer and when they had killed all of them the park was flooded in blood. The robots obviously had an allergic reaction to camera flashes.

When the Simpson family left they all had a day to remember and they lived happily ever after.

Christopher McCann (8)
Shorne CE Primary School

A Day In The Life Of A Tooth Fairy

As Jess went to knock for Nat, she heard a voice saying her name. Jess stared around her but nothing was there. All of a sudden, out from nowhere popped Nat's small head.

'Hey Jessie, wazzup?'

'I told you not to call me that. From now on you call me Jess, it's more *cool* OK? Believe it or not Nat, I just heard a voice when I was coming to knock for you.'

'Yeah right,' said Nat in a disbelieving manner.

'Honestly I did - it said 'Jess'.'

'I think you should get your ears checked out.' Then they both had a good giggle for a fair time.

'Oh, by the way, my tooth fell out last night,' said Jess.

'Has the tooth fairy come yet?' asked Nat.

'The what?' shrieked Jess.

'The tooth fairy,' answered Nat.

'Oh her. No, not yet,' replied Jess, disappointedly.

'Jessie, oh sorry I mean Jess, supper time,' called a voice from the kitchen.

'OK Mum, I'm coming,' said Jessie.

As Nat was walking back to her house, she thought that she could be a tooth fairy when she was older and for a practice, tonight she would go and put some money under Jessie's pillow.

As soon as she got home she dressed up into her fairy clothes and then told her mum that she was going to a fancy dress party. When her mum was hanging out the washing, she sneaked some money out of her purse.

Nat walked out the door and down the alley. When she got to Jessie's house, she got a hanky from her pocket and then pulled out more and more of them until there were thirteen hankies. Nat tied them all together and luckily Jessie's bedroom window was open. She threw all of the hankies into Jessie's bedroom and climbed up the wall to her friend's room. Fortunately, Jessie was asleep, but it was going to be a hard job to put the money under her pillow and to get the tooth. Nat tiptoed over to the bedside and lifted up the pillow slowly and carefully, so that she could exchange the tooth for a shiny, silver coin.

Finally, Nat was tucked up in her own bed, waiting for the next day and of course, it did come. So after breakfast Nat went to knock for Jess. Jessie's dad answered the door. Nat didn't have to say a word and in no time at all Jess was at the door.

'The tooth fairy came last night,' said Jess excitedly.
'Did it?' said Nat, trying to sound amazed.
All of a sudden Nat's tooth fell out. I wonder who's going to give her some money?

Rebecca Pratt (9)
Shorne CE Primary School

A DAY IN THE LIFE OF MATT IN ANTIGUA

On the 8th of November, I was going to a country called Antigua in the Caribbean. My flight was 8 hours in a Virgin Atlantic jumbo jet and when I finally arrived there, I shouted 'Yes! I'm finally here in Antigua.

The first thing I did was to lie on the beach for hours and hours and got swept up by the beach, the blue seas and warm waves. After several days of just doing nothing, my adventure began.

Firstly, I went to a place called Green Island. I had to get there by catamaran. This was called the *Kokomo Cat*. I sat on the front on the netting, so all the waves, fish, sharks and all sea creatures you can think of were directly under me. All the time I was in the Caribbean Sea, things were very calm, but as soon as I entered the Atlantic Ocean it got very rough and I was sick on the bar (not very nice - yuk). Once I arrived at Green Island, I walked onto powder-white sand ready to go snorkelling. Snorkel mask and flippers on, I entered the underwater world of Antigua and there I saw a brown and yellow spotted eel and lots of different coloured fish. Once I had seen the eel, I felt a bit uneasy in the water and swam back to the beach for my lunch. After lunch we made our way back to the hotel. On the return journey the waves were still as rough, my beach towel got blown into the sea and my big brother was sick (yuk).

The next thing I did was to go to Nelson's Dockyard. On the way, we drove through a tropical rainforest. The road was very bumpy, with big holes and bits of road missing. This was due to hurricane Andrew. There were lots of things that you could eat in the rainforest but I did not fancy getting out of the truck, just in case there were big spiders and snakes. Once we arrived at Nelson's Dockyard water, I saw lots of jellyfish and also a bird called a blue heron (my hotel was called the Rex Blue Heron). I then made my way to a place called the viewing platform. The first thing I saw was a very strange looking lizard, called Gizzard. Then a view really caught my eye: I could see the whole Dockyard, English Harbour and in fact I could see the whole of Antigua.

Then came an adventure. I don't know if I really enjoyed horse riding. This was my first time at horse riding. Firstly we had to put on our safety helmets. My horse was called Moron. I think he was a bit of a moron. My mum was the funniest because she is scared of horses, but we all liked the idea of seeing the sunset on the beach on horseback. First we went to a very tiny zoo. There were some pretty peacocks and different sorts of birds. I had to walk through all long grass and trees. This was a bit of a worry as there could have been snakes and spiders. We then reached a compound full of tortoises, some very old, some very young. Then I lifted the smallest one, as they can be very heavy. Then came the return journey. Firstly, Mum fell off her horse. Everyone laughed but Mum did not find this funny. On the way back I carved my name in an aloe vera plant. The guide told me this would be there forever. One of the men we were with then climbed a coconut palm and gave us a coconut. Finally, I was back on my own legs and I felt much safer.

Then I went barracuda fishing. I had to walk through long, flowing seaweed. This was not a nice feeling. I could feel the barracuda swimming past my legs. I did not catch anything so I went shell and coral collecting. Then back to the beach. We then decided to go for a walk along to the end of the beach. On the way I stopped at a bar called O'Jays. To my horror they had caught a hammer-head shark just where we had all been swimming. This was left out to dry as all the local people would then eat it. I purchased a bag of crisps and went on my way, worrying if the next time I went into the sea, there would be a hammer-head shark waiting for me.

Matt Clayden (8)
Shorne CE Primary School

A Day In The Life Of Jennifer Aniston

Dear Diary,

Today I got up as usual. I got dressed and had breakfast. As I was having breakfast, Courtney Cox phoned and said the Friends gang and I had to be in early as the director, Janet, wanted to shoot the first episode of series 7.

That morning I was in quite a rush. When I finally got to the studio I was late, but we carried on as usual. During one of the scenes I had to come into a conversation of Ross and Joey's, but they got annoyed as I kept coming in at the wrong time. It was forgotten at lunch, when we all had a good laugh, especially Matt - he went bright red in hysterics, but not one of us could work out why.

In the scene after lunch, Lisa started crying. It was a love scene between Chandler and Monica, but I must admit I nearly cried too as it was so romantic and they made it seem so real. Janet let us off at 4 o'clock, as we had come in early. It was just as well really, because Courtney, Lisa and I had to go to the MIZZ magazine studio for a photo shoot. We were going to be in one of their quizzes called 'Which Friends girl are you most like?' Lisa was actually a bit excited, but I was dreading it as it is just another photo shoot for me.

I got the photo shoot done with and then the three of us girls went down the pub for a drink. We stayed in the pub for two hours, laughing and joking. I got home at roughly 10.30. It is now 11.00. I am very tired and want to go to bed. Goodnight.

Jasmine Hessenthaler (10)
Shorne CE Primary School

A DAY IN THE LIFE OF A UNICORN

A unicorn is a mystical creature. It is a white horse with a horn and wings. The horn is gold and is what gives them their power. The wings are strong and are white feathers, long and slender.

Once a unicorn is tamed, a gold chain is placed around it. In the middle of this chain is a jewel. This is the symbol of the unicorn's name.
In the unicorn's hair are small beads of ruby, diamond, sapphire, pearl and emerald. Gold and silver flecks are often found on the hooves. The unicorn is called Pearl and has never been tamed.

I wake up in the morning to go to a small magic pool where lily flowers never end their beautiful blossom. I would never leave this place.
Every day a dragon will come and seek me. I toss my head about and shake my wings, then cast a killing spell on it and it vanishes.
But today I had the worst dragon of all to defeat. When I was born, I remember my mum telling me to believe in myself. After all, a dragon is just a fire-breathing lizard. The king of the dragons' name is Yac-e-tat.

I drank quickly from the pool of water, plucked up my courage and walked on to the topmost cliff. I neighed at him for the battle to begin. The first attack came from him. He whipped his tail at me but I froze it with my horn. Then I beat my wings and flew up into the air. I was closely followed by the dragon. Then he started to roar with rage, which meant flames. I concentrated my power to freeze the flames and as I did, his wings became too heavy and cold for him to lift. He dropped down onto the rocks below and I blasted him with the remaining dragon-killing spell before I dropped too and had a long relaxing drink from the lily-scented pool, relieved to know that I would never have to fight a dragon ever again.

Emily Maycock (9)
Shorne CE Primary School

A Day In The Life Of Scampy

I was woken up with the soft, warm, papery bedding being pulled from around me. It was night for me and day for them because I'm nocturnal. Grumpily, I thought to myself, 'Why can't they wake me up in the daytime to clean my cage?'

I came out and saw the big yellow ball at the door. I also saw a delicious chocolate treat. I knew it was a trap, but I could not resist the temptation, so I went in. Before I knew what was happening, the ball had been tipped up and the door was on. I was put on the floor. I sat bolt upright thinking I had seen the door twist! I put the delicious treat in my pouch in my mouth and twisted the door with my paw. It came open.
I was so happy. I ran straight through the door of the room I was in. I heard a scream and a thundering noise. I looked round and saw the humans in hot pursuit. I was terrified and I ran and ran and ran. I dodged under the towering fridge. I heard them run past and the thundering footsteps died away. I felt calmer and was relieved and surprised I wasn't caught.

The door of the fridge was open. I wandered in and saw a lovely juicy carrot. I went over. I thought it can't hurt to have a nibble. I did and it was delicious. I had more and more and just couldn't stop eating it. It was lovely and soon it was all in my pouches and my stomach. Then I realised how cold it was. I was about to go out when the door shut and I was trapped. I thought to myself despairingly that it was worse than my cage, even if it was bigger. I went in search of a wheel to warm me up. I searched the whole place but I could not find one. Just then I had an idea. I pushed myself against the door, trying to open it. I had drained myself of energy before I realised it was the wrong end. I sat down and thought about what I should do in this sticky situation. I even *felt* sticky and then I realised that I was sitting in the jam jar! I wriggled but I only went deeper in. I thought there was nothing to do except wait to be rescued from this awful place. I dozed off eventually, only to have a dream about being a heap of bones left in here and never rescued. I was woken by excited shouting. I was being pulled out of the jam jar and taken out of the fridge. I quickly jumped down and ran up his trouser leg. If I went down I knew I would be seen and caught, so I went further up.

The human went into the garden. When he got outside, I ran down his trouser leg and found myself in the jungle of grass. I walked through the grass and saw something coming towards me. It was a cat! I would've screamed if I could make any noises. I ran for my life but the cat was faster than me. It pounced and picked me up in its mouth. Then a human came, grabbed the cat and took me out of its mouth. I was taken to the vet where I was checked over and the vet said I was fine. I didn't feel fine. I was bruised, cut and bleeding.

I was taken home and put in my clean cage for a rest. As I got into my warm bed, I thought that was not the best day of my life.

Emily Coode (9)
Shorne CE Primary School

A DAY IN THE LIFE OF A WOLF

As soon as I got up this morning, I found my two cubs fighting again. I told them off and then they stopped for a little while, but were soon at it again. It was my turn to hunt today, so I told the cubs to be quiet and that I would be as quick as I could.

In the murky part of the forest I found a herd of anxious deer but they ran off. There was no other meat in the forest that I could smell, so I went to the river and I was lucky - I caught some rainbow trout and some salmon in the fast water.

When I returned, my cubs were fast asleep. Everyone was happy because they hadn't had fish for two months. We all had a bit of rainbow trout and salmon each. It was beautiful and we saved the rest for lunch and dinner. After our wash, which my cubs hate like mad, we all went out for a run around the hill five times. That part of the day is really, and I mean really, tiring! After about two laps I almost collapsed, but I forced myself to finish and we all staggered slowly back to the cave. It did not take me long to drift off to sleep, but I was soon woken by my cubs jumping on me.

Now it was lunchtime and we had some more of the tasty fish, then we went for a drink by the clear blue lake. This was the best part of the day. *Swimming!* It's great fun. All of the cubs go to the shallows for swimming lessons, while the rest of the pack go to the deeper water where we have lots of fun diving on each other.

We had been swimming, washing and grooming for about three wolf hours (one human hour) when the chief called us all for dinner. The chief came to me and offered me the head of the biggest salmon that I had caught, but I said no as I don't like heads and I know that he does.

That night, instead of telling my cubs a goodnight story, I sang a lullaby to them. It went like this:

Go to sleep and close your eyes,
I'll be back in the morning time.
Tonight go off to a dreamy land,
And cover the cave in very deep sand.
You know I love you, you know I care,
I'll protect you from the bear.
So go to sleep and wake up bright,
Because tomorrow will be a more wondrous sight.

After the lullaby they were all fast asleep and slept really well, although this was probably because of all the food they had that day. It was not long before I was nodding off, and my last thought for the day was - I hope I don't have to hunt in the morning.

Rebecca Hopkins (10)
Shorne CE Primary School

A Day In The Life Of A Victorian Chimney Sweep

Today was even harder than usual. My master, Mr Smith, and I had lots of chimneys to sweep. The first chimney was quite easy, going up and up in a vertical line. Such a boring job this is. Mr Smith says, 'You 'ave to be skinny to be a stupid chimney sweep' and he hardly feeds me anything.

Oh, how my elbows ached and how my knees were exhausted, but I still had to finish today's work. Mr Smith always makes me carry the brush and the soot bag from house to house.

The chimney in the next house was even thinner. I could hardly push myself up. That's how thin the passage was and I had to crawl up it. As I was climbing, the passage became even thinner and as I was getting nearer the top. I became stuck once again.

I screamed down the chimney to Mr Smith, who shoved a spare chimney sweeper tool up the chimney. Next, after a very long push and shove up the chimney, I fell from a great height down to the mats below where I got a whack around the face from the master.

For dinner, all I had was one spoonful of peas, one measly spoonful of chicken and one teaspoon of water. Altogether not very appetising.

At seven o'clock I went up to bed and snoozed until six in the morning when I have to get up.

Emilie Ashen (9)
Shorne CE Primary School

A DAY IN THE LIFE OF AN ANT

Hi, my name is Tiny, and yep I'm tiny! In fact I'm one of the smallest creatures around, you've guessed it, I'm an ant.

Let me tell you what it is like to be an ant . . . Firstly it is quite scary being a small guy, there's always some horrid kid trying to squash me! Not to mention the daddy longlegs and beetles and spiders that always want me for supper!

Now let's see, what's in my ant diary for the day . . . lunch with Bob (a mosquito friend of mine). This should be interesting. I wonder what's on the menu, hope it's not me (he, he, he). Now what shall I wear, I know, my best oak leaf tie, my grass trousers and my favourite straw jacket. Oh, I've just remembered, I've got to help build the nest with all the other ants. We have also got to move all the eggs to the new place and the soil. An ant's life is very hard you know. I'm always getting tired. The Queen keeps you busy, she hates to see you sit down. Oh well, I'd better stop daydreaming and lift this big leaf; it's a lot bigger than myself. It won't budge so I'll call my ant friends Bill and Jill to come and help me. They come rushing over and with a bit of ant power we move the leaf. I glanced at my tiny watch and realise it was two o'clock. Time to get my skates on and get my tiny ant body around to Bob's house.

I knock on Bob's door, which is made out of bark and small twigs. His house is made out of straw and the windows are old spider's webs. Bob comes to the door and we sit down to lunch, which h is mud and bug pie followed by bat droppings with spider blood jelly. (Yum, yum). After lunch we go outside for a game of insect croquet. Bob showed off (and cheated a bit) by jumping and hopping about, when I could only crawl. After a tiring and enjoyable day it was time to crawl into my ant bed in the new ants' nest and snuggle down for some serious ant snoring. Night, night, sleep tight, I hope Bob doesn't bite.

Poppy Waller (9)
Shorne CE Primary School

A Day In The Life Of A Super Hero

'Where is our world's super hero, Roony Guy? He's been missing for a day,' asked a little girl from South Africa.

For Roony Guy, the world famous super hero, had flown off to the sun to have a nice peaceful holiday because everyone was taking him for granted.

On Earth there were *wanted* posters everywhere. They said . . .

> Wanted!
> Definitely wanted - alive

The next day a real disaster happened. A dragon attacked the world. It was big and fiery, so the only person who could save them was Roony Guy, by turning on his light bulb hat and blinding the dragon and while it could not see, Roony Guy would throw it in the sea.

But Roony Guy was not there and the world was in real trouble. Up there in the sun Roony Guy was having a great time. The dragon started to eat people and burn down houses.

One day up in the sun, Roony Guy heard screams coming from Earth. He looked down from the sun and saw an awful dragon taking up half of Russia and half of China.

'Oh no, I knew I should not have left Earth,' said Roony Guy.

As quick as lightning, he zoomed down to Earth, turned on his hat which blinded the dragon and he threw it into the sea.

The world was saved again by Roony Guy.

Eleanor Bull (9)
Somerhill Junior School

A Day In The Life Of A Dolphin

'Click, click, wake up seven seas!'
'In a minute, I'm just resting my eyes.'
'Come on, the sun is a lovely shade of primrose!'
'OK, OK, I'm up now!'
'Look!'
'Flipper, we see that nearly every day!'
'Oh yeah! We do don't we!'
'Well, I don't know about you Flipper, but I'm going to go and get some breakfast.'
'I have had mine, so I'll see you later.'

(After breakfast)

'Wow! Look at this thing I have found! It's all shiny and red! I wonder what it is? It could be a red shrimp, or a bit of food another creature left behind, or even something a human dropped! Now that's not something you see every day! I think Flipper might know what it is. Now I have to find him!'

(Later in the afternoon)

'Hey, Flipper, come and see what I found!'
'Wow! That looks so beautiful!'
'I know, but the thing I'm curious about is, what exactly is it?'
'I don't know to be honest with you, but if I had found it I would definitely think it was worth keeping!'
'You're right Flipper.'
'Maybe one day you will find out what it is, but for now you will just have to keep guessing!'

Sarah Parker (11)
Somerhill Junior School

A Day In The Life Of Mrs Bradley

I started my day off with an alarm clock ringing through my ears! I got up and remembered that I had to go to the school today for a new job interview at Somerhill Junior. I'm very excited about it. I've been waiting for this job for a few months now.

I wandered through St Ann's Well Park, judging how far it was from my house to the school and at the same time smelling the lovely smell of the flowers. I finally got there. It wasn't as boring as I thought it would be and was actually very big. As I strolled along, I wondered whether I could ever become a head teacher there. Suddenly I stopped at the gate, thinking how cool it would be if I did actually take over the school.

So I got to the office and I could already tell that the staff were friendly. They gave me a little badge saying who I was. As I walked into the staff room, they were all friendly to me. I walked into the classroom and started the lesson off really well.

The next day all of the teachers were given a letter and there was also a meeting at the school to say that they needed a new head teacher. I filled in the form, thinking what it would really be like and saying to myself that I could rule Somerhill.

The next day I waited for the announcement as to who was going to be the new head teacher. I wondered whether I would be picked. Then I heard a voice say 'Mrs Bradley' and I realised my life had just changed!

Ashleigh Knights & Rochelle Thorpe (10)
Somerhill Junior School

A Day In The Life Of A God

One day in the dark period they call 'the end of it all', a god-like being called Bubuchuck decided that he wanted thousands of little friends. So he tried a little experiment.

He went to his wife and said, 'Shlubasnuk, lend me a needle and thread, oh and some fabric in green and blue.'

So she lent him the things and he said, 'You may miss my attractive beard!' With that he snipped off his beard and the remainders were minimal.

'Oh Bubuchuck, what have you done?' exclaimed Shlubasnuk.
'It's all for your sake, zuggums.' He collected up his beard, put some of it into a bag, muttered a few words under his breath and tipped the bag upside down. His beard was green!

He set to work on the earth.

He set down some material and started to sew. He sewed green to blue, blue to green and so on for a long time. After what must have been hours, he set down the earth and stuffed it with the beard that wasn't green. With the beard that was green, he made some grass.
'Look Shlubbie!' shouted Bubuchuck. 'The earth!'
'Golly, Bubu,' said Shlubasnuk. 'It needs life.'
'Hmmm,' pondered Bubuchuck, 'so what will they look like?'
'I think,' said Shlubasnuk 'that they should look like us, but . . . ' she paused, 'not so hairy!'
'Yes yes, I agree.'
So Bubuchuck set to work on people of all colours for every country, then animals, to produce food.

When he was happy, he put his earth in a cupboard!

Candice Parfitt (11)
Somerhill Junior School

A Day In The Life . . .

Temperature: 0.2 splits per 1 light+ (5.26am)

No Splits. I think I had dog pupil for breakfast. Washed it down with a tear gland (probably). Spawn 2.8 split for the first time. The elder, Spawn 1.1, died after a goggling 26 hours!

Temperature: 0.7 splits P1L+ (per 1 light+) (7.01am):

2 Splits. The new ones, Spawns 2.9 and 2.91 looked so funny after getting trampled by what was probably an ant. Temperature: 0.02 splits P1L+ (a stormy 10.49am)

H e e e e e l l l l l l p! I don't wanna drown! I hate rain.

Temperature: 1 split P1L+ (12.01pm)

I'm s o o o o o o o lucky! I survived a storm! It's not much to say I'm the oldest, seeing as I'm the only one left, but, in any group, I'm almost an elder. The only problem is . . . I don't wanna die . . .

Temperature: 0.47 splits P1L+ (1.48pm):

Nearly the end. Life's short. Why do we exist? No . . . I've got to stop thinking like that. I'm my clan's last survivor and my clan can't die . . . no, I must survive for the clan. I . . . must . . . split . . . yes! Hi, 2.92, nice to meet you.

Temperature: 0.09 splits P1L+ (7.56pm):

The high creature is dark, the world is gone.
The giants turn on their light-givers. The flies seem to like getting fried by them. They obviously don't value life as much as us. I lived for the record-breaking 26½ hours, and now my time has come.

Elder, 1.97, clan 9652, died on May 16th 2001. It's not a bug's life: it's a virus's!

Sam Collard (11)
Somerhill Junior School

A Day In The Life Of Phoenix The Calf

My name is Phoenix and I am a calf. I was born in Devon on Friday 13th April, unlucky for some but not for me. I am lucky to be alive. Sadly, there has been an outbreak of foot and mouth disease on our neighbouring farm and all of the animals had to be slaughtered.

Today some strange men came into our farm with guns. They led our herd up to the top field. None of us knew why we were being taken up there, because we normally went there to graze and the cows had not been milked yet. Suddenly they started shooting. I could not believe it when I saw my mother fall to the ground. All of my friends and relations were crying for help.

Eventually they all got killed but they somehow missed me. When they had eventually gone, I went to lie down next to my dead mother. I lay there for what seemed like forever, hoping she was still alive. I was very hungry and thirsty but I would not leave until my mother awoke.

Eventually the men came back and found me still alive. My farmer stood up for me and would not let them kill me unless they got permission from the court.

Now I am famous for surviving the foot and mouth slaughter and have become a ray of hope for the future. I only hope this means no more healthy animals are killed unnecessarily.

Holly Wells (10)
West Lodge Prep School

A Day In The Life Of A Beanie Kid

I have been put in a box with all my friends to go to a shop. It is very dark but it is a quick journey. I am unpacked and put in another box - this time transparent. I am put on a high shelf but I am a little afraid of heights. Hopefully, someone will buy me soon.

The very same day at about 3 o'clock, a little girl with blonde hair comes in and looks around. I try to look my cutest and it works. She says to the shopkeeper:
'I want that one,' and points to me.
I'm so lucky. The man gets me down and puts me into a paper bag. Once the little girl is outside, she gets me out and cuddles me so hard, I nearly suffocate. I wave goodbye to my friends and hope I'm going to a loving and caring home. We walk along, me in her arms, and I feel the wind rustle my hair.

It begins to rain. The wind is getting stronger. My owner starts to run and I get jolted around. We get home just before the thunder and lightning start.

Now it is teatime. My owner has a sandwich and biscuits. She feeds me some. Chocolate bourbons, I think. They are scrummy. Next we watch some television.

I yawn and stretch my arms. So does my owner. It has been an exciting, but rather frightening day. We go upstairs, brush our teeth and fall asleep.

Helen Freundlich (10)
West Lodge Prep School

A Day In The Life Of A Horse

9.00: I have never liked the sound of the old horse van that woke me this morning. It reminds me of the ship that I was born on, the ship that I made so many journeys in before I came here. For I have not always been a riding pony and it was but a few years back that I was living the tough life of a work horse, chained to a cruel stick, commanded by a rod of metal and harsh words. But the humans that ride me now are not like that.

12.00: I have now finished my first lesson. Some of the horses at the stable complain about lessons, but I find this ungrateful; some of the horses I used to know would think of this as paradise.

2.30: I have eaten all my bran and am making my way to the tack room. At the camp I used to work in, we never had padded saddles or, indeed, any tack at all. The few times we were ridden, it was bareback: humans were greedy there, and a horse's purpose was to gain money and not to lose it.

4.00: I have finished my last lesson and been hosed down and brushed. Back at the working camp, the rain that we were left out in was the only cleaning device we got - we even had to fight over *drinking* water.

8.00: To sleep. And I shall look forward to better than those dreamless nights I have experienced in my past.

Jemma Gurr (10)
West Lodge Prep School

A Day In The Life Of The 60s

I woke up in my 'peace' pyjamas, 9 o'clock on the dot. I put on my groovy bell-bottom trousers and my open-neck tunic and brushed my hair down while listening to a song by the Beatles on my radio. I grabbed a penny and a shilling and set off down Gipsy Road to the hippie hall. I put my shilling in the pot and waited for everyone to come. When everyone had arrived, we all sat round in a circle and started our exercise. First we deep breathed in, next out, for five minutes. Then we shouted 'flower power' ten times. We painted little flowers on our face.

After, I went to the sweet shop and bought a 4-bar KitKat and a snack bar with my penny and ate them on the way home. I danced to some more Beatles' songs. They were really groovy and hip. Then I read about Harold Wilson, the prime minister, in the newspaper. In the afternoon I went to the peace field and sat with my friends and made some headbands using flowers that we had picked.

As the evening drew in, I felt happy and free, like I was floating above the clouds. I went to a groovy disco and danced to songs of peace. At 11 o'clock I went to sleep dreaming about flowers, birds and music. It was a peaceful, loving dream and I was so glad to be young in the 60s. Wouldn't you?

Claire Stevenson (10)
West Lodge Prep School